Sh*t.Falls.Up.

David Deutsch

Dedication

For my kids.
Always follow your dreams.

PROLOGUE

For the past three weeks my life has gone on hiatus. For some reason, I have stopped and the world has continued to spin. I guess the situation I have found myself in is quite prevalent today, or so I continue to tell myself. You see, I am a product of society. Sure, you can tell me I am just a white, upper-class, 30-something Generation Xer crying out about my, "oh so unfortunate" lifestyle, but I choose to look at it in a different light. I represent a new era in the world of former, grungy Generation Xer's. I am a young, downwardly mobile man on the move. I just lost my job, my girlfriend, and my apartment. What they failed to mention in the brochure of life is that I would be thirty, balding, and homeless. Is there still time to get a refund?

I have, after all, been becoming a bit neurotic. You would be, too, if you saw your life slipping away from you. The sad part about my life is that I am not even on sedatives; I couldn't sedate myself if I wanted to since I basically am out of money. To add insult to injury, my girlfriend just left me because we could not fit together on the twin-size, blow-up, air mattress where I am now forced to sleep.

The guy from whom I subletted my apartment selfishly decided that he didn't like his wife anymore and was therefore moving back to New York. Thanks, Bitch.

I now have the distinct pleasure to wake up every morning on the floor looking up at my younger sister sleeping in her bed. She wakes up to go to work while I have to turn over and inhale dust bunnies.

Someone kill me.

Because of my present circumstances, I am rapidly developing a case of the creeps. You might also get the creeps if you were spending every minute with your sister in a studio apartment. There is no privacy in one of these things. I think I may have caught a glimpse or two of some things I have never wanted to see. I may puke.

I can tell you this, I wish I was stoned. Unfortunately, I have to remain clean and sober, just in case I get a job. You never know if they drug test. So I have gone without the aid of nature to enhance my life, which means I can't blame my paranoia on drugs. I am probably the first person to blame my lack of work on myself, but don't whip out the tiny violin yet. I think there is a plot against me, I just haven't figured out whom to blame it on yet. That is why I am obsessed with the evening news, hoping they will be able to inform me who my scapegoat of the week should be. Give me some credit here folks, at least I'm up on current events.

PART I: Before

CHAPTER ONE

There are some very large misconceptions about Hell as we know it. Some people think that Hell is this terrible place in the afterlife where the Devil resides while exerting his fiendish control over his evil dominion filled with people who have done appalling things during their time on earth. Some claim that the heat is unbearable, while others are terrified by the horrible acts of cruelty and torture that await them as repentance for their sins. All of these hypotheses may be true, but my problem with these theories is the fact that Hell does not exist in the afterlife. It exists here on earth.

I've seen Hell. In fact, I've been to Hell. Hell most certainly does reside right here in the living world. Hell is hearing, 'Did you clean your room?' when you are twenty-five years old. Hell is hearing, on a daily basis, 'Did you find a job yet?' while you are confined to the room where you grew up, with music posters from 1986 pasted all over your wall. In short, Hell is moving back in with your parents.

It doesn't seem like Hell at first glance. In fact, it even seems like a great idea. Free rent, your old room back, and a chance to reconnect with the 'rents. Sounds like a virtual paradise, but what you soon discover is a living, breathing, functioning ecosystem filled with all the classic torture and evil somehow confined to a 3,000 square-foot space located in the suburbs.

I was back in my old room, all right. The music posters were still barely covering the seafoam green walls, and the aquamarine carpet was still making me seasick. The difference this go-around was the fact that all the washed-up pop stars on my walls were mocking me.

"Well, well, well. Look what the cat dragged in," some pop star with a fucked up 80's haircut sneered.

"Shut up," I said, sitting on my crappy twin mattress.

The last thing I needed to hear right now was some poster of a singing pretty boy making me feel like shit because I had to move back into my old room at my parent's house after I had just spent $90,000 on law school.

I was trying to piece it all together. What the fuck happened? My sister (who was living with me at my parents') didn't weigh in on the issue yet because she was too busy looking for a man through various online dating services. My Dad had just bought a computer and had actually installed an Internet connection - shocking - welcome to the "future"! However, she was getting annoyed.

"I wish this thing would sort these people by religion. I mean, I'm looking for a Jewish guy and I have to keep flicking around until I find one. Meanwhile, I keep finding all these attractive, Italian guys."

"Well, why don't you go out with one?" I asked.

"Are you kidding? And what, celebrate Christmas? Whatever!"

It was nice that she was so open-minded. I'm sure she'll find someone soon.

I was glad that Michelle was living at home with me because somehow it justified the whole experience. I couldn't be that big of a loser if my sister was sharing the same house with me. After all, she had graduated college and now she was right across the upstairs hall from me. But there was a huge difference between my life and my sister's: she was working.

Every morning, I would awaken to a cacophony, as I tried to remain asleep with springs piercing my skin in my broken twin bed. At 0527, with military-like precision, the alarm clock in my parents' room would trumpet. My father would hit the snooze button and instantly fall back asleep. But I was now up, listening to him snore. Was this man part elephant? How in God's name the sound of the snore could reach my room from the other side of the second floor and through two, closed doors was beyond me. By 0530 the alarm in the room right across from mine would go off. I could hear my sister hit the snooze button and make some weird choking/snorting noise, then silence. At 0532 my parents' alarm would go off again and I would hear my mom shriek, "Richard, will you get up already? I don't want to hear that goddamn alarm again."

My confused father would answer, "What, yeah, okay," and then with lightning speed race into his bathroom to start shaving. In his world, people shave every day. I've known the man for 25 years and I have never seen him once walk around with stubble.

At 0535 Michelle's alarm would go off again and this would rouse her from slumber. By 0540 two showers are running simultaneously, cleansing the occupants. At 0550 both subjects are in the dressing phase, each putting on the proper attire for Mr. Boss. At 0615 - on the dot – Dad and Michelle are out the door on their way to New York City to start their work day.

Their commute is not simple. First stop: the fifteen-minute jaunt to the Park and Ride on Route 16. The Park and Ride is a parking lot where everyone drops off their cars to catch the E-Zee Express Bus that will take them to the train station where they can catch the express train to New York City. The commuters who brave this daily haj have lost their minds. The crowd ranges in age from 21 to 60, but vary little in appearance. They are highly disheveled and half asleep, as they line the curb waiting for the bus. No one talks, and if you turned your head quickly, you'd swear that everyone was in some crappy suit with a sad, white carnation tucked in the lapel.

The Park and Ride is not the worst of it. The real horror show starts at the train station. Here, the commuters have gotten into the habit of standing at the exact spot where the train will stop and the doors will open. They strategically begin boxing out their competition, moving around like caged animals waiting for the exaltation of the 6:47 train arrival. I've even seen some men use their children as obstacles to keep other people from entering the train ahead of them. At that magical moment, the commuters clamber onto the train.

The quest for a seat isn't easy. You run at top speed through the cars but to no avail.

The one available seat is always the same. The middle seat. You're usually wedged between a fat mess of a man who insists on eating his three egg, bacon and cheese on a bagel sandwich and pushing his overstuffed briefcase into your missing legroom. It's a bad habit for him. He's already pushing his overstuffed body into your space anyway so what's the difference if his briefcase jams into your calf? He regularly nabs the window seat.

The guy on your right is usually sleeping. So, you gingerly try to step over his legs on your way to this hell sandwich. Inevitably, you wake him up, albeit briefly. He snorts at you, but then falls right back to sleep. You find your seat, repulsed by fatty to your left, put your own briefcase down and then try to relax for the next 40 minutes. Except, sleeping guy's head starts bobbing and, ultimately, ends up on your shoulder. What can you do? You're so exhausted that you usually just let it slide and accept the fact that for the next forty minutes you've got a commuter boyfriend.

Thank God, I'm not on this train.

I wake up at nine and prepare some breakfast. My mom has already left the house, as well, to teach at the elementary school around the corner. I have six full hours to sit and enjoy the day, but I usually spend the six hours trying to write some stories for publication and pondering where everything went wrong.

Maybe everything went wrong in college. When I received my acceptance letter from Catskill University it might as well have been a judge sentencing me to four years hard labor at a maximum-security correctional facility. I'm not saying this was a bad school, but if you're into friendly people, a beautiful campus, fine dining, impeccable living quarters and brilliant teachers, this was not the place for you. Maybe it was the sheer physical beauty of the school that saved me from insanity. What was not to like? Four, identically beautiful towers of concrete comprised the stunning perimeter, with a lovely, cylindrical skyscraper smack dab in the middle. The Fountain, as it is affectionately called by the students, is the focal point of the campus. This beauty, rained its majestic waters and flowed bountifully at least five days of the school year. What fun! I remember sitting outside by the fountain on the three days of warm weather we had during my senior year thinking to myself, does it get any better than this? And now sitting at home I can confidently say, "No!"

Entry in Journal: After further deliberation I am of the belief that moving home is contributing greatly to my mental breakdown. College is only a minor contributing factor.

CHAPTER TWO

On the first day of law school a professor asked the class, "Who wants to work at a great, big, law firm when they grow up?" 95% of the students raised their hand. He went on to explain that guys who worked at big firms made a shitload of money. 100% of the students salivated.

"Oh, you'll have the big house," he said, "a beautiful wife, a maid, a pool, a gardener to take care of the grounds and a nice car." Yelps of joy erupted from the students, the likes of which I had not heard before or since.

I was sitting in the back row of the lecture hall. My strategy was to always sit as far away from the action as possible. That way you can hide. But I soon discovered that hiding was going to be a bit of challenge. There were only three rows of seating, and the professor had a seating chart with your name on it in bold letters.

From the back row I heard, Dimitri Ananyev, who told us to call him "Fonzi" when he was introduced to the class - the product of learning English from bad 70's and 80's sitcoms - say, in a really bad accent, "When I get one of those jobs, I'm buying a mansion."

Meanwhile, the professor was staring at the class, dead silent, waiting for something. He held his hands up in front of himself, palms facing the ceiling like a television evangelist about to ask the Lord for forgiveness.

Then he started speaking again, "And you know what?" - now he was leading up to the big finish - "your wife, she's going to love the house; the kids, they're going to love the pool. And your maid, and your gardener? They are going to love you because they're getting paid to hang out there. But you're never going to see your wife, or the house, or the pool, or your kids, or the maid, or the gardener. You're never going to be at home because you wanted to work at a big firm and make a lot of money. Have fun. Now, open to Pennoyer v. Neff!"

He was right. I didn't need to work at a big firm to be happy. For God sakes, man, I wanted to come home at night! I'm not very good about sleep deprivation. I had to find an alternative to getting my ass kicked on a daily basis by some stuffy, bow tie-wearing partner. That meant studying really hard for three years, sacrificing my social life, giving up good TV, and getting an A in every class I took. I thought I could do it. There were people who did that all the time. I'd heard about them on television. Summa Cum this, Magma that. I could be that guy.

Turns out, I wasn't that guy. Not only did I blow every chance I had at law review, journal writing, and getting an A in any class, but when I graduated I had amassed a stellar 2.4 GPA. I was guaranteed one thing for sure. I would never work in a giant law firm. But would it also prevent me from working at any law firm?

So when reality set in - and when you are living with your parents reality sets in very quickly - I was off to find my first job. I knew it wouldn't be at one of New York's premier law firms, but I figured a law degree could get me a job somewhere. What that job might be, and where it would be, was a different story altogether. And with my student loan money completely depleted I needed a plan of action.

I was hoping to avoid the whole law office thing since I really wanted to be a writer. But staring at my seafoam green walls, writing in journals and plotting ways out of corporate America, wasn't helping very much. If this year was going to have any silver lining, I had no choice. I needed a job.

I picked up The New York News, newspaper, flipped right

over to the "Help Wanted" section and found an ad:

Recent Grad wanted for work at PI firm.

Will train. Fax Resume: 212.221.1357

I walked downstairs to my dad's home office. His old, oak desk with the leather chair was perfect for a nice, relaxing day of work. Contrary to my way of thinking, my dad was never at his home office because he loved going into the main office for work. I had never, in my entire life, met another person who loved an office so much. In the most hazardous conditions, my father would get in his car and head off to work to be berated by his boss in person. There were times when the entire city - and thus his office – had been shut down, but he would trudge forward. Twenty-three inches of snow wasn't going to slow him down, even if the rest of the world stayed behind at home. After all, there was work to be done and abuse to be collected.

Fax resume, huh? I guess people still fax. I sat down in the leather chair and dialed up the number from the paper. I was nervous as hell, almost too scared to talk. I tried to channel my father's one-track work mentality to guide me through this process, but I still almost puked. No one should be this nervous this early in the morning. Then I remembered that I did not have to talk to anyone and felt like a moron. I managed to fax over my resume to the mystery firm. After I sent the first fax, I sent out fifteen more. I was on a roll. Everything from ambulance chasing to document review, nothing was too menial for me. I needed to get out of my parents' house. This was going to be the start of my legal career one way or another. I could think of nothing worse.

A few days later, it got a lot worse. A mystery lawyer called.

"Can I speak with David, please?" He bellowed.

"This is," I said.

"This is Michael H. Goldberg, attorney. I received your resume the other day and would like you to come in for an interview."

Michael "H". What a fucking tool this guy was.

"Sure. I'd love to come in." This was my ticket out of here.

"How about first thing tomorrow morning? Say eight o'clock? I'm located at 21 Park Row, Manhattan."

"OK. Great, I'll see you at eight."

"OK," and with that Michael H. Goldberg hung up the phone.

Now I had to actually meet him. I was living at home, had no money, and quite frankly, I could see my hair was thinning. And when I ran my hands through it, my hair didn't feel right. That made me very nervous. I had a sneaking suspicion I would be bald before age 30. Since I had moved back home, I've been finding clumps of my precious hair in my shower drain. Why would you want to leave me now, precious hair? I love you so.

My thinning hair made me realize that I didn't have very much time left. I had to get a job, move into my own place in the city, get a girlfriend to marry me pronto, and make it all happen before I went bald. If not, I feared I'd still be living with my parents at 40. No one wants to be that guy. I had to make Mr. Michael H. Goldberg love me.

At dinner that night, I announced my good news to the whole family.

"Well, Mom and Dad, I have some good news. I have an interview tomorrow in Manhattan," I said, as vomit was welling up in my throat.

Dad was the first to congratulate me. "It's about time. All you've been doing for the past two months is sitting around that room of yours writing in that book." Obviously, Dad was excited for me.

"So what firm is it with?" My Mom asked, actually curious.

"Well, it's not exactly with a firm. It's with one guy." It sounded kind of weird to say that out loud.

"One guy? People really work for one guy? Well, one guy is better than no guy. Doesn't really matter to me as long as you go to work and he pays you. He is going to pay you right?" Yep, Dad was brimming with excitement.

That's the odd thing about my Dad. It didn't matter where you went to work as long as you went to work. I could have told him I was going to be spinning a sign on the corner in front of the mattress store, begging potential customers to stop in for the big sale, and he would be happy. Writing at home was not work, that was a dream job that paid nothing.

"We'll see what happens," I said. "I didn't even get the job yet.".

I better get this fucking job.

CHAPTER THREE

I woke up the next day at 4:30 a.m., the earliest I had been up in weeks, perhaps ever. I took a shower and then searched my closet for a certain something to wear and there it was – my only suit. I hated that thing more than myself at the moment. I would have never owned one, but my parents bought it for me when I was accepted to law school. How had it come to this? How could it be that I was about to interview for a law job? I wanted to be a writer, and now I was about to have my dad drive me to the E-Zee Express Bus that would take me to the train that would lead to the subway, so I could get out at the City Hall stop, and walk over to an office where I was going to sit across from Michael H. Goldberg and beg for a job. Holy Fucking Shit!

"C'mon let's get cookin'," my dad yelled upstairs to me.

I walked down the stairs as slowly as possible. "Dead man walkin'," I whispered to myself. "Dead man walkin'."

"C'mon, Dave, the car's all warmed up and waiting for you. Let's go!"

I got in the car and the automatic seat belt locked me in

place. The doors automatically locked, too. I was trapped. My dad turned to me and began his work lecture.

"Son, first, you should hang up your jacket in the back here on this hook," he pointed out the hook like a spokesmodel. "That way it won't get creased while you are sitting in the car. Second, put your tie over the seat belt so that way it doesn't get creased during the ride. Third –"

"Dad, it is six fucking thirty in the morning. I don't care!" Was he kidding me?

He didn't even hear me. "Third, I bought you a combination E-Zee Express Bus/MetroTrain/Subway monthly pass so you wouldn't have to be bothered buying that today. You can pay me back later."

"Dad, I'm going for an interview. I don't have any job yet."

"If you can't get a job from a solo practitioner, then you better re-examine your life." And with that, we were off.

He dropped me off at the Park and Ride at six forty-five.

"Aren't you coming?" I asked.

"Not today. I have a sales call to make in New Jersey. I'll head into the office later," he said.

"But . . ." I just stood there.

"David, you are twenty-five years old. Get your ass in line. I'll see you later." He shook his head and pointed at me to get in line. I heard him whisper to himself, "What the hell is wrong with this kid," as he pulled away leaving me like a kindergartner alone on the first day of school.

I walked over to the line where a fine collection of cretins and misfits stood waiting. I could have made a fortune selling sideshow tickets.

"Step right up, ladies and gentlemen, come see the freaks! Yes, they're here in all shapes and sizes, heights and smells. Come one, come all! Don't miss this show!"

The woman who got in line behind me looked as if she didn't have any lips. The guy behind her was wearing some depressing, shit-brown suit that almost made me dry heave. God, this sucked. Standing there, I calculated the ratio of bad comb-overs to full heads of hair and it was extremely high. Even the bus driver got in on the act. His blue, bus-driver's suit was so creased that one of the wrinkles almost poked out my eye as I showed him my monthly pass. I finally found a seat in the middle of the bus and just looked around. Help.

The EZ Express finally arrived at the train station around seven. The damn EZ bus was running late, so I had to run off the bus like a lunatic in order to get to the platform where the train would arrive in just two minutes. Problem was, a line was already forming on the bus even before it stopped. I didn't have the patience for this. I had to make it to Mr. Michael H. Goldberg's on time. I had to catch the train.

I felt kind of bad pushing some of the commuters aside as the bus door opened, but they didn't go down easy. Disregarding the bad makeup jobs and comb-overs, this was a frisky bunch. They held their ground as I pushed, and I finally made it to pavement after a 300-pound beast, bedecked in orange, rolled her pumpkin ass out of the bus.

I ran for the train, up the stairs, across the platform, and down the stairs. I made the train just as the conductor screamed out, "All aboard!"

To my surprise, there were no seats. I was feeling a bit gamey after the mad dash to the platform, so I decided to take off my jacket and stand at the front of the car. Shit! I had forgotten to put on an undershirt under my starched, white, stiff-as-a-board, fucking dress shirt which had now become see-through since it was riddled with sweat. This was not starting out very well.

I arrived in the city about 7:30, so I ran over to Park Row at top speed, leading me to work up sweat number two in my swanky suit. 23 Park Row didn't look that impressive. It actually looked like a dilapidated tenement with dripping air conditioners hanging out of the windows. I made my way into the "lobby" and found Michel H. Goldberg's name on the roster of disturbed individuals who rented space in this rat trap. When I got in the elevator, and the doors closed, I was filled with fear that I would never move out of my parents' house.

When I stepped into this moving box that was masquerading as an elevator, I feared for my life. The elevator was more of a coat closet that shook violently as it moved. It had faux wood paneling that looked 40 years old, and had a grimy, dirty, linoleum floor. It scared the shit out of me.

By the grace of God, the rickety elevator stopped at floor eleven, and I stumbled out. On the wall was a nameplate of sorts - a laser printout stuck on a piece of cardboard: "The Law Offices of

Michael H. Goldberg, Esq.".

I didn't run, although every instinct in my body said to get away fast. I walked in and went right up to the secretary.

"I have an appointment at eight with Mr. Goldberg," I said.

"Just have a seat. Mr. Goldberg will be right with you."

I sat down and waited. A minute later, a man, who looked as if he had been chewed up and spit out by a dog, walked out. Mr. Goldberg had on a brown suit - and I use that term 'suit' very loosely - complemented with what was once a white shirt and a brown tie.

"David. Please come in," he waved his hand, inviting me into his office.

I sat down in the only available chair: a folding chair. This should have been a red flag for me to run for the hills, but I sat on this uncomfortable piece of shit staring at Mr. Goldberg's law degree hanging on the wall behind him in this 2x2 office. My knees were jammed up against Mr. Goldberg's crappy desk, but he didn't seem to notice or care as he made himself comfortable in a plush, high-backed, leather chair that appeared to be the most expensive item in the office.

"So, David, tell me a little bit about yourself," he jumped

right into it.

"Well, I just graduated law school a few months ago, and now I'm trying to get myself a job, sir."

"Let me tell you a little bit about what we do here. I practice personal injury law - you know, when you get in an accident and want to sue someone, you come to me. You slip and fall and want to sue the restaurant where it happened you come to me. You –"

I had a hard time not staring at this man's comb-over. Did he think he was fooling anyone? He did have it combed in an interesting way. He didn't have the usual part by the ear with the hair combed across the head. This man had hair coming from the back of his head across the top where it was laid to rest. Scary.

"So, does that sound like something you would be interested in?" he asked me. I honestly hadn't heard one word.

"Quite interesting. It's something I could really see developing into a career for me." That must have been the magic answer because what came out next was a shock to me.

"Well, then I'd like you to start Monday. The pay is four hundred dollars a week and unfortunately, I can't offer you benefits because we are a small operation."

"Sounds good. I'll see you Monday," Did I actually say "sounds good?"

It sounded horrible. Four hundred dollars a week. How in the hell was I going to move out of my parents' house on four hundred dollars a week? "Sounds good" - those two words kept replaying in my head as I took the subway to the train, then to the bus, and only stopped when I got in the car with my Dad, who was waiting at the park and ride for me.

"How did it go?" he asked.

"Good. I got the job."

"That's great!" He was excited.

"Yup, great."

That night I called Lisa. I had met her on the first day of law school when she sat next to me and said, "Why did I sign up for this?" I knew we would become good friends. The weirdest part was that she was from my hometown, but I never knew her in high school. She was cute, a slender 5'4", with brown hair and blue eyes, but it was hard to get a good read on her body with her dressed in a professional type get-up for the first day of school. Regardless, I wasn't attracted to her. Maybe it was the fact that she never talked to me for four years in high school that irked me. Maybe she just gave off the "Just Friend's" vibe. Or maybe it was her fat ass. You can't hide that in your slacks.

I mean, I'm sure other men thought she was attractive, but for some reason I couldn't really see it. But she was funny. Very funny. Since we sat right next to each other, she would reach over to my notebook and write me quick notes during class that would crack me up. Her favorite target was "Fonzi." Of course, he was. Who wouldn't love ripping on an immigrant, who looked like Elvis? And not cool, young Elvis, but Fat Druggie Elvis, who spoke broken English in a thick, Russian accent. Any woman who could make Civil Procedure class fly by was all right in my book.

Lisa had recently started a job at a big investment bank working in the legal department. She always wanted to do something with divorce law, but since her father didn't know anyone getting divorced at the time, he did the next best thing. He called a guy he knew at Hobart & Klein. She scored an interview, got the job, and the next thing she knew she was in the "management training program." This was code for reviewing contracts, on the hunt through huge, over-written documents for those few, offending words they were trying to find, and then removing them for $32,000 a year. Fun stuff. In short, she was about as happy as I was.

"You're never going to believe what happened," I told her.

"What?"

"I got a job." I basically let those words fall lifelessly out of my mouth.

"You did! I'm so excited for you! Where? Doing what?"

"It's at a solo practitioner's office. I'm not really sure what kind of law it is. I wasn't really paying attention. I was too mesmerized by the guy's comb over," I said, looking up at the broken clock that I had hanging on my wall - What the fuck?...My parents never bothered to replace the battery?

"What is with you and comb overs? How could you not know what kind of law he practices? You went for the interview, didn't you?" Lisa was perplexed.

"Yeah, but I just said okay when he asked me how everything sounded."

"I know you would rather be writing, but you do know that you have to actually go to work and try to make some money."

Lisa was the only one who knew my secret. While I was in law school I submitted a short story in a country-wide competition, and it came in first place. It was one of the most shocking things that had ever happened to me. After that day, I never submitted another story for publication. This does not mean I stopped writing. In fact, I had written a ton of stories, but I felt that everything I wrote wasn't as good as that first story.

"Believe me, I would rather be doing anything but working at Hobart & Klein, but I have to get the hell out of my parents' house. You'll see, everything will be okay. Just stick with the job and, before you know it, we'll be living in the city. Trust me."

I hung up the phone feeling a little better, but I was not very happy with how my life was shaping up.

CHAPTER FOUR

Monday came so fast that I would swear there was never a Sunday that week. Now I know how everyone else feels about work. I threw on my one suit, and waited for my dad to drive me to the old E-Zee Express Bus so I could catch the train to the city. At 6:30 a.m. things start looking very bleak. Just an hour earlier, I had contemplated suicide as I washed my face and got ready to shave. Holding a sharp, cold blade in your hand at 5:30 a.m. leads you to make one, tough decision: Do I slit my throat or shave off my stubble? I assure you that it is a tough choice, but today it seemed even more daunting. By 5:31, I had made up my mind to shave off the stubble and face the day. Here I come, fellow lawyers. Next stop, two hours later, the city.

I arrived at The Law Offices of Michael H. Goldberg at about 7:55 a.m. I didn't get but one foot in the door when I felt all five feet of Mr. Goldberg breathing fire down my neck. Well, actually it was more like my lower back.

"You're late!" he barked.

Late? It couldn't be later than 7:55 a.m. Could this guy be for real?

"I like my attorneys to be prompt and that means not one minute late. You, dear boy, are five minutes late. According to my watch it is now 8:06, which makes you five minutes late, and even worse you have wasted one minute of my time."

This certainly was an interesting development. This man obviously had set his watch ten minutes ahead so he could be early to work, on time for meetings or just to bust the balls of his employees when they got to the office late. Apparently, he had taken it upon himself to hold the rest of the world to his time-keeping standards. As I was being berated, I looked over and saw another guy around my age sitting at a desk with a look in his eyes that would have made him easy prey for any hunter. His eyes looked dead, and not the kind of dead eyes that you have after dropping too much acid. He had big, brown, lifeless eyes that fixated on me with the innocent look of a deer right before the kill shot.

"Well, now that you're here, let's get started. Come with me," he made a sweeping motion with his hand and we shuffled to another part of the "office."

"Marc, what the hell are you waiting for? Get up and get over here," he screamed at the guy sitting at the table entering data. I wasn't sure if Marc was a lawyer, paralegal, man servant or gimp. I was sure that he liked abuse. "Did you think you were going to sit there all day? Jackass."

Mr. Goldberg continued six steps over to the one other area in this office. This was the other room that, he explained, would be our workspace. Apparently, Marc and I were now sharing a workspace. This space consisted of a collage of file cabinets at different heights, papers stacked and strewn all over like a hoarder's room that hasn't been touched in 10 years, and a desk that appeared to have heaved itself out of the dirt-covered floor.

"This is your desk," he pointed to the dilapidated, fold-up, make-shift desk. "I need you to go through these folders and enter into this here computer the hospital where the client was taken." He threw a stack of folders on the desk. "I'll be back around lunch time. We'll see how you did then," and with that Mr. Goldberg walked right out of the office.

"Let's go, jackass," he barked, and Marc followed him like a dog.

For the next couple of hours, I went through file after file searching for the line on the complaint that specified the hospital. During this mind-numbing exercise, my thoughts drifted to the fact that I lived at home with my parents at twenty-five years old. Jesus Christ. After the first hour, my thoughts turned to the horrible realization that I was being paid ten dollars an hour to do data entry. Ten dollars an hour to sit like an eek, eek, monkey and enter the names of hospitals into a computer program. But here I was eek, eeking along.

Mr. Goldberg returned about noon, "Let's see what we have here." He paged through the folders, cross-checked a few, and proceeded to slowly work himself into a frenzy that would culminate in a human fireworks display.

"Wha – What do we have here?" He pointed at the fifteen-inch monitor. "This says *Jamaca* Hospital. Right here, right here on the screen. I don't see an "I" anywhere in that word. There is no "I". Am I crazy? You do see it, right?" He pointed again at the screen, this time pressing so hard that an actual noise was coming from it.

I saw Marc cower. If he could have dug a foxhole he would have, and then jumped right in. I also sensed that he would not have let me share it with him. Very selfish, Marc. He knew what was coming and wanted to be protected from the shelling that was about to start.

"You see this word is missing an "I". An "I," of all letters," his voice was rising now. "I cannot believe this. This word is missing an "I"," he was now screaming. "YOU SPELL JAMAICA WITH AN "I". J-A-M-A-"I"-C-A. A-I-C-A!" His voice reached a pitch I had not heard to that point in my life, nor have I heard since, "NOT A-C-A. WHAT KIND OF JACKASS ARE YOU?"

He had gotten so excited that he kept repeating himself, screaming, "A-I-C-A" over and over. He was now enunciating every letter at the top of his lungs. "A-I-C-A! A-I-C-A!" This lunatic rambled on for another five minutes, although it seemed to last at least fifteen. As Michael H. Goldberg, Esq., continued to spew his staccato insanity, I got up and walked out of the office, thus closing the first chapter in my new law career.

CHAPTER FIVE

Where else was there to go but home? I found myself back at my parents' house, upstairs in my room, in daily contemplation of my next move. Thus far, law had not worked out as planned. On the bright side, I did have a new record on my hands for the longest time I had ever worked. I was now up to four hours, and if you counted the commute, seven.

The weeks went by, as I stuck to the same routine of faxing and emailing my resume to any and all firms advertising for an attorney. By this time my parents had begun to question my ability to function as an adult.

"What the hell are you doing with your life? All I ever see you do is write in that damn notebook. What the hell happened at the last job? You couldn't stick it out?" This was Dad's typical question.

"I spelled Jamaica wrong. I now know there's an "I" in there."

"That's why you left? You had a job, David. You don't just leave!"

"The guy yelled at me."

"Yelled at you? Yelled at you!," my Dad was now yelling at me, "Grow the fuck up. Everyone gets yelled at. Maybe, one day, you'll yell at someone yourself. If you stay at a job for more than a couple of hours. Everyone starts somewhere."

"But-"

"No 'but.' Get your ass another job, and stop acting like a child."

I was grateful he hadn't thrown me out of the house yet. I would explain that I was trying to get a job, emailing and faxing my little heart out, looking for that big break, but deep down inside I wanted to do something creative. Maybe write a book or a screenplay. These seemed like viable options to me. What seemed almost unnatural, was becoming a lawyer.

I met Lisa at the only bar in our town that had cheap drink specials - a joint called The Donkey. Lisa and I walked in, and looked around for seat, but it's a crowded, quirky, place with 50's style bar stools up against the bar and small booths. There were clothes lines running across the ceiling with figurines of donkeys hanging from it. After pushing our way to the middle of the place, we found a booth and ordered dollar drafts.

"What am I going to do? My parents are flipping out on me," I complained.

"You have to find another job," she said.

"Yeah, no shit. On top of everything, I owe my dad $250 for the super-commuter pass."

"I'm sure you'll get a job. Just keep trying. Look, I'll ask around Hobart for you, and see if there is anything available. You never know."

"Man, I don't know if I can work in a place that corporate. Don't you all just sit in cubicles breathing in the sterile air all day? I'd go nuts," I said.

"Look, if something comes along you better take it. Beggars can't be choosers. Don't you want to move into the city? Don't you want to move out of your parents' house? If you keep heading down the road you're going, you'll be at home forever. Is that what you want?"

"You're right. I need to get a job. Then I need to get a life. If I'm lucky, maybe I can work on getting a girlfriend, too." That was my next priority.

"Well, having a job can't hurt. Moving out of your parents' house wouldn't hurt your odds, either."

Lisa was right. I wasn't going to get anywhere until I got a job. I went home and continued to send out my resume.

As my third month at home drew to a close, I received a phone call. "Ehhhh, this is Avi Chyman, I am, ehh, responding to, eh, a resume you sent in. I would like to talk to you when you get a chance, ehhh, please give me a call back at your earliest convenience. Okay." I had to listen eight times before I could decipher this message.

So, now I had a decision to make. Either I could call back Avi, and schedule an appointment to meet him, or I could ignore the message and live in my parents' house for the next ten years. I opted to call.

"Hello, can I speak with Mr. Chyman please?" I said to the secretary.

"Mr. Chyman is indisposed at the moment. Can I take a message?"

"Yes, can you please tell him David Michaels cal-"

"Ah, Mr. Michaels, Mr. Chyman asked me to set up a time for you to meet with him this week. How does tomorrow sound?" She was an eager beaver.

"Tomorrow sounds okay. Can we do the afternoon? Around one?"

"One p.m., it is. We're located at 37 West 34th Street. Second floor," she said.

"Great, see you tomorrow at one."

Mr. Early got into the city at 12:30, primped and primed, for his meeting with Avi. I headed down 34th Street and figured I'd get there a little early to show how interested I really was in the job. As I walked down 34th street, I realized I couldn't find building number 37. I saw 35, and then I saw 39, but, inexplicably, number 37 was missing. I backed up a bit and then started over. Okay, here was number 35. I took a few steps forward and looked for 37. I didn't see it. All I could see was number 39, Dunkin' Donuts, next door. Mother Fucker. I took a step back to number 35 and looked really hard this time. There was the door to the shit-hole clothing store with the 35 on it. I walked up to the door and to my surprise, behind the grate used by number 35 to close up shop at night, there was a small pathway. I followed the path for a couple of steps. Lo and behold, there was an elevator and a very sad-looking sign under glass that had Avi Chyman spelled out in off-white, block, stick-on letters. Was this guy a squatter? This was definitely not a normal, commercial building. Hey, what the fuck? For the second time, I was about to come face to face with the wonderful world of law.

I got off on the second floor and came to a door. I rang the doorbell, and a 350-pound woman opened the door.

"You must be David. Please have a seat," she sat me down in front of her desk that was littered with paper.

There was the secretary's desk right by the door. Ten feet from her desk was a cubical partition with a hole cut out so the secretary could see right through to what I assumed was the attorney's office that was 15 feet from her desk.

She finally spoke, "David, I'm sorry, but the attorney won't be able to make it in today. He's in court, so if you don't mind I'm going interview you."

"What?" Where the fuck was Avi? I wanted to leave, but that's not what happened. Instead, I pussed out, "I guess that's okay."

She started asking me about my experience. Well, genius, judging from my resume, I don't have any. Then she told me what Avi does here in the office. He practiced general law. Basically, taking any cases with a paying client. Fifteen minutes later, she offered me the job, "This job pays $10 an hour, which will come out to four hundred dollars a week. You'll work nine to five. Is that okay?"

By now, you all know that it was okay, and I agreed to start the next Monday. Luckily it was already Friday, so I didn't have a chance to get too excited.

Since I was a working man now, I bought myself another monthly bus/train/subway pass, which cost a cool $250 with money that I borrowed from Lisa. But I was confident this time. Things were going to last. With my new found independence, I slipped into work at 8:45 Monday morning raring to go. I knocked on the door, but no one answered. I rang the bell or buzzer or whatever the fuck that button was on the side of the door and got the same result. I popped a squat, and twenty minutes later the secretary arrived.

"Waiting long?"

"No, just a few minutes."

"Oh, we don't get here a minute before nine."

Oh, whoop-tee-doo for you.

"Well, let me show you to your work area." She took five steps to the cubicle wall and pointed to the desk barely large enough to hold the computer that sat upon it. "Here you go. You can hang your jacket on the back of your chair. So, have a seat and get acquainted with your computer. There may be some legal stuff on it, so take a look. The attorney also wanted me to give you these folders. He wants you to go through the files and get acquainted with them. I'll be over there," she said, pointing to her desk five feet away, "and if you need anything just dial 477 and I'll be there to help."

Dial 477? She was five feet away. If I stretched my legs, I could make it over to her desk in one step. This woman has got to be kidding. I spent the next hour going through the files and playing on the computer. There was basically nothing in them. One had a bill receipt for $200. The other had a bunch of papers that, when read together, made no sense. I turned to the computer. There was nothing on it. By 10:15, I was ready to kill myself, when in walked a totally fucking, disheveled immigrant. He stopped at the Secretary's desk and and said, "Eh, anything up?" This had to be Avi.

"David, eh, what's happening, my friend. Glad to have you aboard. Give me, eh, a minute, then come into my office and we'll get a chance to, ehh, know each other a little better," he said as he passed by.

I could see him getting settled because there was a sliding piece of glass that separated my "work space" from his office. I was fiddling on the computer when I heard the secretary's phone buzz.

Out came Avi's voice, "Can you send David in, please." I quickly turned to Avi and saw him talking into a phone, then quickly turned to see the secretary talking to him. I was sitting right next to Avi. Why was he buzzing the secretary?

"Yes, Mr. Chyman." Then my phone buzzed. "David, Mr. Chyman would like to see you now in his office."

I sat there utterly bewildered. Then I heard my voice eek, "um, okay. I'll be right there." I got up and made my way to his office. It took three steps.

"You wanted to see me, sir?"

"Have a seat, David," he sat back in his chair. He went on to tell me all about the firm. I was busy looking at Avi. He was a short man, a very tan man and a man that wasn't the best shaver in the world. He had a little bit of stubble left on both cheeks. The few, odd strands looked like cat whiskers. I pictured Avi sipping milk from a bowl on his desk. Then I pictured myself rolling a ball of yarn under his desk and him batting it around with his pudgy, little hand-paws.

He droned on, nothing interesting. Then he tells me that he is going to need me to follow up on the cases that he doesn't have time for. I tell him that sounds great and he says, "I assume Ann has given you the files to peruse. (Oh, that's the moron's name - Ann.) Ehh, First thing is we are going to, eh, need to get back that $200 for Mr. Thomas. He left his wife's fur coat at, ehh, the fur, eh, vault. Now they are charging him, ehh, an extra two bills because he left it an extra week. You are going to write a letter. Got it?"

So I went back to my seat, started writing a letter, looked up some law regarding holding property in one of the 10 legal books he had in his legal "library" and, 15 minutes later, I was done. Avi's shades were drawn on our glass partition, so I couldn't interrupt this man's private time. Ann also made it clear that when the blinds were drawn Avi was not to be disturbed, so I spent the next hour staring into space as I waited for an opportunity to show the letter to Avi.

Finally, the blinds went up. Here was my chance. I knocked on the glass window to get Avi's attention, then asked if he had a minute. He walked over to my desk, and I handed him the letter. He took a minute to read it, hovering over me.

"How did you know how to do this?"

"What?"

"How did you know what to say in the letter? I mean, you say something here about a bailment," he pronounced bailment as if he had never heard of that word before.

"I don't know. I know how to write a letter."

"Yes, but how did you know what a *bailment* was?"

"Umm, I went to law school. You usually learn things like that there. Then I looked up the relevant law and put it in the letter."

"Relevant law? Where did you find that?"

"Umm, right here in the books behind you."

"How did you know how to do that?"

"I told you, I went to law school. You learn things like that. You're a lawyer, didn't you learn things like that in school?"

He looked at me, completely perplexed. He nervously

chuckled, "Of course. Yes, of course, I did. Very good." Then he ran into his office, closed the door and pulled down the blinds so I couldn't look in.

Holy shit.

CHAPTER SIX

The next day didn't start out any better. I arrived at the office at nine on the dot and was surprised to find the door open. Since I had already completed the letter yesterday, I wasn't quite sure what was on the agenda today. The secretary, who today was dressed in a purple sweater, black skirt and black stockings, was sitting at her desk. I was not actually convinced she was sitting at all. She was more like wedged between the wall and her green desk. How was this woman breathing? She looked like she was doing work, so I sauntered over to my desk, sipping coffee. Avi arrived near 10:00 a.m., made a beeline for his office, and closed the door. I had nothing to do but sit and stare at my computer, so I decided that I would start writing a movie script. I was ten pages into it by lunch time. I would have gotten more done, but there was constant buzzing between Avi's office and his secretary's desk. I spent a considerable amount of time trying to eavesdrop.

By the end of the day, I had completed thirty pages of my screenplay. At 5:00, on the nose, I headed home and wondered to myself what had just happened.

The next three days were exactly the same. Nothing changed, until Friday afternoon, when Avi had me make some photocopies. At five, I left. By 7:30 I was in my room talking to my friend, Jon.

"I can't believe your wedding is coming up. You're the first to get married. It's sick," Jon was getting married at the end of the week.

"I know. Sara is going nuts. We have the wedding this week and then we close on the house Tuesday," Jon was moving to the suburbs to be close to Sara's family.

"I'm living with my parents and you're getting a house with your wife! I can't believe I just said wife," I was jealous.

Jon had been working since we had graduated from college together. I guess I didn't really think that things would ever change. I thought that we would tackle each new life stage together, but that wasn't the case. He went right into a big accounting firm, moved into the city and met a wife, who happened to have gone to college with us. All of this occurred, in what seemed like a day, but it was really a span of three years ,while I was locked away in law school.

"Well, I like the city, but Sara's mom is out there and so is her brother. She's very family oriented." Jon sounded dejected, "It should be a good move."

Then my call waiting sounded, "Jon, hold on a second I have someone on the other line." I clicked over to the other call.

"Hi," there was a pause until the person recognized my voice. "This is Ann, from Mr. Chyman's office."

"Hi, what's up?"

"I'm afraid we have decided to let you go. Things just aren't working out. So we'll have your check sent to you."

"What's not working out?" I was shocked.

"Well, you don't seem to be working out," was the best she could come up with.

Come on, lady. Lie, for God's sake.

"So, you're telling me, I'm not working out. You don't find it odd that there is no work to do at your office and the lawyer that you work for doesn't know how to practice law? He didn't even know how to look up anything in his own books."

"David, I don't have to discuss this with you. Your check will be in the mail," then she hung up.

I clicked back over to Jon.

"Who was that?" he asked.

"It was the place where I worked. I just got fired on call waiting. I have to go."

That was the truth. I actually got canned while lying on my broken bed talking to my friend. And what about my screenplay? How the fuck was I going to get that back? All that hard work down the fucking drain. This was now becoming a sad pattern for me. Job number two had ended in a dismissal by a lawyer, who may or may not have had a license to practice. Wait, it wasn't even the lawyer himself who fired me. It was his secretary, which was even more humiliating.

"I knew it wouldn't last," the poster on my wall was getting lippy again.

"Fuck you," I was yelling at the wall.

I had to get a grip here.

Mental note: Rip down the goddamn music posters. They are not good for your sanity.

CHAPTER SEVEN

Most Freudians would trace all the problems in your life back to your days as a young lad. And maybe they are right. I've never been face up on the couch chatting away at a doctor, but when you examine the evidence at hand, they may be onto something. Perhaps the reason for my recent downfall stems from my lack of a pet in my childhood. Maybe I would have learned how to love, thereby keeping the good Chi in constant supply. I bet the Bow Wow, Ruff Ruff would have taught me a thing or two about the transference of love to another living being. Ever a Purr Purr, Meow Meow might have done the trick, but the baffling, muted silence of my parent's pet, a bird, didn't get you very far on the path to altruistic love. Our bird pet didn't do me any justice back then, and she was still screwing with my life.

Jon's wedding was approaching very quickly and I had run into another problem. I only had the one suit, and it wasn't going to suffice since the wedding was black tie. I was the only one going to this wedding that was dead broke, and the only one that was dateless. I didn't want to embarrass myself by bringing Lisa. She knew how pathetic I was, but she didn't need to see the details of this incipient fiasco first hand.

I walked downstairs. I found my mom sitting at the kitchen table eating a brownie and my dad sitting in front of the birdcage "whistling" to our bird, Misty. My blood immediately started to boil.

It is pretty much common knowledge that cockatiels are raised to speak. They learn to mimic the sounds that they hear around them. Some whistle Beethoven, some tell their owners how pretty they are, and then there are those few that never say one word. How this happens, and why, is a mystery. In my childhood house, the mystery was solved with one word - fear. Fear is what stifled the voice of the cockatiel known as Misty.

Misty never had a fighting chance. How could she? My mom would screech so loud that poor Misty ran to the back of her cage and sprouted goose, er, cockatiel, bumps. My dad would always try to calm Misty down, gently muttering to the bird, "It's okay, okay, birdie, birdie. It's okay, shhhhhhhhhhh." It was this contradiction between the screeching and the birdie 'shhhhhh' that marred my early years - and it was now what made my blood boil.

"It's okay. You okay, Birdie? Wheeeeeee Whooooo," every

day I hear this. Day in and day out. Part of the reason Misty never learned how to say anything stemmed from the disturbing fact that my dad didn't know how to whistle. He would stand in front of Misty's cage for hours on end, repeating over and over, like a mental patient, "Okay birdie. Wheeeee, Whooooo." The 'Wheeeee Whooooo' sound was my Dad attempting to whistle a two-tone call to Misty. One note up, one note down. Simple. All that came out, though, with my Father's lips pursed in whistle-like form, was that sound masquerading as a whistle. Wheeee Whoooo wasn't going to cut it.

I had always wanted to hang out with the bird, bond with the bird, maybe shoot the shit with the bird for a few hours, but it would just sit there freaked out by my Dad. All it managed to do was eat and crap all over the cage. This couldn't be a pet. I've seen pets before. Some of my friends had pets. They would throw Rover a stick and he would bring it back, or they would take Rover for walks and runs. I knew how it worked. Even the stupid cats did something.

Once, I decided to see if Misty could do some of the things Rover could do. I reached into the cage and grabbed a hold of her. I took her out, sat her on the ground, took a pencil, since a stick would be too big, and threw it.

"Go fetch, Misty, get the stick, girl." Misty didn't budge. "Go get the pencil, Misty!" I pleaded. Misty scrunched her face and sat there, mute. Maybe fetch wasn't for her.

I decided to take Misty for a walk instead. I looked around for some rope, but Misty was about the size of a glasses case, so a rope leash wouldn't work. I pulled out a long strand of dental floss, made a noose, and threw it over the bird's head. I picked her up and we went outside for a nice walk.

I put her down on the driveway and Misty started to really move. By move, I mean, she must have been pushing 1 to 2 centimeters an hour. That was good, right? Out of the corner of my eye, I noticed my neighbor, Jack, and Jack's mom, watching my bird show on the driveway. This definitely did not look very good to outside observers. I didn't want to be reported for bird abuse.

"Hey Jack," I said, waving. "Just taking the ol' bird out for a walk."

"Oh, OK," Jack said, shaking his head, bewildered. His mom just stared at me stone-faced.

We weren't really getting anywhere. Misty did occasionally

try to take off and fly, but, with clipped wings and a dental floss noose, she couldn't get very far. She did manage to bang her head a few times on the asphalt when she would get some air and come crashing back down.

After Misty banged her head a couple of times, I got nervous, and decided to call it a day. After all, we had given it the ol' college try. "We're going back inside now," I said to Jack, who was still watching, and motioned towards the house.

Both dejected, and Misty possibly brain damaged, we went back inside. I threw Misty back in her cage, then sat down in front of the television.

Moments later, my dad arrived home, "Hello, birdie. Wheeeee Whooooo – Wheeeee Whooooo."

You see? He didn't care if the bird did anything except sit on its perch. There was a man capable of love. He loved the bird even though he expressed it in tone-deaf, vocal spurts. Why couldn't I love Misty the same way?

My mom would sometimes pick Misty up, put her in her cupped hands and kiss the bird all over. Kiss the bird! As if this wasn't repulsive enough, she also wanted me to "give kisses" to

Misty. I couldn't do it. I wasn't kissing a bird that didn't talk, didn't fetch, and didn't go for walks.

"Meeep," some kind of weird sound came out of Misty.

"You see, she loves you, and wants kisses," said my mom, cooing lovingly at Misty.

Here was Mom's argument; if the bird was emitting anything remotely like a sound at you, it meant she loved you. Come on, mom, I would think to myself. Did you ever think the bird was just slow? Maybe the bird has to relieve itself? Maybe the bird wants to be set free? Did any of these reasons occur to you, mom?

"I'm not kissing the bird."

As I walked down the stairs - and heard my father talking to the bird for the ten-thousandth time in my life - my immediate reaction was to freak, but I regained my composure and tried to speak to them nicely and calmly. After all, I needed cash to rent a tux.

"Hey guys," I tried to keep it nice and light.

My mom was in her post-work outfit of a skirt and a frilly, button-down, white blouse. Dad had also changed, and now wore his 10 year-old polo shirt that he'd tucked very snugly into his jeans, with his belt cinched a notch too tightly around his waist. That shirt was not going to escape.

"Weeeeeee Whoooooo."

"I just got off the phone with Avi, and it seems we have a bit of a situation," I broached the subject lightly.

"Situation?" My mom said with a mouthful of brownie. "What kind of situation could there be on a Friday night at eight-thirty?"

"You hear this birdie, weeeeeee whoooooo, we have a situation, yes, we do." This grown man was actually talking baby talk to a bird.

"Dad, can you cut it with the bird?" I snapped.

"Oh, David, is that anyway to talk to your Dad?" Mom asked.

"Mom, why is Dad talking to the bird?" I asked.

"Why not? It's a living thing with feelings. You know you should talk to Misty every now and again. It wouldn't hurt. You know that ignoring her will hurt her feelings. Why don't you apologize to the bird for not talking to her? Give the bird some kisses."

"I'm not kissing the bird," I said.

"David, that is no way to act. Give the bird some kisses," she demanded.

"Mom, please, enough with the bird."

Then my Dad saved me.

"What's the situation?" he asked.

"Well, I was just informed that things weren't working out . . ."

"Weren't working out?! What's not working out?" My mom exploded.

"I don't know, she didn't give me an answer when I –"

"She? I thought you said you talked to Avi?" My dad said.

"Not exactly, it was the secretary that . . ."

"Oh, my God, the secretary! You mean you can't even get fired right?" My Mom screamed.

"Meep," Misty weighed in on the issue.

"You mean to tell me, the secretary called, and fired you on the phone?" Dad asked.

"Yes. That's what happened," I said.

"What kind of operation is this? Who hires someone, then

fires them that same week, and doesn't even have the decency to call themselves? What is with this guy? Isn't he a professional?" My dad was closely examining the situation.

"I really don't know. I'm very upset," I said.

My new strategy was to play the victim.

"Look, don't get yourself all upset," Mom said. "It's not your fault. This person doesn't know how to behave."

"I know, but I have Jon's wedding coming up this weekend. It's black tie, and I don't have any money to rent a tux. I don't know what to do."

I threw out the line hoping for a bite.

"I'll lend you the money for the tux," said my father. "You can't look like a fool at your friend's wedding, but you better take a good look around that wedding and do some serious thinking. Take a look at what grown-ups are like. Maybe you could learn to be a little bit more like your friend, Jon. He has his shit together. Maybe you'll learn something!" My dad put an exclamation point on the day.

"Thanks, Dad," I grovelled.

CHAPTER EIGHT

After begging and pleading, the tuxedo rental store finally found me a tux to rent on short notice. So, here I was, standing in line for some shrimp scampi during my favorite part of the wedding: the cocktail hour. There is always so much hope and promise outside the main dining hall while you are filling your mouth with delectable appetizers. You are free out here. Free to mingle with your friends, free to talk to anyone you please, and free from all the pitiful looks you get when you are sitting alone as the first slow song begins to play.

"I'll have some shrimp," I said.

I was safe here at the scampi station.

"I love shrimp," a woman behind me in line said, "especially shrimp scampi."

"Yeah, I love it too," I said, as the chef put some on my plate. "But the thing about it is, it gives me garlic breath all day."

"Who says that's a bad thing?" She asked.

"Well, most people don't want someone laying a big, fat smooch on them smelling like a pizza."

"I love it. The more garlic, the better, I always say."

"Well, one thing is for sure. You're definitely not a vampire. I'm pretty happy about that." I smiled.

"Don't be so sure. Maybe I'm an enlightened vampire," she said, with a wink. "Are you one of Sara's friends?"

"Actually, I am a friend of Jon's from college. My name is David," I turned around to introduce myself.

"I'm Erica," she said.

"Are you friends with Sara?" I asked.

"No, actually, I'm here with one of Sara's friends from elementary school."

"Really? Who?"

"Do you know Michael Kabe?"

"No."

"I didn't think so. He moved to Portland a few years ago. Sara still keeps in touch. I live here in New York, so Michael thought it would be easier for him if I could come to the wedding as his date."

Erica was beautiful. She had on a slinky black dress, a killer body and a touch of make up. She was naturally pretty, so she didn't need the typical cake-on job. She also wasn't in sequins, so that was a definite plus, as well. So, immediately, I was drawn to her. Her voice had a very feminine, sing-song tone that almost hypnotised me.

"Actually, here comes Mike," she pointed to Michael, who was walking over to the scampi station. Mike was dashing. He appeared to be everything that I was not. For starters, he had a full head of straight hair that was perfectly combed. He looked like a male model in his tux, where as I looked like his sidekick, Boo-Boo. He also looked successful. I didn't stand a fucking chance.

We were introduced, and I excused myself to go eat my shrimp in misery. Erica was amazing. I wanted to get to know her better. She had a sense of humor and was very attractive - and I'm not going to lie, I needed to get laid as well. It has been a while. My parent's house isn't exactly a swinging bachelor pad. If only Mike wasn't in the picture. Although, maybe they weren't a couple. But who brings a friend to a wedding, especially if you are traveling such a long way to attend it? A lot of people. They are probably a couple. And a good looking one, too. Anyway, she was much too pretty for me. I'm broke, dateless and jobless. What the fuck would she want with me?

I was looking for Dan and Pete when I ran into the bride. I always feel awkward in these situations. You know it is the bride's big day and she is ecstatic about everything, but, for me, it is just one more wedding in the endless parade of weddings that I have attended this year. At each wedding, I feel like I'm just another ingredient in the mix, ready to be shaped by the cookie-cutter festivities that are about to commence.

"Hi, Sara," I hugged her.

"David, I am so happy you made it," Sara said.

"Sara, you look beautiful. Everything was perfect. This is such a lovely party." I had the script down pat.

"Thank you so much. You know, I have a little surprise for you at the table. I don't want to tell you now, but you'll thank me later."

Sara loved surprises. The last surprise she sprung on me in college left me with half a sorority throwing dagger stares at me every time I walked into the campus center. Sara and I were at a party during college, and she introduced me to her friend, Kim. We were both very drunk and, well, one thing led to another and we hooked up. After that night, Kim was convinced we were boyfriend and girlfriend. Apparently, in Kim's case, not calling and ignoring a person obviously translates to dating. Who knew getting a little tit could lead to such disaster? Here's the tip that I gave Kim: Just because we hooked up doesn't mean I'm your boyfriend. Oddly, that didn't go over too well, and Sara's entire sorority would stare me down for the next three months every time I had a cup of soup and half of a sandwich in the campus center.

Thank God, Kim's not here.

"I can't wait," I mumbled.

"Anyway, David, I am so glad you are here. I have to go find Jon now. We have pictures to take before we head into the hall." She gave me two air kisses and dashed off.

Hiding behind Sara, about ten paces away, were Dan and Pete. They came running up as soon as she left.

"I don't know what to say to these brides after I see them, even if it's Sara," Dan said.

"I already gave her the prepared speech," Pete followed up.

"Well, that's the same speech I just gave her, and it's the same one your fiancé is going to hear in a couple of weeks," I said to

Pete.

"At least change it up a little. She's heard me use it at least five times," Pete said.

"But, when you are the bride, you think it's special," I said.

As we were chatting, we were joined by Amy, Peter's finance, and Dan's new girlfriend, Tammy. I had become the fifth wheel.

"Hey, Amy and Tammy. How are you guys doing?" I asked.

"Good, thanks. So, did you bring someone? Peter said you might," Amy said.

"I decided not to. I just wanted to have fun tonight hanging out with you guys, you know? Not spend the night entertaining someone," I said, taking yet another sip of my gin and tonic. My hope was that I could drink myself into oblivion by the next question.

"Why didn't you bring Lisa?" Dan asked.

"She doesn't really know you guys, and I just wanted to hang out. She gets all weird at weddings," I said.

What they did not need to know is that I was scared to bring her. I took her to a wedding about a year ago at a yacht club, where she proceeded to get downright sloppy. She was falling all over the place, slurring nonsense at people, until she capped the night off with a striptease act by the marina that concluded with some solo skinny-dipping in front of the entire wedding party. Needless to say, I didn't need a repeat performance.

"How's the job hunt?" Dan asked.

"Bad. Very bad. I've been fired twice."

"Twice?"

"Yeah, once on the phone. I'm never going to get the fuck out of my parent's house."

"At least you can crash with us if you ever make it into the city for a weekend? Where have you been?"

"Dude, I'm broke. I can't even buy myself a ticket into the city let alone go out."

"You need a job," Pete said.

"Fuck," I sighed.

Just then, the lights started flickering and the doors to the banquet hall opened.

"Looks like it's time to make our way in," Tammy said.

Here's where it gets scary.

"What table are we?" Dan asked.

"Fourteen," I said, assuming I was sitting with the fortunate couples.

When we walked into the hall it was everything you would imagine a wedding would be if you bankrupted your father-in-law. There were three hundred people at this wedding. That means there were thirty tables each adorned with elaborate floral arrangements that must have cost $1,000 each. There was a purple hue to the room from mood lighting, I guess. I have no idea how they do this shit. There was a ten-piece band playing jazz as we walked in. At least, the music was amazing.

After about ten minutes of funneling through this hall, we made our way over to table 14. All the couples grabbed their chairs, leaving three seats free. These must be for the only three singles in the place, I thought. At least I was facing the dance floor. So, I would have a good view people-watching while I sat by myself. I sat down, and to my surprise, Erica and Mike joined us.

"Is this table 14?" Erica said.

"You've come to the right place," I answered.

"Well, isn't this funny?" she said, "I didn't realize we would be at the same table."

"Well, that's the magic of weddings, I guess."

"Nothing wrong with a little magic," Erica said, then introduced herself around the table. She then proceeded to sit down right next to me.

"So, are you the surprise Sara was telling me about?" Erica asked.

"I thought you were," I said.

"I'll tell you what, I am surprised about one thing. How handsome you are," Erica said.

"Thanks. You should have seen some of my former surprises," I said, and we laughed for a second. Then I continued, "Before I get too excited, what about you and Mike?"

"You really don't know Mike, do you? Mike's gay," she said, "He isn't seeing anyone seriously right now, so he thought it was easier to just bring a girl instead of bringing a guy."

"Well, I've never been happier to hear someone was gay," I started, "I mean, I'm glad –"

"I'm glad, too," she said, and patted my knee in a definite I-like-you sort of way.

Was this really happening? I hoped so. I liked her. I mean what was not to like. She was beautiful, fun and she appeared to be into me. Now, I'm not the most intuitive guy in the world, but if I didn't know any better, I would say that Erica and I would make a great couple.

Erica told me about the trials and tribulations of being a single girl living in the City. The bad dates, the bad job (she was working at a fashion magazine as an assistant, which translated to: she got her boss a lot of coffee). Then we danced. Let me be clear. I don't dance. But, with Erica leading, I felt like Ginger Rogers. No, I'm not interested in dating Mike. And having a woman lead does not make you gay. After all, a guy can be led sometimes, right? My penis usually does the leading, but, in this case, I let Erica take over, and it was fantastic. At least until I accidentally body checked Sara's grandmother to the ground during one of those line dances. I told you I wasn't a strong dancer.

The family came running and surrounded poor grandma. No one wants to get a broken hip at a wedding. Sara looked at me like I had committed mass murder, and the rest of the family was mortified. I tried to run, but Erica grabbed my arm and kept me on the dance floor.

Turns out, Sara's grandmother has quite a tolerance for physical abuse. She jumped back up like it was nothing, and even gave me a quick shout out, "It's going to take more than this twerp to kill me."

That night I went to sleep happy for the first time in months. I couldn't believe how lucky I had been in meeting Erica. For once, Sara had actually surprised me with something very special. Maybe it was a little wedding magic at work or maybe it was just dumb luck. It didn't really matter. I had a feeling this one was forever.

CHAPTER NINE

When I woke up the next morning at eleven - this was still morning in my world - I was inspired. I couldn't believe the fortune that had been bestowed upon me the night before. I reached for my notebook, which I keep next to my bed, and jotted down yesterday's date. This was the day that I had met the girl of my dreams.

I called Lisa at work.

"Hobart and Klein, this is Lisa speaking."

"Hey, its me," I said.

"How did you know I was here? It's Sunday."

"Exactly, it's Sunday. That's how I knew you were there."

"I'm ready to kill myself. This is the ninth weekend in a row that I've been here. I hate this job."

"Just tell them you're not coming in," I said.

"Yeah, right. It doesn't work that way David. I'm trying to get out of my parent's house."

"Good woman. Hard work. I like it. Keep plugging away there, killer," I said.

"Don't be an asshole," Lisa said.

"I've got myself a new girlfriend," I said.

"What? When did that happen?"

"Well, it didn't quite happen yet, but it's going to. I met this amazing girl last night at Jon's wedding."

"Jon got married? Who did you go with?"

"No one. Anyway. She was –"

"You didn't go with anyone, and you didn't invite me! I can't believe it. You're still mad about the yacht club thing, aren't you?"

"C'mon, don't be silly," I said.

"You are. I told you gin doesn't agree with me, and that bartender was making me gin and tonics, instead of vodka tonics." This was Lisa's sad defense.

"They don't really taste the same, but that's not the point. I don't care. Listen, I believe you. Come on. Let me tell you this news," I pleaded.

"Okay, go ahead," She said, shame in her voice.

"Anyway, she's amazing. I know we met only yesterday, but I can tell. This is something special, and I know she going to feel the same way.

"You sound a little bit like a stalker."

"Oh, shut up. It was magic. I don't know how it happened, but it did. I'm calling her later tonight to ask her out. I can't wait to see her," I was gushing.

"I've never seen you like this. I'm happy for you and – what's her name again?"

"Erica."

"Erica what?"

"Erica . . . hmmmm . . . I don't actually know her last name. I'll ask her later tonight. Who cares? At least I can find her. She gave me her number."

"A woman gave *you* her number? Things really are looking up," Lisa said. "On a different note, I have some more good news for you. While you were gallivanting about at Jon's wedding, I was stepping up to bat for you at work. After countless hours of groveling and promises that I will never be able to keep, I managed to get you a job at Hobart. All you have to do is show up for the interview, and the job is yours! We're going to be working together! Can you believe that? I can't wait. You will show up for the interview, won't you?"

"Really?! I don't know what to say. Actually I do, thank you. Thank you! Yes, of course, I'll show up for the interview. I don't care how corporate it is, or how many commuters I will have to stomach, as long as I can get out of this house."

"Well, my friend, looks like you and I aren't long for this town. We better start looking for apartments - they're hard to get."

"New York City, here we come!"

PART II: Five Years Later

CHAPTER TEN

It's hard working shit out on an air mattress. After careful consideration, I have come to the conclusion that my prior work experience did not lead to any sort of bad Chi. On the other hand, it did lead to excruciating embarrassment. Usually, that's what happens when you are escorted out of your office in front of your friends and colleagues. It's not that I did anything wrong, or so I was told. It was the simple fact that we didn't have the best financial quarter at the firm and they had to downsize. In other words, I was fired. In British lingo, "made redundant." At least the British have a nicer way of saying you were canned.

I was led downstairs to the front door escorted by Timothy McNaughten and Michael Cogden, the co-heads of the crack security staff at Hobart and Klein. After five years it had come down to this. When I got downstairs my desk was packed up in a box and waiting for me right by the door. My secretary must have done the honors, packing everything, while I was meeting with HR on the fifth floor. Very sneaky.

That wasn't even the worst of it. Three days earlier, I had lost my illegally subletted apartment when the owner decided to divorce his Italian wife and move back to the United States. Lisa had warned me about subletting, but it seemed like a great deal at the time. I had been paying close to nothing for a one-bedroom with a water view for the last five years. I was even going to transfer the apartment into my own name this month. I had even started the paperwork.

I was now thirty, bald, unemployed, and living with my younger sister, in her five hundred square-foot, studio apartment. Erica, my once girlfriend, was also gone, but she was kind enough to leave me with some words to chew on.

"What kind of loser loses his job and their apartment in the same week, and then chooses to move in with his sister and sleep on an air mattress? I'll tell you, a pathetic one. You are a pathetic loser." Erica always knew how to make me feel better about everything.

There was some truth in Erica's parting words. I was running pretty close to the line of being a loser. Jon, for one, was already married with a kid, living in his own house on Long Island. I was the same age, but living at my sister's. Things weren't adding up. I was also shaving my head now because it was starting to look a little weird, with an island patch surrounded by a sea of baldness, on the top. I had long since moved beyond the "finger lakes" of patchy hair that had once covered my head. It looked like the cards were stacked against me. Basically, I was back to square one. On the bright side, I was lucky enough to lose everything just after Michelle had made it out of my parents' house and into her own apartment. Otherwise, I'd be ready to kill myself even more that I now wanted to if I had to move back in with mom and dad.

Erica leaving me after five years wasn't the most shocking thing in the world, even though it hurt. We were so right for each other in so many ways, but it had become apparent that we were very wrong in so many more. Erica would tell me all the time that she wanted me to be rich, that she wanted someone who would be a successful professional. When everything came crashing down on me, she left. Her instinctual drive for a successful doctor or lawyer kicked in. Erica wasn't like most women, she was what one would classify as a "Pink Piggy."

Since Erica was now gone, I was free to find a new piggy for my very own, one that would last forever. You see, I wasn't going to just settle for any New York City Woman. Oh, no, I was in search of the elusive Pink Piggy.

There are a lot of piggies running around New York City, but nothing stirs the emotions quite like that solitary moment when your eye drifts across the traffic-infested avenue and you catch a glimpse of the Pink Piggy. Well, you may ask, what does a Pink Piggy look like? This answer won't offer much of a definitive description. The Pink Piggy comes in all different shapes, colors, races, and heights. Why, I saw one the other day, who was just shy of five feet tall, decked out in a snazzy, pink raincoat, her reconstructed nose sticking in the air sniffing for a man. The reconstructed nose is easy to spot. It's looks perfect, almost too perfect. The nostrils flair a bit more than normal, though. That's the tell. I've seen plenty of them. Piggies in my neighborhood usually received their brand new nose around their 16th birthday. Sort of a Sweet 16 present.

My latest Pink Piggy sighting was on the hunt. I could tell. She wasn't wearing a wedding ring. Piggies without rings are kind of like humans without water. You need the ring for survival. A Pink Piggy running around without a ring was sacrilege. They need at least a two-carat, cushion-cut ring in order to survive. So, any Piggy without one is looking for a man.

I was so distracted by this Piggy as she walked towards me, her head at a 45-degree angle between the sky and Fifth Avenue, that, as she passed, I found myself gawking. This one was quite confident for a non-married Piggy. I'm usually a big fan of the Pink Piggy, but the way this one had strutted past me seemed a bit hostile. The weird part was I found myself strangely attracted to this hostile piggy. I wanted to run after her, stop her and introduce myself, which on Fifth Avenue would not go over very well at all, but my senses got the better of me and I just watched that little piggy get away. All you can do is wave goodbye at that point as you continue to walk, rather quickly, away.

"Goodbye, Piggy."

Two traits most - and I stress the word *most* - Pink Piggies share is their love of themselves - their hair, their reconstructed noses, their mani-pedis, their clothes, their shoes - and the color pink. They love dressing up like little Easter bunnies year round. The most bizarre part of the equation is they don't realize they are one step away from being placed in a basket with some eggs.

I admit, there is something strange about Pink Piggies. And, maybe they're an acquired taste. You could be at a bar, minding your own business, when a Pink Piggy comes busting through the crowd, snorting and laughing, bumping and spilling, all along her path. She'll glance at you and your friends, then turn and take a sip out of her Cosmo glass filled with Cosmopolitan feed. This is usually a sign that the PP is on the hunt for a man. Piggies like to drink. They've seen it on TV. Cosmopolitans out with your friends equals fun times and meeting guys. So, too, does dressing up in ridiculously expensive clothing and wearing beautiful shoes on your Piggy feet as long as they cost more than $500. This is the fun Pink Piggy.

Alternatively, you could be at the local frozen-yogurt shop, minding your own business, waiting in line to get your large yogurt, when the PP starts screaming at the poor Indian behind the counter.

"I said a large vanilla, VAH-NILLA, not chocolate with sprinkles," the PP will bark, exasperated. "I mean, how many times a week do I come in here and order the same thing? What are you, retarded or something? God!"

It is this exact situation when you have to try to handle the encounter with the poise of a seasoned hunter. Let me explain. The PP gets very edgy around feeding time. Oh, the PP isn't like you or me, she isn't going to have a normal dinner tonight. She subsists on a diet of frozen yogurt. For most people, this just would not suffice. I, for one, would be passed out, starving, if this was all that I ate every day, but not the PP. In fact, she thrives on this lack of human food.

It seems that the frozen consistency of the yogurt allows piggies to keep their nasty edge. That and starvation - I mean, how many calories can that yogurt really have? Just the anticipation of feeding time gives them the *chutzpah* to verbally berate these poor frozen yogurt workers. Now, of course, if she had a normal lunch she would have probably left out the whole "retard" comment. I mean that was uncalled for, right? But, it is this edge that makes the Pink Piggy attractive, it is also this edge that makes the Piggy a little scary. I don't need Piggy kicking that sort of mud in my face. I usually just stand back and admire this not-so-fun Pink Piggy from afar.

The PP is a very interesting creature. What I really would like to do is shoot one Pink Piggy in the neck using a tranquilizer gun, approach slowly as the tranquilizer works its magic, and then, after she is out cold, tag her with a homing device so I can track the Piggy when she returns to the wild. You only have a few minutes after the tranquilizer wears off until she regains her senses, so I would have to act fast because if the PP wakes up in the middle of a tagging the results could be deadly. I'm pretty confident that a PP does not want to be shot in the neck. That kind of blatant disregard for the Piggy's looks would certainly send the Piggy into a rage. After all, a dart to the neck might leave a scar!

Pink Piggies seem to always find themselves men to date. It's quite a remarkable thing. I have a theory that the Pink Piggy is akin to one of those special pigs that can sniff out truffles from under the earth. If you threw a leash on the PP, and walked it around the city, it would sniff out just the right man for her. I think the PP emits some kind of high-pitched "sue-eeee," similar to the sound one of Homer's sirens would use to lure sailors to their ultimate demise below the rocky cliffs. Thankfully, only some men fall under this spell. The result is usually a marriage that leads them to Long Island, where they will spend the rest of their days in suburban hell. Or to divorce court, where the PP will rake the man over the coals on her way to finding a new man, leaving her discarded husband to ponder what the hell happened as he's lying on his air mattress.

Up to this point I thought I had avoided the Pink Piggy. But

Erica, in the end, was my first taste of the species. I am ready to find my new Pink Piggy, the Piggy that will make me happy, the Piggy that will make all my dreams come true. God, I hate New York.

I was a man of action. I had decided that fact just a minute ago. Meeting a woman at a bar wasn't going to happen. I'll tell you what else wasn't going to happen, meeting a woman through JewDater. What was wrong with my sister?

Michelle had since moved on, from her early online dating days, and was now pursuing JewDater, the online Jewish dating network. I would sit and watch her click through the thousands of men looking for Jewish love over one of the most disturbing inventions ever placed into the public domain. There are thousands of people in New York on this abomination posting pictures and filling out bios hoping to meet Mr. or Mrs. Jewish Wet Dream. Unfortunately, Michelle hasn't found the Jew of her dreams yet. But man, she keeps looking. Oy vey.

I had a better idea. I would just call my friends and have one of their wives set me up. It was the only civilized way.

"Jon, it's David." He was my best shot.

"What's up?" Jon said.

"I need to get set up. Tell Sara to run through her group of friends and find someone perfect for me." I told you I was a man of action.

"Dave, I hate to break it to you, but you live with your sister. How exactly are you going to do this?" He had a valid point.

"Why are you getting caught up in the details? We'll go to dinner or something, if things move along, we'll go back to her place." Ha!

"Dude, you're unemployed. How are you going to pay?"

"You're joking, right? I'll put it on a credit card. Anyway what do you care? Just get your wife to set me up with someone."

"All right, all right. Relax, I'll talk to her tonight."

"Thanks." Mission accomplished.

"Anyway, what else is going on?" Jon said, trying to continue this conversation.

"Dude, just talk to Sara, I have to go. Later."

I was all over this. I now had Jon working on the case. It was just a matter of time before I was off to the races.

Later that night, I was awakened by the sound of a vacuum in my face. I opened my eyes. My sister was pushing the vacuum into the air mattress, then away. Into the air mattress, and then away.

"What the fuck are you doing?" I yelled at Michelle from the floor.

"Cleaning. Someone has to clean this apartment." She was vacuuming in small circles around the couch and myself, which were the only two pieces of furniture in the place.

"I know, but it's . . . what time is it? Oh, God. Three in the morning? Can't we clean this tomorrow?" Was she kidding? Who in their right mind cleans at three a.m.?

"It's very dusty. I'm cleaning now. You can go back to sleep if you want."

"Is that window cleaner I see over there by the couch?"

"I just finished the windows. Take a look, no streaks."

"Michelle, I can't see any streaks. It is the middle of the night. It's pitch black outside."

"I assure you there are no streaks." She was serious.

"I'm sure there aren't any. Don't you have to work tomorrow?"

"I'll be fine. Go back to sleep. I won't use the vacuum anymore."

"You are insane," I didn't know what to say.

Michelle turned off the vacuum, "Nighty, night."

She moved on to dusting. I listened to her softly whistling for fifteen interminable minutes and then I must have passed out.

CHAPTER ELEVEN

After I, The Prince, awoke at noon, I spent the next couple of hours writing, trying to relax a bit. I was getting pretty stressed out about not working. It wasn't that I didn't want a job, I had just come to the realization that it was time for a career change. It was time to follow my dreams - and that was writing. The problem was I didn't know how I could make any money at it. I wanted to write a novel - who didn't - but writing a novel on an air mattress was proving difficult. Besides, I should be out making money, not writing all day, especially while Michelle was slaving away at work.

My mom called, saving me from my pity party for one, "Yeah, so, what's going on?"

"Nothing, same old stuff," I said, getting up from the air mattress and moving onto the couch.

"Michelle is at work?" She asked.

"Of course, she is. You know she is. Where else could she be?" I snapped.

"I don't know. One day, you were at work, the next day, you weren't. I'm glad she's there," she said. "Anyway, I called to tell you Daddy has someone he wants you to talk to, so maybe you can get a little advice and straighten out your life."

"I'm straightening it. I don't want to talk to these people," I said, cringing at the idea of calling anyone my father thinks could help.

"What people?! Call Dad's lawyer friend. He said he would be willing to talk and see if he could help you. What do you have to lose? Give the man a call. Don't make me beg."

"Okay, I'll call the mystery man who should be able to help because he, like five thousand other people, is a lawyer. Who is the guy anyway?"

"Dad met him while he was getting the oil changed at the garage," said mom. She was serious.

"Dad tells everyone he meets my business?" I was horrified.

"Just call," she barked.

"Okay, okay. I'll call him in a few minutes," I said, purposely banging my head against the couch. Then I hung up.

I walked over to the bathroom to splash some water on my face. Why do they torture me? Why? I sat back down on my air mattress and found the piece of paper where I had written down this guy's name and number.

I dialed the number. Mr. Hofstein answered.

"Ken Hofstein," he said.

"Hi, Mr. Hofstein," I said. "My name is David Michaels. You met my father the other week and he said to give you a call."

"Yes, yes. Good to hear from you. So you want to be a lawyer, huh," he said.

"Actually, I am a lawyer," I said.

"Oh, I thought you wanted to be one. Anyway, what kind of law do you practice?" he asked.

"Well, I used to do compliance stuff, but then I was let go. I would really like to change over to something interesting like art law or entertainment," I said.

"Everybody wants to be an entertainment lawyer. It's hard to become one."

"Well, that's what I would like to do," I said.

"Let me give you a little advice here, son. You know what you should be?" Dramatic pause, "You should be a cop."

"Why? I'm a lawyer. I don't want to be a cop," I said.

"Mike, when you're a cop, you get a pension and you'll

always have food in your belly. Best thing you'll ever do with your life," he said.

What was with this guy and cops?

"My name is David. Why would I want to be a cop if I spent three years and all that money going to law school? I don't want to be a cop. That's just silly," I said.

"Well, that's my advice for you, Mike. I have to run. Best of luck to you."

That was the worst advice I had ever received. My plan of writing a novel was looking a whole hell of a lot better after talking to him.

I called my Mom back, "This guy told me to be a cop."

"What? A cop? I thought he was a lawyer," she said surprised.

"I don't know what he is. I couldn't believe what he was telling me."

"RICHARD!" my mother screamed in the background, "WHAT KIND OF FOOL DID YOU HAVE DAVID CALL? HE TOLD HIM TO BE A COP!"

"Mom –" I tried to break in.

"YOU AND THESE PEOPLE YOU MEET AT THESE STUPID GARAGES. YOU'RE A FOOL," she continued to scream.

"Mom, I'm going to go now." I slowly hung up the phone.

Before I knew it, Michelle was home.

"Hi, big Bro. Whazzz up?"

How could I possibly explain what had been going on? That I had decided writing a novel was my best bet, that I should be a cop, that I was having a nervous breakdown in this minute apartment. I would tend to think that most people, including my sister, would think all of that was a bit disturbing. So I told her, "Nothing really. You?"

Michelle hustled to the computer to see who emailed her on JewDater.

"Let's see who emailed me," she shouted.

This was my entertainment. I was forced to not only sleep on my sister's floor every night, but now I had to watch her sift through men. This was killing me.

Michelle and I were at the computer going over potential dates when Jon called. I hadn't even gotten the chance to make fun of anyone yet.

"You want to meet me at the diner? I have some time to kill. Sara has the baby at her sister's and won't be done for an hour or so. I can't stand that we have to take the train home together. We do everything together. Man!"

"Yeah, I'll meet you there in ten minutes."

Michelle and the rest of the New York, single, male Jews would have to wait.

I ran out of the apartment and walked the three blocks to the diner. You never know what you are going to see in New York when you're walking the streets. Today, on my walk over to meet Jon, I saw a couple fight right on the corner of my sister's apartment. It was great. I love watching other people fight, and this one had screaming, not just the usual stern talking by people with pursed faces that generally occurs in public. This was the "Fuck You Asshole!" and hands flying kind of fight. I lingered a few minutes to try to catch the gist of it, but this couple was wily. They kept walking and screaming. They were quickly out of range after a few minutes. Unfortunately, it wasn't the all-out brawl where the people are stopped dead in their tracks shrieking at each other.

When I arrived at the coffee shop Jon was already at a table, "Where the fuck were you?"

"I saw a couple fighting on the way here. I got a little distracted," I said.

"You want to see a fight? Just wait until Sara gets here. I hate waiting for her, she's such a pain in the ass. So what's up with you? How's the job hunt?"

"Not too good. Some guy just told me to be a cop," I confessed.

"A cop? What guy?"

"My mom had me call some lawyer, who my dad met, for advice on how to change my life, and he told me to be a cop. A fucking cop."

"Well, there's nothing wrong with being a cop. That's not a bad job."

"I'm a lawyer. I went to law school. If I had wanted to be a cop I would have been a bully in school and dropped out of college."

"Maybe you could be a detective or something?"

"Or maybe I could be a fireman or a doctor or an astronaut – Fuck!"

"What are you going to do?"

"I don't know. I guess check out the help wanted section of the paper again like I did when I was twenty-five. It's so pathetic. Can you believe this all hit at once? I mean Erica, the apartment, the job. Sick. I've been trying to figure it all out."

"And what did you come up with?"

"Not too much. I figure I must have done something wrong in the past, otherwise the bad Chi wouldn't have hit all at once. But then, I thought back, and couldn't come up with anything."

"Maybe it's just time for a change? I mean, you were with Erica for five years and you obviously weren't getting married. You were at your job for five years and it was the same old, same old, every day. But the apartment, ah, the apartment. That's the killer. That was one great place."

"Thanks. Aren't you trying to make me feel better? But you have had the same job and the same wife for the last five years. How come it isn't time for you to make a change?"

"Dude, look at my life. I want to change. I'm trapped. Let me fill you in on something. The trap is marriage. Don't do it. Because you know what happens if you do? The trap gets deeper and wider and then you can't get out. You see it in action. Look, now I have a kid, and one on the way. I love Sara and all, but, c'mon, man. Do you think I want to live like this forever? I'm cleaning up baby shit on a regular basis. This is your big chance. You have to live it for the rest of us. I'm going to talk to Sara again and get you laid."

"Yeah, but isn't there more to life then getting laid?"

"Listen to me here, Dave. You have to sleep with as many women as you can right now. Believe me. That will make you feel better. You also have to tell me about it. I have to live through you at this point. You're all I got, man. This is it. This is the big chance. Erica gave you a new lease on life. Don't blow it."

"Living on my sister's floor on an air mattress is a new lease on life?"

Jon's cell phone rang. "Yes. But I thought you said an hour – I'm sitting here with David . . . Okay, okay!" He turned to me obviously pissed, "I have to go. You see! Do you see? I'm trapped," his voice was shaking, like he was about to cry. "I don't know what happened to me. Fuck. I have to go or Sara is going to kill me. I'm a mere shell of the man I used to be. A shell." Jon picked up his laptop bag and ran out of the diner petrified with fear. This was certainly no way to live.

CHAPTER TWELVE

The next day I awoke with a new sense of purpose. I was going to be somebody. My talk with Jon really set me straight. I looked up from the air mattress and saw my sister all wrapped up in her twin comforter, sound asleep. Again, I realized I was sleeping on the floor. The good feeling quickly subsided.

Michelle got up around ten and hopped right on the old laptop. She wanted a desktop so she could see the guys better on JewDater, but there was nowhere to put it. As it was, I was occupying most of the available floor space. She even had to move a sad, little, cocktail table into the building's basement storage, so I could have somewhere to sleep.

"What are you doing up on the computer so early?" I asked.

Michelle was no computer wiz. She was nearly 28, and had only used a computer for the sole purpose of finding men to date. Her most recent accomplishment was her adaptation of primitive emailing skills. Michelle was now capable of two things, surfing for guys and sending email. That's what I call progress.

"I'm on JewDater. Looking for a hot man to go out with

tonight," she said in a bouncy tone. "You have to see JewYorker33. This guy is hot, and he says he's sarcastic. I love that in a guy."

I had to see this. "Yeah, he's good looking, I guess. Don't you think there is something wrong with guys that sign up for this thing? They've got to be a little socially off." I scanned the dude's bio. "Did you read what this guy has to say? He wrote 'I typically hang out downtown because if I go above 14th street I turn into a pumpkin.' Are you kidding me? A pumpkin? Holy crap." All I could do was laugh.

"We'll, I'm emailing him, to see if he wants to go out with me." I think she was really interested. "You know, you shouldn't laugh. I don't see you with anyone," Michelle added.

"I'm getting over Erica. I need time. Anyway, there are better ways to meet people. Why don't you meet someone the old fashioned way?"

Just then the phone rang.

"Are you up yet?" It was Jon. Isn't 10:30 a little early? "I've got good news for you. You're going out with Sara's friend, Nicole, tonight. How do you like that?!"

"What does she look like?" I mean, come on. I'm not

desperate here. I need to know these things.

"What does she look like?! She's pretty. What does it even matter? You wanted a date and now you have one."

He was right.

"But what does she look like?" Like I said, I'm not desperate. Well, maybe a little.

"Okay, let's see. She has blond hair and a cute body. Do you want her number or not?"

"All right. Give me the number. I'll give her a call."

"Now, if I give you the number you have to call her right now. She is expecting your call. If you don't call her Sara is going to kill me. You understand? You have to call her," Jon was laying it all on the line.

"Yeah, yeah, I'll call. Give me the number."

I arrived at Agean, a new Mediterranean fusion restaurant, at 9:00. It was dark, yet perfectly lit for all the wannabees that wanted to think they were eating in an important place. I knew the food was great here. It wasn't listed in any restaurant guide yet, but you couldn't get a reservation. Luckily, I knew the owner so I was able to get one at prime time. In New York City, you don't eat dinner out before nine, especially not on a first date. I waited by the bar, and ordered myself a G&T after I let the hostess know that I had arrived. I was staring at every blond that walked in, hoping that a good looking one named Nicole would walk right up to me. There goes a hot one. But she's with someone. Fuck. There's a cute one. She's walking this way. Then right past me and over to her boyfriend. I was slowly getting annoyed; every cute girl that walked in was with someone. I sucked down that G&T in under two minutes. I ordered another one and, as I was paying the bartender, I got a tap on the back.

"David?"

I nearly spilled the drink when I turned to view Nicole for the first time. This was not anything resembling anyone's definition of cute. This was cute if cute got kicked in the face by a mule after standing out in the rain for five hours. Her hair looked like plaited rope. Literally, rope. She had little, beady, brown eyes. And that wasn't even the worst part. As my eye continued to drift downward I saw a pouch. A pouch of stomach that looked like she was housing a Joey. Beady eyes, rope hair and a pouch?! That's quite a trifecta.

What the Fuck was Jon thinking? He'll pay for this. Oh, he'll pay.

My first drink was taking effect so, I figured, what the hell? How bad could dinner be? My understanding of what dinner should entail was pretty simple, some food, maybe some nice wine, and some pleasant conversation.

"Would you like some wine?" I asked.

I always like to start the dinner off with some wine, usually just to loosen up. In this case, I needed to drink myself into oblivion.

"I don't drink wine," she barked.

Oh, good. I ordered myself a bottle and started to get hammered.

"I love television. I mean, I love it. I have four TVs in my house."

Thrilling.

"You know, I love everything on TV, but I really love reality shows. They're so much fun to watch. I even tried out for a couple."

"Which shows?"

"Pretty much all of them."

"All of them?"

"Yeah, I figure if I get on one I'll be famous. And I'm pretty interesting, right? I mean, who wouldn't want to watch me on a show?"

Well, me for starters.

"You know the coolest part about being on a reality show? You learn so much about yourself. All the ups and downs. You can figure so many things out. I'll totally grow as a person."

"Maybe you should try therapy," I sarcastically suggested.

"Therapy? Isn't that for depressed people? No, I'll stick to TV, thank you very much."

I took a slug of wine. I wasn't bothering with sipping it at this point. As I was intoxicating myself, I was thinking that this woman could be the dumbest person that I have ever shared a meal with, or, for that matter, I have ever met. I looked over at the couple directly behind Nicole. They were sharing a bottle of wine. Yes, yes, that's normal. This is not normal. Not even close.

"Oh, you can learn a lot from television," she explained. "For example, I learned that chopping basil into little ribbons is called a chiffonid".

"You mean a chiffonade," I corrected her.

"Yes, a chiffonade. You're right. How did you know that?"

"I like to cook," I said.

"I know, but where did you learn that term?"

"I don't know. Probably on the cooking network."

"See we have something in common," she said.

"What? We both like to cook?"

"No, we both like television!"

This date was terrible. I choked down my dinner in record time and sat around waiting for Nicole to finish. I spent the next fifteen minutes just staring at this woman, watching her eat. She ordered a roasted leg of lamb, so I had to watch her navigate pulling the meat off of the bone with a knife and fork. It wasn't pretty. Her knife kept slipping off of the bone as she stabbed at this poor lamb leg. She seemed so hungry that I was convinced she was going to just pick up the leg and start gnawing on the bone. But, to her credit, she didn't. When she finally placed the knife and fork down on her plate, I was relieved. This nightmare was coming to an end.

By the grace of God, the waiter came over, "Can I get you two anything else?"

I was just watching Nicole in utter disbelief. She kind of

looked normal, despite the rope hair, her face and the pouch. She was dressed sort of normal. She had on cool jeans and a cute white top. She did take a page out of the Piggy playbook and was sporting some cute shoes. Nice move. She also had nice tits. I'll give her that. But even nice tits couldn't make up for the rest of this package.

"No just –" I couldn't get it out fast enough. All I wanted was the damn check and the chance to end this horror show.

"I would like some dessert," she demanded.

"Very well," said the waiter. "We have some desert specials. We have a heavenly tiramisu tonight, a lovely chocolate velvet cake-"

"We'll have the tiramisu, thanks," Nicole said.

"I'll bring two spoons," the waiter said.

Why? Why are we having desert? We were now sitting in silence waiting for our desert to arrive. I was on a mission to finish this bottle of wine. While I was sipping my fourth glass, I peered over at the table next to me. There was a cute girl, about twenty-five, sitting with her father. Well, I guess it was her father. Who knows in this fucked-up city. Anyway, she was cute. Why wasn't I dating someone like that? This father and daughter were talking, laughing, touching hands. For Christ's sake, these two are a couple. This old fuck is dating someone that I should be dating and I'm stuck here with Tiramisu. This is fucking evil.

The waiter promptly brought over the delectable dessert with two spoons. Piggy dug right in, and shoveled forkful after forkful into that mouth of hers. You know where that's going don't you? Right down into the pouch. I caught a glimpse of some tiramisu on her lip. I motioned with my hand to wipe off the crumb on the corner of her lip, but she wasn't paying attention. She just continued to shovel it in. I looked a little closer, angling the small candle to shed a little more light on the situation. What I saw unnerved me so much that I shot backwards in my chair almost falling over. I grabbed the table in a last ditched effort not to fall, shaking the table causing the silverware, china and glasses to rattle. It was loud. As I composed myself, the entire restaurant stopped for a second, turned to toward our table, collectively murmured, and then resumed eating. Even the cute twenty-five year-old dating the old fuck stopped to look. Nicole barely lifted her head from the desert plate, "You OK?"

Not really. I'm trapped here with you.

I stood up, repositioned my chair, and sat back down. Nicole didn't have tiramisu on her lip. No, no, no. She had some kind of mole that was sprouting hair dangerously close to the middle of her lip. I was completely freaked out.

"Check! Please!"

"Dude, what are you trying to do to me? What have I done to you? Did you ever see this woman, and I use the term 'woman' lightly?" I asked Jon the next morning.

"What do you mean?" He asked.

"What do I mean?! This girl has a pouch for starters. Jon, kangaroos have pouches, not women. That wasn't even the worst part. She has some nasty, hairy mole on her lip. That's it! You and Sara are never setting me up again. It was a complete nightmare."

"She told Sara she had a good time."

"Are you kidding me? All she told me was how much she loved television. It was completely fucked up."

"You have to call her and ask her out again."

"No! There is no way I'm ever calling that thing again."

"Sara's going to freak! You have to call her!"

Panic was setting in.

This guy had to get a grip. Nicole would never be receiving a call from me. What was his problem anyway? He needed to come back to reality. I can't believe he was so scared of his wife that he would even suggest that I call this monster.

"No way!"

"You have to."

"No way!"

"Please," Jon said.

In the background I heard Sara screaming at him to have me call Nicole. It was piercing.

"Do you hear that? She's going to kill me," he whispered.

Fuck.

I dialed Nicole and actually heard myself say through gritted teeth, "Hey, I had a good time the other night. Do you want to do it again sometime?"

Fuck you, Jon.

"I'm pretty busy this week and next week, so I'll take a rain check, okay?" Nicole said.

Was she blowing me off? I couldn't believe this.

"Okay. Bye."

Jon's a dead man.

CHAPTER THIRTEEN

I was somewhere around 65th Street when I caught a glimpse of a Pink Piggy in all her glory. I was walking south and she was walking north. She was the picture of beauty. Head held high, nose nicely reshaped, walking as if she owned the joint, and yes, of course, dressed in a pink jacket with blue jeans. "Wait, Pink Piggy!" I screamed. I had to meet this girl. I started to run down Third Avenue, trying to cross. She turned on 64th and disappeared by the time I got to the other side. These piggies are wily. Where did you go, piggy, where did you go?

I decided to continue downtown to meet Lisa for a drink this fine afternoon. Lisa had graciously agreed to take a very long lunch. Surely, there would be some other Pink Piggies out for a good time, even if it were the middle of the day. We found this great place downtown that offered dollar drafts and two-dollar mixed drinks. The bar was a bit of a dive. Maybe it was the biker decor and the actual bikers that frequented the joint, but what did it really matter? I was quickly becoming white trash, anyway. Living on pre-taxed unemployment benefits of $405 a week puts everything into perspective real fast.

I walked in and grabbed a seat at the bar. "What's up, Nance?" I asked the bartender. I've gotten to know Nance pretty well since Lisa and I began frequenting this joint at least once a week. Nance isn't bad on the eyes, either - in a trashy sort of a way. She's always in a black tank top and jeans. She's got dirty blond hair and a great body, but she's got a sleeve of tattoos down her left arm. The jury is still out on how I feel about the tats. It's definitely sleazy, but I think I might be into it.

"Not much," answered Nance. "What can I get you?"

"I'll have a beer until my friend gets here."

"Meeting Lisa again? How come you don't go out with her? You guys seem like you get along so well," she placed the beer in front of me.

"We're just friends. I wouldn't want to spoil our friendship," I said.

"That's nice of you. But take it from me, sometimes girls want a chance to spoil things," she winked.

Lisa walked in the door.

"What's up, Lisa?" I asked.

"Nada. I can't believe how long it takes me to get from 57th and Park to down here. It's unbelievable. I can't stand the fucking subway. We stopped for fifteen minutes for no reason."

"Do you want a drink?" I asked her.

"After that trip, hell yes! I'll have a Cosmopolitan" I know, possible Pink Piggy scenario. But don't worry, Lisa's not a Pink Piggy. She just frugal. The Cosmos are $2 down here, so why not?

Nance walked over after a few minutes to take our drink orders. "Hi, Lisa."

"Hey, Nance. I'll have a gin and tonic," Lisa said. She had changed her mind.

"A woman after my own heart," Nance said, as she reached for the gin.

"I thought you don't drink gin since the wedding incident," I said.

"Well, guess what? I do now. It agrees with me," Lisa said, taking a sip.

"Well, well, well, looks like you've come a long way from stripping in public," I said.

"It really was the gin, David. But now I can handle it," Lisa claimed.

"Hey, if you want to drink gin, be my guest. I won't bring it up again. But promise me there won't be any stripping today," I said.

"You are such a goddamn wise-ass."

"I know. I can't help it. You bring it out in me."

Lisa rested her chin on her hand and fluttered her eyelids at me. "So, what's up, sweetie?" She said.

That was her new thing now. She used the word 'sweetie.' I don't know when it started creeping into her vocabulary, but I do know where she got it. Lisa lives with what I can only describe as a "special" girl. Her roommate is a party promoter, who throws parties that no one attends. She has a mix of ADD, general confusion about life and a nightmare habit of talking to you with her eyes darting everywhere around the room except where you are standing. I'm always thinking to myself who are you waiting for to walk in? She also claims to be some kind of star. She once actually said to me, "Sweetie, you don't realize it, but I am very visible. People know me and expect to see me" Oh, yeah? Who?

She was dating this guy, who lived in Philadelphia. He was forty-five, fully mustached like a Seventies porn star, gold chains hanging out of his shirt, and hair so thin that it looked like an old robin's nest. She, on the other hand, was thirty-five, gaunt, very dumb, and desperately looking to get married. She actually met this guy on JewDater. The first time I saw him I asked her if she saw a picture of him before they met.

"Sweetie, of course, I did," she told me.

Hey, looks aren't everything. I was even beginning to learn that lesson. So maybe I was missing it, maybe his personality was what it was all about. Well, that's what I thought until these words came out of his mouth the first time we were introduced:

"So, Boss, how the fuck are ya?"

Not too good, Chief. I had a problem with people addressing me as, chief, boss, slick, haus, my man, friend, jefe, etc.

"Ain't this chick just fucking great?" That was his second line.

You get the point. And now, for some reason, Lisa felt the need to mimic her roommate using the word "sweetie" every chance she had.

"Nothing, still looking for a job, apartment, and a girlfriend. I actually went out on a date the other night with this girl Jon set me up with."

"So, how was it?" She said, leaning in. She loved the romance stories.

"It was definitely interesting. Let's put it this way, the girl had a mole on her mouth that seemed to increase in size as the light got brighter, and it actually started to grow hair right before my eyes." I was actually sickened retelling this story.

"Are you going to see her again?" Lisa said, taking a swig of her G&T.

What? Did she hear me? My eyes drifted over to Nance. She was bending over grabbing a beer out of a bucket of ice behind the bar. She has a nice ass.

"No, she had a hair-sprouting mole."

"Disgusting. Doesn't sound like a good catch," Lisa finally admitted.

"You have to help me. Don't you have any friends to set me up with?"

"You had your chance, but you didn't want to date Stephanie, you wanted to stay with Erica. Look where that got you."

She did want to set me up with Stephanie, but I was way too

into Erica for that. I was an idiot.

"I know, I know. But is there anyone else?"

"Nope, they all got married and moved out of the city," Lisa said.

Everyone was moving out of the city. That was the new thing. You get married, move to Great Neck, Long Island, or some other suburb, get pregnant, and get a house. All of this before you turned 30. But shit, I was 30, and so was Lisa, and both of us were getting smashed in the middle of the day at a dive bar.

"Did you try JewDater? I've been on it for a month, and went out with some very nice Jewish boys."

Fuck.

"No, I didn't try it. Michelle also loves JewDater. I just thought since she liked shopping for shoes she might as well shop for men," I said.

I looked over at Nance serving a biker a drink. She was cute. Now, a few drinks in, I was beginning to really like the ink. Jewish girls aren't that into tats. Maybe that's because every Jewish mother tells their children that if they get a tattoo they can never be buried in a Jewish cemetery. Nothing like a little Jewish guilt and fear to stifle any creativity one might have. I was pretty sure that I'd never find a girl like her on JewDater, but maybe that's the kind of girl that I wanted. Maybe I'm just drunk.

"You have to try it. Just go to JewDater and fill out the biography. You'll see, you'll meet plenty of women," Lisa said confidently.

CHAPTER FOURTEEN

I arrived home before Michelle and went onto the JewDater website thoroughly intoxicated. In fact, I was shaking as I typed the address into the browser. This is what it had come down to, huh? I hit the 'new user' button and began one of the most degrading experiences of my life. Step one: create a user name. How about 'NYCMediocrity?' That's eye-catching. I filled out the basic info, and then came these questions:

Ethnicity?

I had a choice: Ashkenazi, Mixed, Sephardic - I'll tell you later. Do you think I know what I am? My parents pulled me out of a religious Hebrew school when I was six because they thought I was becoming brainwashed. I'll chose: I'll tell you later. Which translates to: I have no fucking idea.

Religious background?

All the choices were there, Orthodox, Modern Orthodox, Conservative, Reform, Hassidic, Unaffiliated. As if those weren't enough there were another five choices that I didn't even understand. Where was the dysfunctional guilt choice? That is what I practiced. I have a hard time remembering there are holidays until my mom calls me up on the phone and guilts me into coming home so I can sit at the table and get harassed about my life. 'Will tell you later' seems like the best choice.

I keep Kosher? I go to Synagogue?

What the fuck is up with this dating service?

Then came the essay about myself. Here was my chance to really shine. I was born the son of a toothless sharecropper. I walked to school uphill both ways. I finally settled down in New York City to seek my fortune, instead I lost my hair, my job, my apartment, and my last girlfriend. Despite this tragic twist of fate, I believe I can find love. Where? I don't know, but I'll find it.

The person I would like to meet?

Help! Please, help me. Look at this situation. I live at my sister's apartment on an air mattress. If you have a real bed, then you are someone I would like to meet.

My ideal relationship?

My ideal relationship would be someone who will have sex with me on a regular basis and let me sleep in their real bed. If you have an air mattress this will lead to immediate rejection.

Your idea of a perfect date?

A perfect date would be me deflating my air mattress, meeting you at an inexpensive restaurant for some interesting conversation and, hopefully, some therapy for myself.

What I've learned from past relationships?

Don't lose your hair, job, and apartment in the same two-week period. It's not good for any relationship.

I didn't even finish typing out half of my new JewDater biography when I got a phone call from Jon and an instant message from CityChick34.

"Jon, hold on a second. Someone is instant messaging me," I said, and looked at the little box that popped up on my screen.

CityChick34: Hi

NYCMediocrity: I'm on the phone. Give me a minute

CityChick34: I like your name. Mine is City Chick.

NYCMediocrity: I didn't hang up yet. I'm still on the phone.

CityChick34: Damn! You're worse than a girl!

NYCMediocrity: I just got the call when you IM'd me.

CityChick34: What do you do?

CityChick34: What do you look like?

CityChick34: Do you live in the city?

CityChick34: Why aren't you answering me?

CityChick34: Do you want to grab something to eat for dinner?

At this point I had to evaluate the situation. Reality would dictate that this might be the only response I would receive. The problem was, based on my bio that clearly states that I have no job, hair, or apartment, she wanted to talk to me. I feared that this could be desperation at its worst. I hadn't even finished with my answers yet. Wouldn't she want to wait to see what foods I liked or what I liked to read? Maybe I shouldn't be hasty.

NYCMediocrity: I have to pass. I'm not that hungry.

CityChick34: Oh, I see how it is. Lead a girl on then just slap her in the face.

NYCMediocrity: I wasn't even talking to you. I'm on the phone.

CityChick34: Look asshole, I don't need your sympathy or your excuses. Why don't you go fuck yourself!

NYCMediocrity: Nice talking to you CityChick.

CityChick34: Die!

Well, this was starting out really well. Dejected, I hung up on Jon, closed the instant message window and crawled back into my hole to finish my bio.

Michelle walked in and saw me sitting at the computer.

"Ha! Ha! Who's the loser now?" She was hysterical.

I caved. I knew I did, but what choice did I have? Apparently, I had no game. I think that was pretty evident. I was a bumbling jackass. Let's face it, I couldn't even seal the deal two minutes ago. Nothing was working. I was now being forced into the fun and exciting world of online dating - and I was failing at it. But after filling out that form I had to re-think what I was getting myself into. Who bothers to ask what sect of Judaism you practice? And Keeping Kosher? I should run. How did dating become a job search? It's like you walk up to the manager behind the counter and ask for an application, fill it out, interview a little, and wait for the call-back. I have a graduate degree! Why am I filling out life applications? I have become 'that guy.' I shouldn't get excited here. Calm down. Calm down. I should embrace this moment. The moment I took my pride and self-respect, spit on it, threw it in the gutter, and then stomped on it repeatedly just for good measure. Calm down, my ass!

Now came the piece d'resistance. I was going to post my glorious picture on the website. If I was going to do this (and since I had already taken twenty minutes filling out the biography), I was going to do this right. Come, Piggies, come to Papi!

"Michelle, how long does it take until women start talking to me?" I was curious.

"You know you can contact them, right?" Michelle said from the bathroom.

Hmm, I could contact them. That was still hard for me to get used to, but it was like an epiphany. Yes, yes, I could contact them, couldn't I? Mental note: do not, I repeat, do not use cheesy pickup lines in email or instant messages.

"Just go to 'change your search' and fill in what you are looking for," Michelle was a JewDater genius.

So I went. Let's see here. Age: blank to blank.

I've always liked younger girls, oh excuse me, *ladies*. So let's say age 18 to, hmmm . . . I don't know. Lately I've been fantasizing about older woman, like 45. You know, some divorcee who wants to have a good time, but doesn't want a relationship. She would invite me over to her Park Avenue apartment, feed me glass after glass of wine, get me sufficiently drunk, and then take full advantage of me. 45! 45! I quickly typed that in.

I ended up searching for a woman between 18 and 45, any marital status, any education, unaffiliated with any particular sect, any ethnicity, who goes to synagogue, always, sometimes, or never, and doesn't keep kosher. Of course, she can drink and/or smoke. I hit the search key and - like the plagues from the sky - a list of fifty women appeared out of nowhere, with photos.

Up and down, I searched for the right Piggy to induct me into the mysterious world of the JewDater. Then I was floored. There she was. There was a real life Pink Piggy right there on the screen. My heart went aflutter and I didn't know what to do. PrettynPnk4821 - it was like music to my ears. And it was true. She was dressed in pink, right there in the left hand corner of my screen. She had it all right down to the rebuilt nose and the flaring nostrils. Could this be real? I read her bio, intrigued.

About Me: My profession does not allow for me to meet many people. This will hopefully be a great opportunity to do just that. I look forward to seeing where this may lead me.

She has a profession. I really don't have a profession. I don't see this as being a problem.

Perfect Match: I am interested in a man who is kind and loving to all. He should have a big heart and be socially aware. He should be motivated and driven. He should smile a lot and laugh with me.

Hmm. Did you hear the one about the loser on JewDater? She'll love that one.

Ideal Relationship: There is an understood balance between myself and my partner. Things are 50/50. We never stop learning from each other. If we aren't looking in each other's eyes, we are on the floor, hysterically laughing.

50/50, huh?

Perfect First Date: We meet for a glass of wine, which turns into two or three more, because the conversation is just flowing and we are already enjoying each other.

I like to drink.

Learned from past relationships: Don't hold things in if they are bothering you because the anger will build and continually resurface.

This meant sharing feelings. Hmm, I'd have to think about

that one.

After careful review, I realized that we both really didn't have too much in common, therefore, it should work perfectly. All I had to do was send her an email. Type something a little catchy to PrettynPnk4821. That shouldn't be very hard. Should it?

I got really nervous. Panic was setting in fast. What if PrettynPnk4821 didn't write back? Could I handle being rejected online? I felt like I was back in high school. My hands were clamming up and I was slipping deeper and deeper into a state where I would bail on this idea completely. I had to act - after all, this was just email. My voice couldn't crack on email. Email is light and breezy. IM on the other hand could get nasty. Breezy, that was the key.

Try this Breeziness on for size PrettynPnk4821:

PrettynPnk4821,

I sat at the computer for fifteen minutes and this was all I could come up with. Think, man, think.

PrettynPnk4821,

If you were a letter in the alphabet I'd put U and I together!

P.S. I like wine too

I liked that. It was fun and breezy. WAIT! WAIT JUST ONE MINUTE! This wasn't going to work. I can't use some line. I have to write something interesting, engaging and breezy. This was not, I repeat, NOT breezy. Wow, this is hard. Okay, okay, let's try this one on for size, Ms. PrettynPnk4821.

PrettynPnk4821,

I liked your bio. Just wanted to say hi. P.S. I like wine too.

-NYCMediocrity

I could deal with this. It was light and breezy. I hit the send key and waited. It didn't take very long until I got this response:

NYCMediocrity,

Do you really live with your Sister on an air mattress at 30??? That's really sad! You sound funny, if you want give me a call at 212.543.9876.

- PrettynPnk

Sure she was mocking me and thinks I'm a pretty sad individual. But I was in the game. It was time to bag this piggy.

Pink,

Yes I live with my Sister. And the air mattress is quite comfortable. I'll give you a call in a few.

-NYCMediocrity

I gave Pink a call and we decided to meet for drinks the next day. It turns out she works with kids and adults suffering from strokes. She teaches them how to speak properly. And as luck would have it tomorrow would be her day off. I lied - I told her, it was my day off as well. My first JewDater date was just hours away.

CHAPTER FIFTEEN

We met at Front Porch at two. Piggy was waiting for me at an outdoor heated table under an umbrella, already working on her first beer. 'Under an umbrella' was a Pink Piggy's favorite place to park themselves. They could sit for hours, usually with other Pink Piggers, human-watching, searching for a man. You can sometimes hear the snorting when a cute guy walks by, but, usually, it's just them commenting on another woman. They use their time penned under an umbrella to check out other Pink Piggies. Pink Piggies are always comparing themselves to other women. Sometimes, they are so engrossed in the hunt for similarly dressed piggies that they actually eat something. The fare of choice is usually some kind of pub food, like nachos. These are the "rule breaker" piggies. They know they shouldn't be eating until their yogurt dinner, but they can't hold out. They scarf it down in record time to avoid any pink-piggy, friend backlash that may occur if they are spotted by another from the drift of swine.

After I examined the situation, and determined that this blond-haired Piggy in her snazzy, pink, velour jumpsuit was a nonhostile piggy, I strolled over and introduced myself.

"Piggy?" I asked, dressed in my finest ratty t-shirt and jeans.

Piggy looked at me, confused. "David?" She said, "Nice to meet you." She got up and gave me a kiss on the cheek.

I sat down, and we exchanged some general information. Then the date took a turn for the worse when we started playing 'Jewish Geography.' For all of those not familiar with the game let me fill you in. The rules are simple. You randomly call out the names of high school friends, college roommates, fellow summer campers, folks who grew up in your hometown or state, who might know the other person.

"You said you went to CAT U, right?" See how she was teeing that ball right up.

"Yeah, I did."

"Oh, do you know Jon Carrol? He was in Alpha Sigma Zed."

When it came to names at my college there was almost certainly a fraternity or sorority attached to the end of it.

"Was he my year?" This is where it all goes downhill.

"Well, let me see. Either he is your year, or two or three years older than you," she said.

Sixteen thousand people went to CAT U. Unfolding before your eyes, is the stupidity of this game.

The sun was shining in my eyes, so I was forced to squint. Fuck, I didn't need a headache today. I turned my head a bit to avoid the sun.

"Yeah, I probably don't know him," I said, quickly losing patience.

"You have to. He was really cute. ASZ, all the girls loved him."

"It's not ringing any bells." Please just stop.

"He was so cute. I fooled around with him once when I visited Catskill my freshman year. He was hot."

I don't care. Why would she tell me that? What she really wanted to say was, "Hey faggot, I like to hump real men, guys that were in fraternities, not guys who live at their sister's apartment on air mattresses."

I had to get off this subject. Usual custom provides for the person to volley back with a possible common link for the other person to ponder. I couldn't handle it, plus the sun was really in my eyes.

"Do you mind if I move my chair?"

"Sure," Piggy said.

It was a sunny day and unseasonably warm. I was actually getting a little hot under the heat lamp. I shifted my seat a little more and was now staring out at the avenue. I saw a tall girl walking down the avenue in a cool jacket and knit dress that stopped at the top of her knees (you could see a bit of the dress peeking out from under her coat) with thigh-high boots on and a gigantic bag that looked like it probably cost $6,000. Jesus, she was hot. Showing a little skin in the middle of winter. Bold! Then I looked at Piggy, the sun no longer an issue. She was cute, too. She wasn't quite the model that I just saw, but, hey, I am sitting here with a Piggy. One in the hand is worth . . . well, you know.

"So, you work with people learning to speak again?"

"I work with people who need help learning how to speak again because they were in an accident, or had a stroke, or have some serious medical condition," she said.

"That's funny. I had a teacher once, Mr. Comstock, who had Bells Palsy. He would always get water on his shirt when he tried to get the water from the water fountain in that unfrozen hole left in his mouth. Do you help people like that?"

"Was that supposed to be a joke? That's not very funny. But yes, I would help people like that."

"He was a dick, though," I added.

The waitress stopped by and asked if we needed any more drinks. We both passed.

"What is wrong with you?" Piggy said in an uppity, piggy pitch. The voice goes up at the tail end of each word. This is the first sign that a piggy is about to turn violent. I had to soothe the piggy.

"I'm just kidding. Well, sort of. I mean I think he is a prick, but I hope his palsy went away by now." Dude, I was blowing it.

"Look, let's just end this charade. I think you have a lot of problems and you are probably an idiot, but this is my day off and I don't have that much time to date. I'm pretty sure you aren't going to kill me, so if you want to come back to my apartment we can sleep together. I need to relieve some stress, anyway."

Did I hear that right? We can go back to her apartment and have sex. This was like a dream come true. Score one for the piggy hunter.

"Yeah, yeah, let's go back to your apartment," I was like a

ten year old and the ice cream truck was heading down my street.

Yeah, ice cream!

CHAPTER SIXTEEN

The rest of the day was magical. We connected in a way that I didn't know was possible. I knew Piggy despised me. That was pretty obvious from our "date." But when we got to her apartment the sparks started flying. Before we even had a chance to sit on the couch Piggy attacked. We made out for ten minutes and the next thing I knew we were in bed for the next three hours. Physically, everything was working. This was the best sex either of us had ever had. If only we didn't have to talk to each other.

I'm chalking this up to physical attraction. There was nothing else it could be. Piggy did have an awesome body. Although I couldn't quite tell how awesome it was at Front Porch with her all covered up in winter clothes. But, when I got her naked, her body was even better than it looked in clothes. I mean what red blooded male is going to turn down nice full tits and a tight ass? In addition, making out doesn't require any talking, and that was a good thing. I mean, the conversation at Front Porch was fine, but the sex was definitely better. It was so good that I needed to make Piggy sex a regular thing. Plus, it got me into Piggy's much roomier apartment and into a real bed, if only for a little while.

I started seeing Piggy about twice a week, strictly at night. We would never go to dinner, we would never grab a drink together, and we would never talk. The rules were pretty simple. Piggy would call when she had some time, and I would go over to her apartment, open the door, rip her clothes off and we would make love for about an hour or so. After we were finished, I would throw on my clothes and hit the road. This went on for a month. In short, I was a booty call.

One night that all changed. We had just finished having sex and I was taking my ten-minute breather. Piggy had allotted me ten minutes to hang out before I had to leave. Who was I to argue? Ten minutes in a bed, just lounging, was heaven when you regularly sleep on an air mattress. I was lying down in the bed catching my breath, when Piggy caught me by surprise, "Can you come with me to a Christmas party?"

Piggy was inviting me to a Christmas party? Surely this must be some kind of joke. Was this Piggy getting involved?

"When is the party?" I figured it was some sort of work party.

"On Christmas Eve," Piggy did have a persuasive way of saying things. I was a bit shocked, but I figured, what the hell? I wasn't going to be doing anything.

"I guess. What kind of Christmas party is it?" I was curious.

"Just a regular kind of Christmas party. It's out of the city, so I'll have to rent a car. We have to stay over as well, so pack a change of clothes."

With the holidays just a couple of weeks away I was looking forward to being able to partake in some festivities. That's what I was beginning to miss most about not having a job - the holiday office party. A free night out with the people you work with. The camaraderie, the drinking, the hope that someone will do something totally embarrassing. This party was going to be great. I'd get to meet other women, get trashed, make an ass out of myself and then have sex in the hotel room with Piggy. JewDater, why did I ever doubt you?

Piggy pulled up in front of Michelle's building in her rented car. Bobby, the building doorman, rang me up, "Mr. David, your ride is here."

Excellent. I gathered my bag and told Michelle to enjoy her free night.

"What do you think I'm going to do here?" she asked.

I was going to party my ass off. She'd probably watch television and pass out by 10. There's nothing to do anyway. Everything is closed! If she was smart she would hit the Matzah Ball, the big Jewish party that always takes place on Christmas Eve, usually Downtown at some club. She'd probably meet an eligible, single Jewish guy there, but I doubt that is happening. Meeting someone in person? No way, that's way too traditional for my sister. I'm sure she'll revert to JewDater at some point. Anyway, I'm sure it will be blowing up tonight with other bored Jews. Who's up for some exciting Jewish chat over instant messenger? Ugh.

We were on the road for an hour, or so, on our way to the suburbs. We were killing time chatting, a rare activity for us. Piggy was telling me about her clients. One dude was learning how to pronounce the 'TH' sound. Another was learning how to swallow. I never want to work in a hospital. What a fucking drag. I don't think I have the patience to work with these people. How the fuck did she do this every day? She must be a caring person. I, apparently, was heartless. We finally pulled off the highway, and turned into a residential area. Four-bedroom colonials everywhere. We pulled into the driveway of a house. Piggy killed the engine.

"We're here," she unbuckled her seat-belt and threw open the door of the car, "Come on."

"Where are we?" I asked.

Some work person's house?

We were at the front door, bags in hand, when Piggy says, "This is my parent's house. Oh, and one more thing, you're my boyfriend."

"What!?"

Ding, dong.

The door opened, and 'Merry Christmases' started flying. There were two people standing in front of me dressed in red cardigans. Turns out they were Piggy's parents.

"Is this him?" Her mother was asking. She had a reindeer embroidered in her cardigan. And were those snowman earrings? Holy mother of God. Who were these people?

"Looks like a fine, young lad," said dad, sticking out his hand. "Pleased to meet you, son. Come on in."

"He is a adorable," cooed her mother, then she put her hand to her mouth and whispered to Piggy, while pointing to her head, "but a little light on top."

We got five steps in the house when Piggy's 96 year-old aunt exclaimed, "Happy Birthday, Baby Jesus! I am just tickled you two are here to help us celebrate the birth of our Lord and savior. Praise his name!"

I stood there in utter confusion mumbling back to these people 'Merry Christmas' and 'Praise Him,' sometimes even throwing in a 'Hallelujah' - just to be safe. I got introduced to 30 Born-Again Christians, each very excited about the birth of the Lord. My head was spinning. I wasn't sure if it was from the shock of the situation or from all the green and red playing tricks on my eyes.

Of course, they had a Christmas tree. It was in the corner of the 100 square-foot living room that somehow managed to fit all thirty of us. I've seen one of those on TV but never in real life. There was an actual star on top. I discovered that people really do that. And there were ornaments on the tree. Interesting. Where were the stockings? I scanned the room . . . and there they were, right where they should be, lined up on the fireplace mantle. This really looked like a Norman Rockwell painting. I do not belong in one of those paintings. I walked over to the tree to get a better view. Yes, different types of ornaments. There was a snowman, reindeer, a manger, stars, balls, etc.

"I bought that for my mom when I was seven," Piggy said pointing to the ornament in the shape of a deer. "She loves deer."

I guess that's how it works. You buy ornaments for parents?

"This one is from my Nana," she held up a baby Jesus ornament in Mary's arms.

I was wrong. Your parents and grandparents can buy ornaments for their children, too.

Suddenly, Joshuah, Piggy's insane uncle, accosted me. He shoved some creamy, vile drink in my hand. I took a sip. This must be eggnog. Piggy walked over to her Aunt.

"Is this eggnog?" I asked.

"Of course it is, spiked eggnog, with a touch of nutmeg," Uncle Joshuah said to me, winking.

Nutmeg, of course. That is what tastes like shit. At least this vile concoction had alcohol in it.

"So you own a house there, Dave?"

"I live in the city." I left out the part about my sister.

"Well, one thing you have to know about your house is the windows. One piece of advice for you, get storm windows. They're not that bad to put in yourself, although you don't look like much of a carpenter, like our savior, Jesus Christ, so just hire someone to do it for you there, kid. But go get yourself some quality-grade windows, you won't be sorry, and I'll tell you why-."

"I don't have a house, but thanks for the advice, I guess."

Get me out of here.

"But when you do, son. Treat yourself. Don't skimp on the windows."

This man kept droning on about construction. Do you know how much experience I have with building things? None. I once heard a snippet of a home improvement television show, and I think that was ten years ago, only because my Dad had it on. Why he was watching it was beyond me. The man couldn't fix himself a drink, let alone install storm windows.

Piggy re-appeared.

"Uncle Josh, are you talking about windows again? David

doesn't even own a house. He lives with his sister on an air mattress," Piggy offered.

Jesus Christ, she didn't say that, did she?

"What is he? Some kind of pervert?" Uncle Josh asked.

"Jesus Christ," I blurted it out. I couldn't hold it in.

"Son, you just took the Lord's name in vain." Gasps filled the room. "We don't take the Lord's name in vain in this house."

"I'm sorry, I just got a little carried away," I didn't know what the fuck to say.

"What kind of Christian are you?" Uncle Josh was pissed.

"The Jewish kind," I said.

Apparently, Piggy left out this detail.

"Jewish?" Uncle Josh went from pissed to completely confused.

"We'll be right back," Piggy frantically pulled me outside, "What the fuck are you doing?"

"What am I doing? Are you kidding me? First you lie to me about going to some party. Then you take me to your parent's house for Christmas Eve, where apparently the entire family is now gathered. Plus, you failed to mention that you were a Born Again.

Apparently, you didn't think I needed to hear that Good News. And, if that is not enough, I have to pretend I'm your boyfriend, oh, but not just any boyfriend, your Christian boyfriend! So don't talk ask me what I am doing!" I went crazy.

She started crying.

"I know. I am a terrible person. I am sorry for everything. It's just that my parents want to make sure that I'm taken care of, and you are so nice and kind that I started telling them you were my boyfriend to get them off my back. But the more I lied about it, the more I started falling for you. I kept our relationship at arm's length because I didn't want to get close to you. I'm sorry I didn't tell you about any of this. I couldn't."

"So you lied about everything, including being Jewish? Why?" I asked.

"I really like Jewish guys. I knew I could find one on JewDater. And I did. I can't help it if I'm attracted to balding, thirty-something, Jewish guys. I do wish I picked one with a job, though."

"I can't believe what I'm hearing here. You are standing here telling me you lied about everything and then you are insulting me! You have to take me home. I can't be here."

"You can't! You have to stay! Please! I'll do anything."

Whoa! Really? I switched gears. "Anything, eh? One, I don't want to talk to Uncle Josh anymore. That guy scares me. Two, I'm not pretending to be Born Again. Three, I want to have a lot of loving tonight. Four, when we get back to the City we are going to date like normal people. Agreed?" I was laying the law down.

"Date like normal people. I think I would like that," she smiled. We went back inside and braved the holiday, this time together.

The next morning, when we woke up, we all ran downstairs to see what Santa had left for us. Piggy was now in girlfriend mode, hugging and squeezing me like a little kid as she opened up her presents. Her parents were okay with the fact that I was Jewish, and that their daughter had lied to them. After all, this was Christmas, and they jumped right into the Christmas spirit. As Piggy was opening up her presents I surveyed the scene, and thought to myself, 'What was a nice Jewish boy doing opening up presents on Christmas?' I mean, I was a nice Jewish boy from a nice Jewish town. I never even saw Christmas lights on a house until I was in college. And here I was, running down the stairs to see what Santa had left for me under the tree. I hoped it was a job. I knew that I had been good all year. I mean, I went to synagogue on Yom Kippur to repent for my whole year of sins. I hoped that Santa cross-references the Book of Life to make sure he didn't leave anyone off his list.

When all the Christmas songs faded, I came away with a new outlook on Piggy. I actually enjoyed spending the holiday with her. I was looking forward to the times we would have together back in the City.

CHAPTER SEVENTEEN

We returned to the city the next day. Piggy dropped me off at Michelle's apartment, gave me a kiss on the cheek, and waved goodbye. I waited for a couple of days for the booty call, but it never came. In fact, I never saw Piggy again. Who knows why? She certainly didn't give me any explanation. But, I learned a long time ago not to question these sort of things. I knew myself too well. When I wasn't into someone anymore, I just stopped calling. No need for confrontations. They can get ugly. Avoidance was the best medicine. Unfortunately, this medicine being dished out to me tasted pretty shitty.

Luckily, I had a party to go to at Jon's house in a few days. The Jon and Sara Annual New Year's Eve Bash. Days earlier, I had actually considered bringing Piggy to this party, but now those hopes were shattered. I would have to ring in the New Year with the couples. The thought of it sent shivers down my spine. It didn't bother me that all my friends were married and living outside the city. In fact, I kind of liked it. I was able to go out with anyone I wanted, I had the freedom to do what I wanted, and there was no one in the city to judge me - especially not the wives. What scared me most about this party was the fact that it was going to be all couples. Everyone would look at me and comment, "Who's the single guy? Can we set him up with someone? It must be sad to be single on New Year's Eve when you're that old." Fuck.

Everyone was going to be there. Jon and Sara, of course, Peter and Amy, Matthew and Jen, Dan and Tammy. This was my college group. I had left the high school group behind a long time ago. At least 30 more couples would also be in attendance, all ready to ring in the New Year. Last New Year's Eve, I was a couple. Now I was entering into the lion's den, flying solo. All I kept thinking was: this is a bad move.

The Jon and Sara Annual New Year's Eve Bash always started out with drinks. After all, it's New Year's Eve. Guests would imbibe drinks that were way too strong for them and subsequently get hammered while Jon and Sara fixed dinner. For some reason, Jon and Sara loved fixing a seven-course feast. They loved the preparation, the cooking, and I think even the cleaning. But that was before the kids came. Since Jon and Sara moved out to their new house on Long Island, the cocktail hour was now catered and a bartender fixed your drinks. Jon had a bar built in his house - for entertaining, of course. That's why Sara allowed it to be built. If it were there just for fun . . . I think you know where this is going: no bar.

Ten o'clock would usher in the inevitable dinner. Each person would be assigned a seat that was indicated on a handcrafted place-card that one received upon entering the party. Last year, the place-card was a picture of their two year-old. Apparently, this is what Sara spent her time doing, as she no longer worked. The two year-old was cared for by a nanny, which left Sara with plenty of time to plan. I wondered what this year's place-card would be. By 11:30, the party would actually be in full-blown shindig mode, the obligatory kisses at midnight, and then the party would slowly dwindle by 2 a.m.

This New Year's Eve, I arrived at Jon and Sara's at four in the afternoon. I was completely bored at my sister's, and I needed to get at least an hour jump on the drinking if I was going to have any shot at making it through the night. I brought a bottle of wine and handed it off to Sara as she opened the door, "David, what a surprise, you're here early."

"Yeah, well, I was a bit bored at my sister's."

"Thanks. Can you be a dear and bring that over to the bartender?" She asked, handing me the wine back and pointing to this year's bartender. "Oh, I almost forgot, here's your place-card. This year's theme is revenge." She handed me a nine of clubs that had my picture in the place of Jamal Mustafa Abdallah Sultan Al-Tikriti, the Deputy Head of Tribal Affairs Office, from one of the Iraqi most-wanted cards. "You're the nine of clubs. Wait till you see who the 10 of clubs is sitting next to you at dinner."

"I can't wait." I needed a drink.

This house was huge. The entire downstairs appeared completely open. It must have been some sort of architectural trick. It looked like a kick-ass loft, but it was really a house. There were marble floors and two circular staircases at either end of the house. There was a formal living room and multiple, additional sitting areas lined with couches and plush chairs, Jon's built-in bar in one corner of the downstairs, and a dining area with a table that could seat at least fifty. Even with this gigantic table it looked like there was plenty of room left for the wait staff to serve dinner.

The cool thing about this house was you could see into nearly every area at once. In fact, you could see the gourmet kitchen from the living room, sitting areas and from the dining room. It was crazy. I walked over to the bar. The bartender was setting up shop. I bellied up to the brand new cherry-wood bar and handed over my bottle of wine to the barkeep. "I've got this bottle of wine for you."

"Thanks." I sensed he was less than thrilled about my wine offering.

"I'll have a G&T." My standard.

"Getting an early jump on the night?" he asked, as he mixed.

"Might as well. I don't really have anything better to do and, believe me, I need a drink. So, how come you're bartending instead of ringing in the New Year?" I asked.

"I need the money. I've been unemployed for the past ten months. My unemployment just ran out." Sucker.

"I'm unemployed, too. Actually, I kind of dig it."

"You must be in the honeymoon period. I loved it, too, the first month. I was able to finally take a break from work for the first time in over three years. I was psyched." I suspected a 'but' was coming.

"Three years? What the hell did you do?"

"I was an investment banker. I even have an MBA. Now I'm tending bar. The fucked up thing is I kind of like just being a bartender. It's therapeutic."

"Shit! I'm a lawyer. I used to work at an investment bank, too. Let me run something by you. I was thinking about writing a book instead of getting a job. You know - follow my dream. I just don't think I can go back and work in a cubicle. It will kill me."

"I guess that's okay. Only problem is making money. I wanted to write movies, but here I am - bartending - because I need the cash. I wish I were stuck in a cubical."

"I guess the next stop for me is bartending," I said, feeling suddenly depressed.

"If you're lucky. I had to interview for this job four times. It was harder than getting my job at the bank. I took $250 out of my $405 a week and went to bartending school."

"Holy Shit!" I said, baffled.

Sara walked over and pulled me away into the living room. I could see chefs in their white hats way off in the kitchen busily preparing the night's feast. I liked the layout of this house and I liked that chefs were working out the menu. Dinner was going to be good.

"Now you chit chat with the help? What the hell has happened to you?" Snooty Sara asked.

"Did you know that your bartender has a MBA, and was an investment banker? It's sick!" I still couldn't believe it.

"Forget about that. Who cares? I have a surprise for you tonight - you want to guess what it is?" Sara asked.

Ladies and gentlemen, playful Sara, ready to wreak havoc on my life.

"Did you get me a job?" I was terrified to hear the real answer.

"Better. It's so exciting. I want to tell you, but I'm going to wait."

Goody Gumdrops. I can't hardly wait.

Sara scampered off - probably to yell at the chefs. "You'll see," she called back to me, giggling to herself.

"Jon!" I yelled, walking back to the bar to have the bartender fix me another G&T. "Jon!"

Jon suddenly appeared. "Dude, relax. What's with the yelling?"

"Your wife, that's what's with the yelling. She just told me she has some sort of surprise brewing for me. That makes me very nervous. What the hell is it?"

"I have no idea. She won't tell me, either. Believe me, I begged her to tell me, but she won't budge. It can't be that bad."

"Or that good."

"Dude, relax and have a few drinks. Everyone will be here soon," Jon ordered a G&T for himself, drained it in thirty seconds and declared, "God, I hate throwing these things."

People started to filter in around 5 o'clock, bearing alcoholic offerings to Jon and Sara. I sat at the bar and continued to get sufficiently trashed. Peter, Matt, and Dan finally all arrived with their wives in tow. It didn't take very long for us to meet at the bar.

"Michaels, what is the deal?" Peter asked.

"Deal with what?"

"Dude, you've been living on Michelle's air mat for the past three months, you pretty much disappeared for the last month, and we haven't heard a peep about any girl since you and Erica split up. What the hell have you been up to?" Fair question.

I told them the story about Piggy, conveniently leaving out

the parts where I met her on JewDater, that I was her bitch, and then was dumped by her. I happen to like my new version much better. In my new version, I met "Alison," the 21 year-old with a tongue ring, at a club one night. We were immediately into each other, so we went back to her place to fool around. After that, we started seeing each other. Of course, I would sleep at her place. No one even got to the end of the story, they all stopped at the '21 part,' and gasped.

"No fucking way," Peter said.

"That had to be amazing. I wish I fooled around with a girl with a tongue ring. Somehow we missed all that piercing and shit. We were born too early. Today all these girls have tongue rings and eyebrow rings, tattoos and have threesomes. God damn it! I want to have a threesome with a tongue-ring girl," Matt said, trashed.

I went on to explain that we saw each other for a couple of months. I would call her when I wanted some sex, go over to her apartment, and get some. Eventually, I told them, I got sick of her and the tongue ring, so I called it off.

"What the fuck is wrong with you? You were with a 21 year-old, who liked you, no less, and then you dumped her?! Are you out of your fucking mind?" Peter was pissed.

"You must be," Dan added, bewildered.

"It just wasn't right," I said in my defense.

"Wasn't right? Wasn't right! Take a look over there at Tammy. I'm married to a woman who doesn't bother closing the door to the bathroom when she takes a shit, has gained thirty pounds, and hasn't given me a blowjob in the last three years. Wasn't right! You better start making it right and start giving out some details," Dan yelled, fully inebriated.

"I'm telling you. You would have done the same thing. It just wasn't right," I was pleading my case.

"Oh, my God, he's gone mental," Matt exclaimed. "Buddy, get a grip."

We went on joking around for an hour or so, wife-free. But, of course, all good things must come to an end.

Tammy was the first wife to mosey our way, "I couldn't take it over there anymore. Those women are nuts."

Tammy was the one wife I could handle being around.

"All they talked about were manicures. Manicures! For an hour and a half! It didn't matter how much I drank at that point, I just couldn't sit there anymore."

Dan and Tammy were the last couple to hold out and live in the city. They were married about a year ago and were still fun to hang with. The others usually went home around 10, claiming that they had a long drive ahead of them. Yikes! My dad would say that exact same thing when we were at my grandmother's house. My friends really were becoming like my dad.

Dan and Tammy moved out of the city three months after they were married. After all, Peter and Matt were already living in houses. Dan and Tammy couldn't just sit idly by and let other people pass them on the social ladder.

"Hi, David. So, what's going on?" Tammy asked.

"Nothing much. Just looking for a job and stuff," I said, not bothering with details.

"Any girlfriend yet?" They loved that question.

I said with a sad face, "Not yet. I was seeing a girl, but we just couldn't quite connect. I need the connection," I said.

"Oh, that's too bad. I'll keep my eyes open for you."

I feigned some sort of excitement, and thought, 'Wow, that's just super, Tammy!'

"Please do," I said.

I saw the other wives making their way over to the bar. I couldn't have this conversation two more times. I got up and walked around a little. The three strong G&T's were settling in quite nicely. I knew about half of the people here. Everyone was accompanied by their significant other. I could get used to living out here in the suburbs, I thought. Especially if this was my house. Maybe all these couples were onto something. You get the car, the property, the peace and quiet. It was nice. I was waxing poetic in my mind about the virtues of suburban life, meandering about in a daydream, although some might say a drunken stupor, when I tripped over a some leprechaun doll. Somehow, I had wandered into a play room off the living room.

"Are you okay?" this gorgeous girl asked me.

"I think so. I can't believe that doll tripped me, what a prick," I said.

The leprechaun doll had an evil smirk on its face. It freaked me out.

"Forget that whole pot of gold thing...leprechauns are nasty sometimes," she laughed, while she helped me up.

Once the spinning stopped, I was awestruck. This girl was beautiful. "What's your name?" I asked her.

"Karen," she said, as we shook hands.

Good thing I was dressed up for this party and not in my usual uniform - jeans and a t-shirt. I had on a black casual suit - no tie. Karen was impeccably dressed, too. She had on a little, black, revealing dress, a pretty diamond necklace, diamond earrings and black shoes with a very high heel. How do women walk in those things?

"Karen, eh? I'm David Michaels," I was enchanted.

We sat down and talked about life for a bit. I was explaining the finer points of being unemployed, when she interrupted me and explained that she, too, was unemployed.

"I actually kind of like it," she said.

I couldn't disagree. Actually, I was so mesmerized by her that I was set to agree with anything she said. Her blond hair and green eyes had a spell on me.

"You know I live on an air mattress," I confessed.

"What?" she looked very confused.

"On an air mattress. On my sister's floor."

There, ladies and gentlemen, is the straw that would most assuredly break the camel's back. Good thing we were isolated in the playroom. I didn't need everyone at the party to know what a loser I was.

"I used to live in this amazing, one-bedroom sublet in TriBeCa for six-hundred a month. It even had this incredible balcony that overlooked the Hudson River. The guy who owned it lived in Italy with his wife. He was actually going to give me the apartment, but then he decided to leave his wife. Then he kicked me out."

"Sad story," she said. "I would kill for a one-bedroom apartment."

"The worst part is he called me about three months after I moved out and told me I owed him $300 for the cable bill. I told him that was impossible since I canceled the cable. Then he told me I owed him $150 for the phone bill. I told him that was a lie. Then he said I owed him 250 for a shower curtain. I said, '$250 for a shower curtain? He said, 'no, $2.50. I said, 'cash or a check?' He was nuts."

"Oh, my God," Karen laughed. "He does sound crazy."

Karen was laughing and acting a little flirty. Granted, I was drunk, but she was flipping her pin-straight hair and touching my shoulder, especially, when she said, "You're so funny."

While I was enjoying Karen's praise of my comedic skills, Sara came running into the playroom looking for me. No! Go away, Sara! Karen and I are going to fall in love and live happily ever after! I tried hiding under the princess castle, but she found me.

"I've been looking all over for you. C'mon! Your surprise is here."

Sara dragged me out of the room. She pulled me through the living room, past the bar over to the kitchen where my surprise was waiting for me. And man, was I surprised! I heard, "I'll cash that rain check now," and nearly fainted. Standing before me was Ms. Tiramisu. Why the fuck was she here?

"David, look. It's the ten of clubs, Nicole. I know you guys have been trying to get together for a few months, but Nicole has been a busy, little girl. I thought this party was the perfect opportunity for you two to catch up," Sara said, beaming.

Yeah, Sara, I see who the fuck it is. She looked even worse than I remembered, except this time I was completely fixated on the mole. The light in the kitchen did her no justice. I could see clearly that the mole hair had grown longer these past few months. Shit.

Fuck. Insert expletive here. What the fuck was I gong to do now?

"I'm so happy to see you. I had such a great time on our last date, and when Sara told me you were going to be here I just had to show up," Tiramisu was utterly excited.

I didn't know how to respond. I know I wanted to ask Sara what the fuck she was thinking by inviting Tiramisu here. I also wanted to tell Tiramisu that she made my stomach turn. Thank God, I was liquored up.

If I was in the wild, and this piggy came sniffing around the camp after I shooed it away once, I would go back in my tent, get the12-gauge shotgun, and put two craters the size of Tiramisu's mole though it's head. Unfortunately, this was the civilized world. All I could do was stand here and take it like a man.

"Hi, Nicole," I said, looking for an exit.

"You two look so great together," twittered Sara. "Okay, you kids have fun. I have to go play hostess." Sara left me standing there with the pouch-ridden Tiramisu. This was a nightmare. I looked over to the chefs for help, but they just stood there chopping shit up. Help a brother out, I pleaded with my eyes.

"Oh, my God, this is going to be so much fun. You know I

was watching this great show last night and the funniest thing hap -,"

"Do you want to get a drink at the bar?" I had to interrupt her. She was killing me.

I couldn't stand here alone with her for one more minute listening to her drone on about television. She was sad proof that people really did sit in front of their televisions all day watching sitcoms and reality shows.

We strolled across the kitchen, living room and multiple sitting areas until we found our way back to the bar. This house was beautiful. What the hell was I doing on an air mattress? When we got to the bar, a chorus of comments rang out from my now drunken friends and their wives.

"There he is," Pete yelled out.

"Where've you been?" Dan asked.

"Oh, you are a bad boy, where'd you pick this one up?" Matt said, laughing.

Jon was sitting at the bar, and when he saw who I walked over with, his eyes almost popped out of his head.

"Hi, Jon," Nicole jumped in.

"Oh, hi, Nicole. I didn't know you were coming," Jon blurted out.

"Yeah, I know. It's a surprise for David." She looked everyone over. "You know, me and David went out a few months ago, and now we finally get to have our second date tonight. Isn't that romantic?"

I spit my drink out. Actually, the drink sprayed out of my mouth in a manner you would see on a really bad television show. How apropos. Second date? What the fuck!

The girls, upon hearing the news, reverted back to their single days and were swept away by how exciting it must be to have such a romantic second date. The guys stared at the mole. Then Matt's wife, Jen, jumped in, "The best part is you know you two are going to kiss tonight. After all, it's New Year's Eve. It's so romantic."

There was no way a kiss was going to happen. Maybe I'd try to trim the mole hair if I could find a hedge trimmer.

I left Nicole talking to Lisa and went around to Jon's side of the bar to order a drink.

"Dude, what the fuck is she doing here?" I asked Jon.

"I have no idea. I can't believe Sara invited her," Jon pleaded with me to believe him.

"We have to get rid of her. I can't spend the whole night with her." Then it hit me, "Oh my God, I left Karen. I have to find her."

"Who is Karen?" Jon asked.

"This beautiful girl I met when I tripped over some doll and landed in your playroom. I have to find her."

"Karen, what? I don't think I know anyone named Karen?" Jon said, perplexed.

"I'll find her, and then show you," I said. Tiramisu was waving to me and mouthing "I miss you."

Miss me? What's next, she loves me? How did this happen? I think Sara has a way of setting me up with needy women. At least in college I fooled around with Sara's friend before she thought the friend and I were a couple. This one was fucking nuts.

"I'm going to kill Sara," I grumbled, sucking down my G&T.

A bell started ringing throughout the house. Then came Sara's voice over an elaborate intercom system: "Everyone, dinner is now served. Please make your way to the dining room. Dinner is now served."

Dinner indeed. I knew one thing for sure. I wasn't having

Tiramisu for dessert.

CHAPTER EIGHTEEN

Jon and Sara were seated at the head of the massive dining table. I was next to Tiramisu, and across from me were the King and Queen of diamonds, Jim and Sandy McBride, from Jon's firm. I frantically searched for Karen. This was one, goddamn, long table. I looked up and down the table, person by person. After a few minutes, I located her at the total opposite end of the table. She was fifteen couples away from me, sitting next to some good-looking guy I had never seen before. Where the hell do Jon and Sara meet these people?

"I love nice dinners," Tiramisu whispered in my ear. She put her hand on my leg.

"That's nice," I told her, removing the hand.

"I'm so happy that we get to sit together," she told me.

Sure, you, me and the mole make three. She better not touch me again.

The servers, bedecked in snow-white, brought out the first course, lobster bisque. When everyone was served, Jon stood up to make a toast. I don't know how we were all supposed to hear him. I felt like the other end of the table was miles away. I looked over at Karen, hoping she would see me. But she was staring at Jon.

"I'm so very happy that all of our friends were able to join us tonight to usher in the start of a wonderful new year. This past year has been wonderful for myself, and Sara, and our growing family of Zac, and our newest addition, Edith. We are truly blessed. We want to wish each and every one of you the best in the coming year. Happy New Year! Cheers!"

Glasses chimed and everyone shouted, "Hear, hear!" We all returned to our bisque.

"That was so nice. I love Jon and Sara," Tiramisu said, getting sentimental.

"Oh, I love them too," I said, but not so much at this very moment. I wasn't going to let this night degenerate into any kind of long, drawn out, exclusive conversation between Tiramisu and myself. I had to bring the unsuspecting Jim and Sandy McBride into the picture.

Jim was about 45, but looked about 60. He had grey hair, wrinkles galore, wore glasses, and had on expensive, though ill-fitting clothes. Jim, we have tailors to fit your blazer, pal. To top it off, he was as stiff as a board. Sandy, on the other hand, was hot. She was dressed to kill, adorned in diamonds, and was quite possibly 50, but looked like a sophisticated 40. That made her a few years older than Jim - way to go, Jimbo! I did a quick scan for the reconstructed nose, but I think hers was genuine. She was the epitome of a WASP. And to be honest, I was really digging it. She was the socialite daughter of an ex-curator of the Art Museum, so she possessed this very dignified air. Quite the opposite of the thing I was sitting next to.

"So, Jim, how's life at the old firm?" I asked, sipping on the bisque.

"Well, I tell you, Dave . . . it is Dave, right?" Jim started to answer.

"Actually it's David, Jim. I don't go by Dave," I informed him.

"And I'm Nicole," Nicole said, jumping in uninvited.

"So, you and Dave are . . . " Jim started.

"David," I interrupted.

". . . Going steady?" Jim asked.

Who goes steady? Ummm, heads up there, Jimbo, this isn't

1955. Amazing. Jim not only looked 60, he acted 60.

"We met at a sock hop. Nicole was in a real nifty poodle skirt," I answered.

Sandy laughed.

Nicole looked at me like I had ten heads. Then she looked over the folks at our end of the table and announced: "No, we didn't, silly. We met on a blind date. It was so romantic. Can you believe this will only be our second date?"

"I still can't," I threw in, perhaps a little too forcefully.

I knew one thing thing for sure this will certainly be the last.

"Isn't he funny? That's what I love most about him," Nicole was droning on.

"He's cute, too," Sandy said in a sultry voice, winking at me.

Did Jim see the wink? God, I hope not.

"I know, so cute," Nicole added.

She then started babbling on about how it was destiny that brought us together, when, actually, it was just Sara making a really bad mistake. As Nicole continued to talk, I felt someone's foot rubbing up and down against my leg. I looked up and saw Sandy intently listening to Nicole. Was I crazy? Maybe someone was wiggling their leg around and accidentally brushed it up against mine. That was definitely it. But this person didn't have a shoe on, and that puzzled me a bit. I pretended that I didn't feel anything, and listened to Nicole babble incomprehensibly.

"So, when I was watching this dating show the other night, I couldn't believe my eyes -"

Why did I bother? What a twit. I can't even listen to this girl when I'm trying to avoid a very awkward situation. I thought a sip of wine would calm me down. Perhaps the four G&T's had me a bit edgy. I took a sip of the wine when I felt someone's foot smack dab in the middle of my crotch. I nearly jumped out of my seat, and I spilled some wine on my pants. Sandy looked at me and smirked. Holy Fuck! It was Sandy!

"Excuse me, I need to go to the bathroom for a moment," I said.

In the bathroom, I looked in the mirror. What the hell was going on here? I was standing there, considering these absurd circumstances, when Sandy busted in. Suddenly, things got more absurd when she pushed me up against the sink and started to make out with me.

"You are adorable," she said, in between tongue thrashes. "Jim is such a bore. He acts like an old man. I love it that you just made fun of him to his face."

"Sandy! You're married," I couldn't do this. "I can't do this, especially not in the bathroom! Didn't Jim and Nicole wonder where you were going? I just got up one minute ago?"

"Jim is entertaining your young lady friend with some stories about Jon at the firm. Don't talk. Let's just neck."

Neck? What was with this couple? Those two were meant for each other.

"Sandy, I can't do this."

"Why? You don't want to break little Miss Annoying's heart?"

Hmm, maybe Sandy and I had something in common. "Actually, I can't stand her," I said.

"Then let's make love, right here, right now. Give it to me," she was stripping.

When she took her bra off, I couldn't help myself. She had nice, firm, big tits. They've got to be fake. But who cares!

"Not bad for a 49 year-old, huh," Sandy said, seducing me.

I didn't want to degenerate any further this year, but, apparently, I was about to add 'adulterer' to my list of accomplishments. I helped Sandy out of the rest of her clothes, and, before I knew it, we'd had sex. Sex in the bathroom. Public sex. It was my first time having sex in a bathroom with a stranger at my friend's house, and it was amazing. I got my pants back on and watched Sandy get dressed. She was lean and thin and had the body of a woman 20 years younger - if, like Sandy, she were in great shape. Her ass had just the right amount of umph, and those legs. Oh those legs, they went on forever. Sandy was right. She was pretty hot for a forty-nine year old.

"I'll go back in first," Sandy said to me.

I sat in the bathroom for another minute or so, and splashed some water on my pants to give the appearance that I had just removed the wine stain. Then I rejoined the party.

"Everything all right, Dave?" Jim asked upon my return.

"Fantastic, Jimbo." I paused for a second - was he suspicious? - then added, "Got the wine stain out."

"I missed you," Nicole said to me. "I told the waiter you were done with your bisque, I figured you didn't want it anymore."

I still wanted the bisque. I looked at Sandy, who was freaking me out with her goo-goo eyes, and then said to Nicole, "Whatever." I looked over at Sandy calmly talking to Jim. I wonder if she's done this before.

The rest of dinner was a bore. Jim told us about Jon at the office. Nicole talked about television, and I was just too drunk and spent to carry on any kind of conversation. What the hell just happened? Did I really just have sex in the bathroom? How fucking degenerate is that? Not just sex in a bathroom, but sex with some lady that I don't even know at my best friend's house. In fact, it's his boss' wife. Shit! I've fucked things up big time and I'm pretty sure I can't go back in time to correct it. Now, I have to sit here and have a celebratory dinner with these people. I can't even look poor Jim in the face. Granted, I thought he was a douchebag, but fucking his wife in the bathroom is pretty low, even for me. He can never find out. And, what's with Sandy? Who does that? Cheating on your husband is wrong, but cheating on your husband at a party - that he's at - in a bathroom is despicable. Even I know that! And why the hell was she making eyes at me. That's pretty fucked up.

And what the fuck was I thinking? I like that girl Karen. Why was I trying to blow *that* before it even started? There's something very wrong with me. I was never going to see Sandy again. That much I knew. Sandy was married and sitting right across from me with her husband. Karen wasn't married. Hell, Karen could be my future. So, every now and then, in the middle of one of Jim's stories, I would peek down to the end of the table to see Karen. She was always laughing and smiling. Once, during dinner, she caught my stare, and smiled back. I had to talk to her again.

With about a half hour to go before midnight, dinner was finally wrapping up, and we were all heading to the various sitting areas. I was trying to find Karen, as I made my way over to the bar area, leaving Tiramisu lingering somewhere by herself. Dan, Peter, and Matt cornered me at the bar.

"Michaels, over here," Matt called me.

"Hey, I'm trying to find this girl -"

"Why does Sara seat us at opposite ends of the table every year?" Matt asked. "It gets so annoying."

"I think she wants to torture us for being friends with her husband," Dan said.

"I was next to some freak that Sara knows from Kiddie Gym. The woman wasn't that bad, but the husband kept picking his nose the whole time, and wouldn't shut up about how the kid can do a somersault. Who gives a shit, pal?" Matt looked like he had gone through a war.

"Well, I was next to this guy that Jon knows from Kiddy Music class. It turns out the guy is gay, and has a kid with his partner, but the partner is away on business, so he brought his sister here. She was fucking hot," Dan said.

"Was her name Karen?" I asked.

"Yeah, I think so. I didn't really talk to her, she was talking to some other freaks that Jon knows."

"Dude, I was talking to her earlier. That's the girl I'm looking for! She is amazing. Where is she?" I asked in a panic.

"She said she was leaving after dinner. She had to go to some other party," Dan didn't even realize the news would crush me.

"Shit. Shit. Shit!"

Midnight was quickly approaching and I had stayed in one place too long. Nicole had located me, and the rest of the wives had found their way back to their men as well. I took a second to look around at the crowd, everyone with their wives content in their suburban world. I had just committed adultery, fell in love with a woman who left before I could get her number, and was about to kiss a woman with hair growing out of her mole. The coming year had to be better.

PART III: Decisions

CHAPTER NINETEEN

January started with the realization that I was going to have to get a job. Despite the fact that I thoroughly enjoyed being unemployed, the money was going to run out soon. My initial attempts to find gainful employment through The New York News had proved unsuccessful. I had only one choice left, and that was to network. This meant calling people I despised and asking for a job. This would, of course, lead to the inevitable "no, I'm sorry, but let me look around for you" speech. Eventually, I would be back to The New York News, and sending resumes out to headhunters and bullshit artists, hoping that one of them would call me back, not even necessarily for a job, but just to let me know that someone was actually reading my resume on the other end.

I called a few people that I used to work with, and grovelled a bit, just to get back in the swing of things. They all said they would check around for me, but they also pointed out that, "The market is tight right now."

It was this type of talk that had me sitting on my sister's air mattress, petrified to go back into the corporate arena. Phrases like "the market is tight," "let's touch base," "we need to get our ducks in a row," "gotta make sure we dot all the I's and cross all the T's," make my stomach turn. In my former life, these were some of the phrases I would use on a daily basis. You would know what I am talking about "if we are on the same page."

A couple of weeks later, I got a call from Valerie Feinman, a woman from my prior life at Hobart. Evidently, she had forwarded my resume to a woman in the legal group at R.J. Smith & Company. She said they were interested in meeting with me and would get in touch shortly. The wheels were in motion.

However, when Valerie presented me with this opportunity to go back to work I felt sick. I didn't think I could handle practicing law every day, twelve to sixteen hours a day, for the rest of my life. There had to be a better way. But after my conversation with the bartender at Jon's party, I wasn't so sure anymore.

Eventually R.J. Smith & Company called and we set up the meeting for the following week. I had to go on this interview. The reality was I was living on an air mattress at thirty.

In order to see Constantine Beeka on the thirty-eighth floor of the R.J. Smith & Company building, I had to sign in with security in the lobby. Once I was cleared, I got a paper ID tag that I had to place on my upper-right lapel. I tried to place it on my left, but security was all over me.

"Sir, I'm going to have to ask you to place your identification on your upper-right lapel. Preferably, in the upper quadrant," he said.

Thanks, Mr. Security. These guys were top-notch. Once I negotiated through security on the ground floor, my next step would be the 'elevator meet and greet' on floor 38. This is where I would first meet the head of the compliance legal group.

Constantine was waiting for me right at the elevator bank as the doors opened onto floor 38.

"Hello, David. I'm Constantine. It's nice to meet you. Please follow me."

Constantine looked as if she had stepped straight out of 1987. Shoulder pads are out, Constantine. And so is teased hair. Just a heads up. And one more thing, just because you're a lawyer doesn't mean you have to look like a fucking mess. I should have hit the "close door" button and returned to the ground floor.

We entered an office of sterile air and cubicles. The cubes

were all arranged in a frighteningly, orderly, symmetrical pattern. I heard nothing except the pounding of my heart as I contemplated my future here. I didn't know why I was shocked by what I was seeing. I had been escorted out of a similar office less than six months ago.

I sat across from Constantine in her cookie-cutter office. Desk in the middle of the office, one green plant in the corner, book shelf behind her and another off to the side, computer on the right of her "L" shaped desk. I was sitting in a typical, leather, guest chair, one leg crossed leisurely over my knee. I was repulsed by this whole scene, though I was not sure why. Sure, Constantine looked straight out of an 80's movie. And yes, her hair was some sort of friz fro incapable of being brushed neatly in any direction. And, of course, it struck me odd, that she was as pale as a glass of skim milk with a slightly blue hue. But that wasn't it. Constantine was just part of the problem, there was something more that was making me sick.

"So David, you're a lawyer," she said.

"Indeed I am," I said, still staring.

"I am looking at your resume, but I don't see where you are admitted to the Bar."

She seemed confused, but it was hard to tell. Her eyebrows

weren't moving. Botox? I don't think so. I looked a little closer. I think her eyebrows were drawn on with some sort of makeup. Can you do that?

"It's there," I said.

She flipped over the resume, cursorily scanned the reverse side, and then looked at the front of it again, "Nope. I don't see it. You must have accidentally left it off."

"No. I don't believe I did. It's there," I said.

"Well, if I can't find it, it must not be there," she said, with a little attitude.

"It is definitely there. I'll point it out to you."

I reached over and pulled the resume out of her hand, put it on the desk between us and pointed to the first line. Experience: Member of State Bar.

"Well, it is in the wrong place." She mumbled.

At this point, the interview was not starting off with a bang. Besides that, I was confused and I could not figure out why. And what was confusing me the most was my complete lack of interest in getting the job.

"Let me tell you a little something about the position," she began. "We are looking for an attorney to work with . . ." Bla, bla, bla.

I didn't have a clue what she was talking about. I was mesmerized watching her 'eyebrows'.

"I'm highly organized and I expect everyone in my group to be, as well. We have an online database that keeps track of the entire work product being created by the attorneys. That way we know where each document is at any time and what stages of the negotiations they are at. I personally invented this system."

Who gives two shits?

"My boss, the head of legal here, is a patent lawyer," she said, throwing this line out there hoping, perhaps, that I would be impressed.

"Wow, he must really be organized."

I shut down at this point. At first I didn't know why, and then it dawned on me. I hated corporate America, and everything about the stifling, soul-stealing, time-robbing, greedy, life-destroying philosophy it represented. Constantine was the just the messenger; the corporation was the culprit.

"Oh, no. No, no, I'm just as organized, if not more so. He

may be the boss, but I'm organized."

This was the moment of my epiphany. I could never work in an office again. Life had to be about more than just getting a job, or telling potential employees how organized you are. I didn't want to be Constantine when I was forty. Hell, I didn't want to be her now. I stood up, thanked Constantine for her time, and ran out of R.J. Smith & Company as fast as I could.

CHAPTER TWENTY

I decided that I needed a colonic. Or maybe I needed to fast. Somehow, I needed to purge myself of the evil that was festering in and around me. Only then would the gods provide me with the energy that I needed to get a job.

Some serious thinking had convinced me that I was not cut out for the legal life. I know what you are thinking. Just five years ago, he spent $90,000 on a law degree, and now he's not going to use it? What's the problem? Who does something like that? Believe me, I've thought plenty about that myself, but the freedom to be a degenerate was far outweighing my desire to work as a lawyer. I could eat spaghetti out of a can, and I could wear the same pocket T's for another ten years, if I could follow my dreams. It was actually a pretty easy decision. I could not spend one more day of my life talking to, working for, working with, or even looking at someone like Constantine. I knew that would kill me.

This decision did not come without any consequences. I was getting calls of support from across the country.

The Parents (New York): "What the hell is wrong with you? You're killing us. What are we supposed to tell our friends?"

Grandma (Florida): "Mommy just called and told me you're not a lawyer anymore. How does that happen? I thought you had graduated. If you needed money, why didn't you tell me?"

Great Uncle Simon and Great Aunt Carol (Somewhere. I don't know where they live. I don't even know who these people are. I think I met them twice.): "Listen, you have to be a lawyer. You're just confused right now. Come over and we'll cook you a nice Shabbat dinner and talk about things. Don't do this to your parents. What's wrong with you? Call us back."

Aunt Anne (Connecticut): "You're killing your mother. Is that what you want to do? Kill your mother? Kill her after she raised you? That wouldn't be very nice."

Uncle Mikey (New York): "Before you stop being a lawyer can you lend me $1,500 so I can get a motorcycle."

Despite the showering of goodwill, I had to go on with my plan. I was going to spend the rest of my time on this planet following my dreams. I did have to make some money in the meantime, but I could work anywhere. That was the new plan. That was the right plan.

Now came the tricky part, I had to find a place to work that matched perfectly with my new outlook on life. Ultimately, I settled on the mall. It was perfect. Low stress, cute mall girls, food court. An entire ecosystem under one roof. It would be like I was living in an 80's movie. I thought about where I would like to work at the mall and it hit me like a bolt of lightning. Caps. Caps was a baseball hat store. I loved hats. And, since my hair had started thinning, I loved hats even more. I was partial to baseball caps, but, hey, I could sell any kind of hat. I imagined a paradise of no stress and apathetic co-workers, where everyone was free to ignore the customers and daydream their life away. Sometimes you have to follow your dreams. There was no time to delay. I hurried over to the mall, pen in hand, ready to tackle the application process. First stop: Caps.

"Do you have any positions available?" I asked the 16 year-old behind the counter at Caps. I waited anxiously for his response. I didn't wait long.

"Sorry, dude. We're all filled up," he said.

My heart deflated. Could this really be happening?

"Nothing?" I asked in a last ditch effort to sway the young man's mind.

"Sorry, dude, nada," he said.

Nada. I heard it, but I couldn't believe it. My dream job had slipped away. But this was the New Dave. The Dave that sets his goals higher, the Dave that strives for job happiness. Surely, I could find another job in the mall that would suit my requirements. Don't you worry, pen, you'll get some good use yet. This new Dave doesn't give up so easily.

I meandered aimlessly through the mall, looking at store after store, gauging which retail establishment would be right for me. Then, I passed Sneaker Heaven, a women's sports shoe and apparel store. The blue-green sign that hung above the store glowed like a halo, albeit an off-color halo. Ladies shoes. Yes. I would like to sell ladies shoes. I assumed that ladies would be traipsing in and out of the store all day long. Sure, they all wouldn't be cute, little twenty-somethings, but I could deal with that. Sneaker Heaven is where I needed to be.

I gathered my thoughts, entered the store and prepared to get myself a job. Sneaker Heaven was a decent-sized store. Various women's sneakers ranging from tennis sneakers to running shoes lined the two walls with a register for check out sitting in the back of the store. There was clearly an entrance into the back area. Shoe stores have always been a mystery to me. People are always walking in the back, and then re-appearing with boxes. If I was a betting man, I'd bet there was a little warehouse back there. Insightful, huh? After a few deep breaths, I strolled up to the register and asked Peaches – that actually was the name on her name tag – if there were any positions available.

"Yeah. What do you want to do?" Things were looking up.

"I'm looking for something in sales."

"Sales? You mean you want to work the floor? Help people try on shoes? Aiight, aiight. You have to fill this out," she handed me an application, "then you'll talk to my manager, Jim. Just bring it back here when you are finished."

This was perfect. I got out the old pen and got to work.

Name: David Michaels (piece of cake)

Address/Phone: C'mon this thing was too easy.

Education Completed: J.D. Degree

Work Experience (last job first): Associate Director, Hobart

That should suffice. I finished the rest of the application, and sauntered back up to Peaches at the register, "Here you go." She said she'd see if Jim had a minute to talk with me. A minute later, she walked out with a kid no more than twenty-one.

He walked out of the back. Hmm, there must be more back there than a little warehouse.

"David?" Jim said to me. I nodded. "Do you want to come back here so we can talk?"

Did I? Did I ever! I followed skinny, frail, pimply Jim into the back where we sat down at Jim's little desk and the interview began.

Ah, there was an office back here. Jim was living the life. Lucky fucker. Off to the right was the warehouse. It was kind of disappointing. It was a lot smaller than I had imagined. The office wasn't bad though. It wasn't the biggest office in the world, maybe 8x8. I sat in the fold up chair across from Jim in my jeans and t-shirt. He must not get very many visitors back here. Maybe I should have dressed up a bit. Jim was in khakis and a polo shirt. He looked chain restaurant chic.

"It says here you have a J.D. degree? Is that some sort of high school equivalency?" he asked, very confused.

"Actually, Jim, that's a legal degree. I'm a lawyer."

"Ummm, well, if you don't mind me asking, David, why would you want to work here?" said Jim, absolutely perplexed.

"Well, Jim, I took the last few months and really took a look at my life, you know, where I was at and where I was heading, and I didn't really like what I saw. I mean, sure I could sit at a desk making over $150,000 a year, but that's not what I wanted, Jim, you know?" Jim stared at me like I was smoking crack. "I want to be happy. I'm really interested in selling sneakers."

I knew you had to sell yourself. That's how these things worked.

"Dude, you're more like a manager or something," Jim didn't know what to say.

"I want to be out there selling. I know I don't have any retail experience, but I really think I could do a great job."

"It says here that you worked at a law firm, or some kind of bank. For real?" Jim said, stunned.

"I know, it's not the best experience, but if you give me a

shot I won't let you down, Jim."

"I mean, if you really want it, you can have the job. You know, it pays eight dollars an hour, right?"

"I sure do. Wow! Thanks Jim. I can't wait to start," I was psyched.

"You can start next week if you want. Let me look at the schedule here for a sec. How does Monday from opening to three sound to you?" Jim asked.

"Perfect."

"You'll need to wear a pair of black pants. When you get here, I'll give you two Sneaker Heaven referee shirts to wear," Jim filled me in.

"Great!"

"OK, then, we'll see you Monday," Jim shook my hand.

"I can't wait."

That night, I went back to Michelle's with a new found sense of purpose.

"I got a job," I declared to Michelle.

CHAPTER TWENTY-ONE

I quickly found myself settling into my new job at Sneaker Heaven. Each day, I had a chance to wander around the store, talk to potential customers and look out into the mall. One of my pastimes was focusing on Coffee Kiosk. This kiosk, directly across from Sneaker Heaven, was a chick magnet. Cute women and MILFs, in particular, seemed to hang out there. It seemed they shared a common interest, they liked whipped cream on top of their drinks. They also really liked what looked like iced coffee. I always secretly prayed that the hot ones would walk in here looking for some athletic gear.

Peaches and I were becoming very close friends. When I wasn't staring out of the store at Coffee Kiosk, we would usually just hang out talking around the yoga pants carousel. Peaches made me laugh. Well, that is, when she wasn't pissed off. I had no idea why she was angry sometimes.

Occasionally, I would hit on Peaches. All in good fun.

"Peaches, I can't believe you are working here," I said.

"Why?"

"You are just too fine, girl, uh-huh" I said, imitating a black girl.

"You're crazy," Peaches said, "You think *I* shouldn't be here. You're a lawyer. What are *you* doing here? What, you're so rich you just want to work at Sneaker Heaven and hang out with the Sisters? See if you can get some black bootie?"

"I wish . . . you offering?" I said.

"Hell, no!"

A customer walked into the store. Not a MILF or a cute, young, mall rat. Just your ordinary, fifty-something lady. Peaches sauntered over and asked the customer if she needed some help. She held up a pair of powder-blue Trail Sneakers.

"Do you have these in a five?" The lady asked.

"Let me check," Peaches said.

"You don't have to, Peaches. Miss, we usually carry these in a five, but we are sold out. We'll be getting a new shipment in on the twenty-sixth, but may I suggest the Lightning Trail Blazers? They are actually better than the one in your hand, cost less, and I happen to think they look nicer."

This was how you sold sneakers. Shocking, huh? I've been

studying up on this sneaker stuff. I can't help it. I've got knack for numbers and spreadsheets. I had been following the incoming shipments since I started working here, and I've been spending some time in the back warehouse getting acquainted with the store's current stock. I've got a pretty good memory, and it was proving beneficial, because I knew what we had in stock most of the time and what was coming in on the next shipment.

"Do you have the Lightning in a size five?" The woman asked.

"Indeed, we do. Have a seat, and I'll be back in a second," I said.

Peaches was looking on - and fuming.

The woman tried on the sneakers, walked around the store a bit, stared at her foot in the little mirror on the floor, and then said. "These feel great. I'll take them."

"Great choice, miss," I said. You never want to use the term "ma'am." "Miss" makes ladies of a certain age feel young. "Ma'am" makes them feel like their mother.

When the woman left, Peaches went crazy, "I can't believe you stole that customer from me."

"C'mon, I didn't steal her. I just knew we didn't have any more of the regular Trail sneakers. I suggested a different pair, that's all. That's how you sell shit."

"But, damn, I need to make sales so I can make money for college. You think eight dollars an hour is going to cut it. I need the commission. I don't have a law degree like you," Peaches said.

"Look, I don't want to take away your sales. You're damn good at selling sneakers. I'm sorry," I patted Peaches on the back, "I want you to be able to pay for college. I'm really sorry."

Jesus. Office politics. What are you gonna do?

I was quickly becoming well-acquainted with the latest styles of female athletic footwear, as well as apparel. Without so much as asking a fellow co-worker for help, or even strolling to the back of the store, I could tell a customer if we had their sneaker size. This skill was saving me energy, and making quite an impression on my manager. Jim even told me that he was impressed with both me and my work. High praise from a pimply, twenty-one year-old.

By the end of my first month on the job I had achieved the coveted 'Employee of the Month' title. I was well on my way up the old corporate ladder, this time on my own terms. Peaches, who had been an employee at Sneaker Heaven for the past nine months, had never lost Employee of the Month. She had been the undisputed queen of sneaker sales since she joined, but not this month. This month she sold more sneakers than she had ever sold before. Unfortunately, that was the second largest number of sneakers sold that month. Yours truly had sold over 150 pairs of sneakers in a thirty-day period. I think that it is a record.

Jim called me in his office to have a chat, "David, you did very good this month. I mean, you sold the most shoes any single employee has ever sold in a month. You should be real proud. I called you in here because I have some bad news. I'm going to be leaving here at the end of the week. I decided to go back to school and do something with my life. And I owe it all to you. You working here showed me that if I wanted to get anything in this world I had to work for it. I couldn't just waste my time standing in Sneaker Heaven, smoking pot in the back and listening to music. I had to take control of my life and go back to school. But anyway, that means there is going to be a manager position open, and I wanted to know if you wanted to apply for it. Of course, I can't guarantee anything."

Hmm, pot. I never smelled it. How did he do that? I did hear the music, though.

"What about Peaches?" I asked, "She's a great salesperson."

"Peaches doesn't really have what it takes. Sure she can sell sneakers, but she doesn't have a grasp of the big picture," Jim answered.

"What kind of big picture could there really be? I'm sure Peaches could handle it," I said.

"David, let me level with you here. I don't like Peaches. She always annoys me when I'm in the back, high, trying to listen to some tunes. I don't want her to become manager. I want you. And if you don't want it, I'm going to let Corporate decide. I don't think you would want that."

Damn, a promotion. I knew that was code for more work. "Will that mean that I have to work more hours?" I asked.

"Well, yeah, but you can just sit in the back if you want. You don't have to stand out there in front of everyone and help people try on sneakers."

"You mean I can just sit in the back and do whatever I want?" I asked.

"That's what I'm telling you. Dude, it seems like you have some demons you might want to work out. A little quiet time might just do the trick," Jim was dead-on.

"Yeah, I want to apply for the manager position. I want to sit in the back." I was getting excited.

"All right then, now we're talking. I'll just put your name in when I talk to Corporate later today. They should make a decision by tomorrow. I'll let you know," Jim was on my side. "Oh, and David, thanks again for showing me the light."

"Yeah, no problem. Thanks." I'm glad that my misfortune was your impetus for change.

On the bright side, this was a golden opportunity. I couldn't believe it was falling in my lap.

CHAPTER TWENTY-TWO

"Michelle, you're never going to believe this. I got a promotion at work," I said, basically out of breath, as I walked through the door to her apartment.

Michelle was sitting on the couch watching television and surfing the JewDater website on her laptop, "You work at a sneaker store in the mall. Did you hear what I just said? You are a lawyer who works at a sneaker store in the mall for eight dollars an hour."

Michelle was trying to knock some sense into me, I guess.

"Not any more, I'm not. I'm getting . . ." I paused for dramatic effect, " . . . a promotion to Manager! First, I scored Employee of the Month last week, and now I'm getting a promotion to Manager," I couldn't hide my excitement.

"You should be the fucking manager. David, you should be in Sneaker Heaven's legal department, for God's sake. What - are you beating out other twenty-one year-olds for the job?" She was nasty tonight. "You work at Sneaker Heaven, helping people try on sneakers."

"I'm not helping people try on anything. I'm going to be a

manager," I barely got that out.

"You sleep on an air mattress on my studio floor. And, you've been doing that for the last six months, and that's not even the worst part. You don't seem to care. You are 30 years old, David. You have to get a grip on your life and start doing something worthwhile," Michelle was laying down the law.

This verbal dress-down was hitting home as I sat on my air mattress looking up at Michelle. What could I say? I was following my dreams. It must look like some sort of 'cry for help' from the outside, but that wasn't going to stop me. I was going to have an office now. An office with a door on it. A door that could shut. That would prove to be indispensable, as I could shut out anybody I didn't want to deal with.

"I like my new life. I like working at Sneaker Heaven. I'm happy with myself. I'm going back to Sneaker Heaven tomorrow and I'm going to get that Manager position," Ha! I told her.

"That is just pathetic. Are we done with this conversation? I have a date tonight, and I have to get ready," she said, and she stormed into the bathroom.

Later that night, and a few drinks in, I was lying on my air mattress and thinking about what Michelle had said. She was pretty much right on. If I wanted any kind of future, I would have to do something other than selling sneakers at the Mall. I walked over to the coat closet where Michelle piled the 20 notebooks that I had filled with story ideas. I sat down and read a few pages. Apparently, after 30 years and 20 notebooks filled with thoughts, I couldn't figure out anything about my life.

I must have passed out drunk in the closet. Because the next thing I remembered was Michelle waking me up. I was laying in a wife beater and boxers and I could feel something imprinted down my cheek. I must have passed out on a notebook because the spiral rings were all bent.

"Are you fucking kidding me? Wake up! What are you doing in the closet?" Michelle blurted, as she slammed the door behind her.

"What?" I said from the closet floor. I was shocked.

"I just had the worst date of my life," Michelle said, "It was so bad I don't even want to talk about it."

Holy shit, give me a minute to recuperate here. I felt dizzy.

"Where did you meet this guy?" I asked, trying to gather my thoughts.

"JewDater. Where else?" She had a point. She had now been on JewDater for the past year, totally giving up on actually meeting someone in the flesh first. But what she may have actually realized in this moment was that JewDater might not be the answer. It only took her 55 dates to figure it out. I personally thought the low point came when she met a guy for two minutes over coffee at some diner. Michelle didn't even get a chance to sit down before the date was over. Apparently, the young man had put cream in his coffee. This set off a chain reaction in Michelle's head that equated cream usage to heart attack, meaning Michelle would be a widow by the time she was 40. Michelle was honest with the guy that it wasn't going to work out, and she left. So I ask you, why should this guy be any different than any of the social misfits Michelle has met on JewDater?

I climbed off the floor, climbed onto the couch next to Michelle, put my arm around her and tried to talk some sense into her for a change.

"Michelle, I think it's time you get off JewDater and get out there in the real world. I mean, every date you've been on has been a disaster."

"Get off JewDater? Where am I going to meet somebody? And that's not true. Every date has not been a disaster. What about the guy that I went to the Cuban restaurant with? He was okay."

"Michelle, he didn't talk to you during the whole dinner. You said he kept his head down and made noises resembling words into his napkin."

"Yeah, but he asked me out again," Michelle said.

"I guess, but could you even tell? He was a mute."

"But this guy was different. I really liked him. There was something there."

"I'm sure he was . . . different. Most people can tell after a couple of hours if the person is perfect for them," I was getting a little sarcastic, "Michelle, c'mon. Every one of these guys has some bizarre, social issue that has forced them onto JewDater. Forced them into a world where they pick out women by clicking on them, instead of talking to them. You are better than that."

"I know. You're right." I think she was starting to see the point. "I just get so upset living here and not meeting anyone that I want to be with. I figured JewDater would at least get me out there meeting people. I just didn't realize that everyone I would meet would be some kind of freak. I just want a boyfriend already. I mean, I like living with you and all, but you're my brother. I want a guy living here that I want to be in a relationship with."

"I know. I wish I knew someone to set you up with. But you know my friends. They're all married. It's sad."

"I'm just emotional. I'm sorry. I'm sorry that I yelled at you earlier today. I don't really think you are a loser. I mean, I think it's a little weird that you want to work at Sneaker Heaven, but that doesn't make you a loser." I could sense that Michelle really was sorry.

"That's okay. We're both trying to work some shit out right now." Boy, was that an understatement.

"Thanks."

Michelle gave me a hug and then walked into the bathroom. I rolled onto my air mattress and closed my eyes.

The next day was my day off, so I met Lisa at the Fox Hole, our favorite dive bar downtown. I was still impressed with the $2 mixed drink special. I pulled up a seat at the bar next to Lisa and beckoned the bartender, "Nance, get me a gin and tonic. Make it a double."

"What is going on with you," Lisa asked. "You look terrible."

"I passed out last night in Michelle's coat closet. I was reading some stuff that I wrote and just blacked out," I said.

"Blackouts are not good, David. How about you start lightening up on the drinking - says the lady meeting you for a drink in the middle of the day."

"Yeah, yeah. Give it a rest. I know the deal."

"How's Sneaker Heaven going?" Lisa asked, as if she couldn't believe the words were actually coming out of her mouth.

Nance was looking good today. Same old jeans and black tank top. Maybe she did something with her hair?

"Yes, in fact, I'm pretty sure I'm getting a promotion to manager," I said, as I finished my first G&T.

"Wow, a manager. You are quite a mover and shaker," Lisa said. "David, what are you doing with your life?"

"Working. Pursuing my dreams. I don't care if that means working at Sneaker Heaven."

"Your dream is to work at a sneaker store? I don't know how

to say this to you, but you smell. And look at your hair. You haven't even shaved your head in weeks. Are you trying to grow your hair out like a clown? It looks like you don't even take care of yourself. You don't even look like the guy that used to work at Hobart. You don't even look like the guy that I knew before you started working at Hobart. You're a mess. Why don't you look for a real job and clean yourself up? You're a professional."

"I can't do it anymore. I have to try this for a while. Law will always be there," I said, as I ordered another G&T.

"I'm sure your new managerial position will really help with the ladies." Lisa was just mocking me now.

"I'm sure it will. In fact, I have a very nice lady that I am friends with at work. I'm hoping I can turn it into something a little more," I said.

"Well, maybe when you are manager you can abuse your authority and bag the 18 year old that I'm sure you have a crush on," Lisa said clearly disgusted.

"I actually met a girl at Jon's party that I want to meet up with. Problem is, I can't find her," I said.

"Another one! Didn't you learn your lesson? Stay away from

women you meet at Jon and Sara functions."

"It's different. She doesn't really know Jon and Sara. She came with someone else. I've been trying to find out a way to get in touch with her, but I never got her last name and Jon has no clue who I am talking about."

"Maybe you want to try a little harder to find her. Ask Jon again. He must know someone who knows her."

"I guess. I'll ask again. Nance, can I get another."

CHAPTER TWENTY-THREE

I eventually became the manager of Sneaker Heaven in the Mall. This meant that I would have to be in the store from 8:00 a.m. until 11:00 p.m. seven days a week. My new position also meant that I would be earning a salary. No more eight dollars an hour for this guy. I was suddenly propelled into the big time. I would be making a stratospheric $32,000 a year. Read it and weep, boys. This could actually get me out of my sister's apartment and into a fifth-floor walk-up studio in the middle of Harlem, if luck was on my side. I wasn't going to allow myself to dream such thoughts. Right now, I was going to bask in the glory of having an office with a door.

In my former life at Hobart, I had an office with a door. The catch was, the door rarely stayed shut for very long. It seems the more you get paid, the more rights you have to relinquish to your surroundings. I was entrenched in a daily battle at the office. I would close my door the moment I arrived at work. Within minutes, people would throw the door open with careless disregard for my wishes to remain a hermit, asking me question after question.

'Get out of my office and while you're at it, shut the door

behind you.' This is what I was thinking most of the time at Hobart. What usually came out was: "I'll have that on your desk by 3." God, I was such a pussy. The beauty of Sneaker Heaven was the fact that I was the boss. This was my kingdom. When that door was shut, someone had better knock before they dared to open that door. To ensure my privacy, the door had a lock, and I would enjoy using it.

As I stated, my typical Sneaker Heaven day would begin at 8:00 a.m. I would open the store, let the employees in, then head over to my office where I would shut the door and really begin my day. I had stocked the 64 square-foot box that served as an office with cereals, ranging from granola to Froot Loops, that I would eat dry (I had not yet managed to get a refrigerator in there) for breakfast and lunch. I wanted to use my time writing. The cereal enabled me to stay self-contained in my office. There wasn't going to be any of this, "Hold on, I'll be right back guys because I'm grabbing something at the food court" shit. I wasn't about to come out of my office.

After my morning cereal, I would start working on my short story. That was the beauty of the door. I could write without distraction. Since I had only started the story a few weeks ago, I was surprised that I was making excellent progress. I attributed the progress to the 8-10 hours that I had every day to work on it. There *were* times during the day where I actually had to do some work. I'd check out the invoices, refresh the stock, and make sure everything was running smoothly. I also would occasionally stroll out into the store itself and check on the employees. Too bad they all couldn't be like Peaches. She was a good worker. Sixteen year-old Emma, on the other hand, appeared to have a limited future at Sneaker Heaven. She was OK with the customers, but the finer aspects of the job had her confused. I mean, how hard is it to find sneakers in the back? You look for the brand and then the size. Trust me, it isn't brain surgery. Thank God, she only worked after school from 4-9.

My appearance had certainly deteriorated to a new low - even for me. I had selected one referee shirt and one pair of khaki pants that served as my daily uniform. One of the new manager perks was I didn't have to wear my old black pants. I had long since stopped washing my clothes. I'm sure that I reeked of body odor, but I was too self-absorbed and focused on writing at the time to realize it.

It was about five in the afternoon - and about two months later - when I first received a knock on my door. It was Kim, the other full-time employee.

"Uh, Mr. Michaels," She mumbled through the closed door. "There's something going on out here that you should probably check out."

One of the things that I have neglected to tell you so far was that I occasionally had a drink at the office. Nothing crazy. Just a scotch or two. I deserved to relax after a long day of writing. Writing was hard work! Hell, Jim smoked pot back here. What's the big deal if I had a drink? Well, I was in the middle of one of those drinks when Kim rudely interrupted me. I put the scotch down and headed out to the floor.

There were two customers in the store. One at the register, and one browsing the clothing racks toward the front of the store. Peaches was at the register.

"Ma'am, I cannot give you a refund for these sneakers. Look at the sole. They obviously have been worn outside. There are pebbles stuck in the treads," Peaches explained.

"I didn't wear them. I tried them on in my house and they were uncomfortable. Now I want a refund," the lady countered.

"You have pebbles in your house? I doubt it. Anyway,

ma'am, I already explained to you, I cannot give you a –" Peaches got cut off at the pass.

"I want to speak to your manager," the woman demanded.

"Well, you're in luck. He's right over there," Peaches pointed to me standing by the new running shoes display.

As the woman approached me, I almost fell backwards in utter disbelief. There stood Sandy McBride!

"Well, I don't believe it. Is that you, David?" Sandy asked. Apparently, she was excited to see me.

"Yup," I was mortified, not to mention, deeply embarrassed.

"What in God's name are you doing here? Are you the Manager? I thought you were some kind of lawyer?"

Peaches was listening, and so was the one, other customer, pretending to be browsing the cross trainers.

"Yup. I'm the manager."

Fuck!

"Aren't you just the cutest in that referee shirt," Sandy complimented me. "Do you want to go into the back over there and –" Sandy said whispering. I don't think Peaches heard that, but the nosey customer might have. She was inching closer by the second.

"Miss, what seems to be the problem?" I said loudly, so the whole store could hear. I was also trying to cut Sandy off before she got totally out of control.

"I'm a 'miss' now? Very nice. Look at you, Mr. Manager." Man, she was seductive. "I love a man with power," She brushed against my arm.

Peaches just looked at me and smiled. She probably thought this woman was just some nut case. Nosey customer was now strolling back towards the front of the store, pretending to look at clothes.

Sandy changed her tone and addressed her sneaker issue, "Well, I wanted to return these sneakers since they didn't fit very well - and your extremely rude salesperson here," she pointed to Peaches, " - told me that that I couldn't because the soles have pebbles in them. And that, of course, would be impossible, since I never wore these sneakers out of my apartment. I guess we both just need a man to decide."

Peaches almost flew into a rage, "I don't need a man to – ". I guess she was listening.

Sandy and I started walking to the register.

"Peaches, I'll handle this. Go ahead and take care of the other customer," I said, even though Kim had already asked the nosey customer if she needed help. I picked up the sneaker and examined it. "Miss, it appears that these shoes were worn outside the store. But I'm going to make you a deal. I'll take your word for it, and I'll be happy to credit you a full refund."

Peaches was listening from across the floor. I heard her mumble, "What the fuck?"

I continued, "I'm going to offer you a full refund, but on the condition that you do not shop at any Sneaker Heaven for the next six months," It was good to be the king.

"That would be quite a shame since I know at least one thing I would like to pick up at Sneaker Heaven very soon," Sandy said, slyly.

I ignored Sandy's comment and continued, "Six months. No sneaker purchases. Are we clear?"

"Absolutely. So that means I can still get my hands on cute boys in referee shirts?" She winked at me.

Kim was busy moving closer and closer to Sandy and me. She was definitely eavesdropping.

"Thank you for understanding. Now, if you'll please fill out this return slip, we can credit you for the sneakers." I handed Sandy the slip.

Sandy leaned over the slip and whispered,. "I've missed you. I think about that night in the bathroom all the time. I even tried to get your number, but since my husband is Jon's boss it was a bit tricky. I couldn't exactly say 'Hey Hon, when you're at work today can you ask Jon who that cute guy was that I fucked at his party. Thanks'."

"Sandy, I'm at work. These people are listening. This isn't the place to talk about it."

"But, you did fuck me. And very well, I might add. I want to sleep with you again. Can we just hop in the back and –" she continued to whisper, ignoring my last comment.

"You're married. That night was a big mistake. I think we both had way too much to drink. I should have never even done so much as kiss you. And now you're here, flirting with me again. This is just wrong." I whispered back.

Peaches and Kim were onto me. The one other customer was probably onto me, too. She has been looking at the same pair of yoga pants for the last ten minutes.

"Oh, stop being such a goody two shoes. Stop worrying about him. We're about to get a divorce anyway. Why don't you just meet me for a drink? That's all I'm asking. Judging by your breath, I assume you're not opposed to that."

"Okay, I'll meet you for a drink." I needed to get her out of here.

"Come to my apartment at 7 o'clock tomorrow."

"I can't, I'm working here."

"What time do you get off?"

"Eleven."

"Then make it 11:30. Jim is out of town, so there is nothing to worry about. My address is on the return slip. See you tomorrow, oh," she raised her voice, "thank you, sir, for your help." And with that, Sandy turned and waved goodbye.

Peaches walked over to me, "Drama. White-boy drama." She shook her head.

Of all the shoe stores in the entire world, why'd she have to walk into mine?

CHAPTER TWENTY-FOUR

Sometimes you just can't help yourself. Especially when it involves free sex. I didn't want to meet Sandy for drinks. I knew it was wrong. I also knew that 'drinks' was just code for sex. There was no avoiding it, as sex was something that I couldn't pass up. Call me weak. Call me stupid. I just can't turn away free sex. And before you go passing judgment on me, think about it yourself. This pitch was being lobbed right over the plate. It's hard not to take a swing, especially when you know you are going to hit a home run.

The sex we had on New Year's Eve was great. But maybe it was the excitement of being caught that made it so intense. Maybe it was the fact that I was plastered off my ass. Cheap, meaningless, bathroom sex was good. What was so wrong about trying to relive a little of the that magic?

I met Sandy at her apartment at 11:30. When I walked through the door, Sandy was dressed in a French maid outfit, holding two glasses of scotch. She looked even better than the last time I saw her. She filled out the outfit quite well and her legs were just as fantastic as I remembered. She handed me a scotch, and downed the other. Now, I am no connoisseur of fine liquor, but I'm pretty sure 25 year-old scotch is not for throwing back, shot-style. But I'll cut her some slack since she was wearing a French-maid outfit. She slammed the door shut, unbuttoned my pants and went to work.

"I'm here to please," she whispered, as she moved down my body.

We spent the entire night having great sex. Apparently, it wasn't the excitement of getting caught or the liquor that made it so great. It was Sandy and me together. There was some kind of raw, sexual magnetism - and I was digging it big time.

After that night, we began to see each other regularly. If Jim was out of town, we would meet at her place after I got off work. Many times, she would meet me at the store, and venture into the back for some scotch and a quickie after everyone was gone.

I was beginning to actually like Sandy as a person. We were having great sex, but we were also having fun. She told me funny stories about mingling in the upper stratosphere of New York Society. She made fun of Jim all the time. She could be hilarious. We would talk on the phone and share laughs between sexual escapades, but, all the while, in the back of my mind, I knew she was married. This simple fact was killing me slowly.

The more we hung out the more I found myself drawn to her. Things were getting pretty serious. We started meeting for dinners about twice a week. That was a huge step since this was in public. Usually, some Chinese food in Chinatown, so we could avoid prying eyes. We figured different little hole in the wall joints were the best spots since we wouldn't run into any of her socialite friends. I have to admit that I did like the excitement of it all. The sneaking around and the fear of being caught was definitely adding to the whole experience. The endorphins created over roast pork lo mein were somehow blocking out the fact that Sandy was a married woman when I was with her. Once, over chicken with broccoli, I broached the subject.

"You know, I love hanging out with you, and the sex is great, but I can't help thinking about the fact that you are married. It really upsets me because I'm falling for you," I said, as I picked up some chopsticks and threw away my manhood.

Sandy turned serious. She leaned in to me and said in a definitive tone, "I know, but I told you, I *am* going to leave him. He doesn't know how to make me feel like a woman. All he cares about is work and making money. He never has time for me. You know," she paused, " I actually think he's cheating on me."

This was an interesting development. Two adulterers.

"Cheating on you? You're cheating on him. You've been sleeping with me for over a month. That's not even taking into consideration New Year's Eve."

Sandy got upset. She leaned in even closer. I could really get a good look at her face. Her teeth were really white. I wonder what toothpaste she used. I needed to get myself a tube. Her eyes were really green, too. They were piercing right through me when she again reassured me, "I *am* going to leave him. I want to be with *you*. Just give me some time."

And there you have it. I couldn't believe what this affair was turning into. I was the pathetic, lead character in a bad, made for television movie, trapped in an uncommitted relationship. I had become the other woman. In this case, the other man.

"Can we drop this?" Sandy implored, " I just want to enjoy our dinner together. You know I love you."

She loves me. Well, that was a revelation. In fact, the second big revelation tonight. Did I love Sandy? I definitely loved sleeping with her. But, did I love *her*? And what do you say after someone says 'I love you'? I wasn't going to say 'I love you' back, but I had to say something.

"Yeah," I answered lamely.

I was indeed, the sad 'other man' listening to my lover tell me everything was going to be fine. "Just give me a little more time and you'll see, things will work out." The really pathetic part was, I was buying it hook, line, and sinker. These conversations became the standard exchange for us over the next few months. We would have sex, or go out to eat at some hidden dive away from everyone we knew, and I would start bitching about our 'relationship.' She kept telling me that she was going to leave Jim, and though I believed her, I was getting desperate. I wanted some assurances. I wanted some proof that this was actually going to happen. Up to this point, all I had was lip service. That's when she dropped the bomb on me one night at her apartment.

I was sitting on the couch, sipping a scotch, looking out the window admiring the sun setting over the Park. It must be nice to live here all of the time. What a view. I could actually see the model boats on the pond. That's crazy! Then Sandy just blurted out, "Look,

I'm tired of sneaking around with you. Going to unknown restaurants and late nights at my apartment when Jim isn't home. I want to see you more. So I got you an apartment on 72nd. Just a few blocks away from me, so we can have some fun without any fear. Anyway, isn't it about time you moved out of your sister's studio apartment? Why don't you start moving some stuff in it this weekend? Then we'll christen the new apartment all night."

I was shocked. I was stunned. Was I really going to allow myself to be a kept man? Where was my pride? Where was my manhood?

"When did you decide this?" I was shocked. I didn't know what else to say.

"The other week. I was just walking along Madison Avenue, doing some shopping, and I said to myself, 'why are we sneaking around when we could just spend time in our own apartment.' I called a broker and told him we were looking for something to keep for friends when they visited. He showed me a few, and I bought the place on 72nd that day. I just knew it would be perfect." Sandy was brimming with excitement.

"Well, I guess that's cool," I said. Holy shit! This woman just bought an apartment like I buy dinner. Well, actually Sandy buys dinner. I'm nearly broke. "How about I just sleep there a few nights a week, instead of completely moving in?" I wasn't sure if I was ready to completely emasculate myself yet.

"Sweetie, you can do whatever you want. It's your apartment," Sandy said, coolly.

I could do whatever I wanted. This sent me into a bonafide panic. I actually had a Sugar Momma. There are some guys who are my age, who have other women on the side. They are the Sugar Daddy. I, on the other hand, was a sad mess.

I agreed to accept the apartment.

That night, back at Michelle's apartment, I called Jon and came clean about the whole affair. I was sitting next to Michelle on the couch, so I'm pretty sure she was listening to every word.

"You've been what?!" Jon exclaimed.

"I've been seeing Sandy for the past six months," I said.

"Seeing Sandy for the past six months. I can't believe what I'm hearing. She's married!" Jon cried.

"I know, I know. I don't know how this happened?" I said.

"I do. You keep sleeping with her. Oh, my God. Does Jim know? How did it start?"

"It started at your house New Year's Eve. We got a little intimate in the bathroom during dinner."

I was ashamed.

"Intimate in the bathroom?? I can't believe what I'm hearing. Sara is going to kill me when she hears this. You have to end it. End it right now," Jon said with a shaky voice.

"You can't tell Sara!" I said.

"Of course, I'm not going to tell her. I just mean, if she knew, she would kill me," Jon said.

"Good. Anyway, it might be a little hard to end it right now. She just bought me an apartment."

"Are you trying to kill me? Dude, listen to me. Jim is my boss. You cannot move into an apartment with Sandy. He's going to fire me," Jon was pretty nervous.

"Jim doesn't know. Anyway, Sandy told me that she is going to leave Jim pretty soon. They're basically separated," speaking this out loud really confirmed for me that I was indeed delusional.

"Do they still live together?" Jon asked.

"Yes, but – " I answered.

"Then they are not separated!" Jon was screaming at me, "Separated people don't live together. She's using you, or having fun, or doing whatever. She's not going to leave Jim."

"I'm starting to really like her. I think I really want to be with her. She keeps telling me that she is going to leave Jim, so I started believing her."

"Dude, you sound like a fucking bitch. Do you hear yourself? Putting that aside for now, considering she does leave Jim, don't you think she will want some kind of commitment from you? After all you're talking about someone leaving their husband." Jon put it all out there.

"Yeah, I guess."

"You guess? Well, you better think about that," Jon said. "Shit, okay, okay, David, I have to go because the baby is crying. Just promise me you'll think about what I said." He hung up.

The truth was, I didn't know what I wanted. I know I was complaining to Sandy about her being married, but that didn't mean I wanted her to leave her husband so that I could marry her. I figured the best thing I could do was to take everything day by day.

Michelle, just shook her head and sprayed cleaner on the windows, "You never told Jon? Patheti."

I inflated the air mattress and went to sleep.

CHAPTER TWENTY-FIVE

The next weekend began Part Two of my personal saga: The Kept Man. I began sleeping at the 72nd Street apartment. It was a beautiful place. I had a balcony that overlooked Central Park, a fully furnished pad complete with giant screen televisions, leather couches, club chairs, a beautiful dining room and a fully-stocked, amazing kitchen with top-of-the-line everything. I was in heaven.

Sandy would stay there with me most nights. We would spend the majority of our time having sex and ordering in. It was nice not having to worry about Jim coming home, or having someone espy me when I did the walk of shame from Sandy's place in the morning.

Within a few weeks, I began to move some things into the apartment to make life a little easier. At first, it was the small stuff, such as a toothbrush and a razor. Soon, I brought my two referee shirts and then my laptop. After a while, I moved in my entire clothing collection that was comprised of a few pair of jeans and some ratty t-shirts.

Before I knew it, I found myself leaving work and making a

beeline for 72nd Street. I was staying there every night. Sandy would spend about three nights a week with me, and the other four nights she would come by for a couple of hours to get laid and to talk. She would tell me about her day, talk about the charities she was working on (me being one of them), and crack jokes about Jim. She was a riot after a few drinks.

When Sandy wasn't around, I worked on my story. I would write a little, and then edit what I had done until I passed out at the desk. I was falling into a sad cycle of a kept man. The troubling part was I didn't care very much. I had gotten to the point where I had no I idea what else I was going to do with my life?

One night, Sandy came over with two shopping bags full of clothes she had bought that day. She made a grand entrance into the apartment, dressed in a cute short beige skirt and a tight-fitting white blouse. Her tits looked great. And her legs, well, they always looked great. She had on a red, large-brimmed hat and was carrying the bags limply in her hands. She walked briskly over to the bedroom.

"C'mon," she said, motioning for me to follow. She sat on the bed and pulled out an expensive button-down shirt and threw it at me, "Here, try this on." I took off my ten year-old pocket T and tried on the shirt.

"You look great," she smiled, and dug back into her bag, coming up with another shirt, "Here, try this one on, too."

I changed into the new shirt and stood there motionless.

"Nah, too big in the shoulders," she concluded.

She continued to pull out articles of clothing, one after the other, for me to model for her. Finally I said, "What's with all the clothes?"

"They're for you. I was shopping for myself, and thought I would pick some stuff up for you, too. I want you to start looking nice for me when I come over. I'm sick of your smelly, old t-shirts and referee jerseys. I want you to look classy," she explained, as I sunk to a new low.

"Thanks," I said, feeling anger rise up within me.

I stood there mute for a moment, and then walked into the bathroom.

I slammed the door shut and walked over to the mirror. I stood there in my $300 shirt and $200 jeans and saw someone that I was not proud of. How did I let this happen? This wasn't me. Taking handouts, mooching off of some rich lady, messing around with married ladies. I had to find a way out. I sat down on the toilet, put my hands over my head, and stared into space. I had to get out of this nightmare. It was one thing to stay in your sugar momma's apartment, but it was another thing when you were being dressed like a real-life man doll.

I don't know how long I was sitting there, when I was pulled back to reality. Sandy shouted from the living room, "What's this story here on your computer?"

I jumped off the toilet, and ran into the other room, "You're not supposed to be reading that. Who told you that you could use my computer?" I was livid. At least the computer was mine.

"Relax, I was just going to check my email. And then I stumbled upon this. It's really very good. Actually, it's excellent. Did you write it?"

Was this validation for something I had actually done? I could hardly believe it.

"Really, David, this is very good. It should be published. Did you write it?" She asked again.

"Yeah, I wrote it. I've been working on it for the past few months." My mood shifted from desperation back to semi-happy.

"You really like it?"

"I'm serious. This is excellent. Is it finished?" Sandy asked.

"Well, I tweak it almost every day. You know, change a word here or there, but it's pretty much done," I explained.

"Can I show it around? I might know some people who would be interested in reading this," Sandy was excited.

"I guess. If you really think so," I said.

"Let me see what I can do," Sandy said, and then she laid a red-hot kiss on me.

CHAPTER TWENTY-SIX

Work was still comprised mainly of writing and spending a little time on the floor, hanging with Peaches and Kim. Because Sandy and I would occasionally meet at the office after hours, I had begun to compile a bit of a liquor collection. I had some scotch and a bottle of gin. I also installed a television in my office, another reward for a hard day's writing, with the mother of all time killers connected to it: The G-Circle, gaming system. I needed something to do when I wasn't writing or on the floor, right? Once and a while, I would relax with a drink and play a little football. I did learn that drinking while playing would drive me to psychotic fits of rage when I would lose to the computer. More than once I found myself standing over the television screaming, "Fuck you, you mother fucker," at the G-Circle.

I was in the middle of one such game when a voice peeped through the door.

"Peep – David – Peep," something said.

I could barely hear it since I was in the middle of a therapeutic scream, "That was out! FUCKING OUT! YOU

FUCKING MACHINE!"

"David," the voice repeated, a tad more audible.

"Whatta fuck you want?" I slurred. I was drinking this day. A little too much.

Kim, the other full-time employee, said, "David, there is someone here to see you. She wants to come back here. She says she knows you. What should I do?"

"I don't know," still slurring, "Send her back here, I guess. And another thing, next time you come back here, you knock!" I was nasty today.

A moment later, Sandy walked in the office, "God, it reeks in here. Is this what you do all day? Drink and play video games?" Her face was scrunched up in disgust, as she looked around the office.

She looked great today. It must have been work-out day. She had on black yoga pants and a tight, work-out tank top/sports bra sort of thing. The guys must love her at the gym.

"Whatta you care?" I said, pointing at her. Then I stood up, and did a little twirl in front of her, so she could see my wrinkled khaki pants and my nasty referee shirt.

"Did you come here to check up on what I was wearing? Is

this okay with you, Miss Officer of the Fashion Police? Or should I get my Fancy pants on-" I unbuttoned my pants, which fell around my legs.

"Whatever. Listen up, Honey. I have some great news, I called a few friends of mine and showed them your story. And you're never going to believe this –"

"C'mon. Out with it already," I was still standing there with khaki leg warmers.

"The Manhattan wants to publish it!" She was so excited.

"What?" I was in shock.

"The Manhattan magazine wants to publish your story," she repeated.

"The Manhattan wants to publish my story," I had to say it out loud to confirm that it was true. "The story you read on my computer? The Manhattan wants to publish that?"

It was sinking in. Well, not totally, but it was beginning to.

"Yes, baby! They want to publish your story and they want to meet you. Carl Greenman, the editor in charge of fiction, wants to have dinner with you tomorrow night to talk about your story." Sandy was jumping up and down with excitement.

"I can't believe this. I can't believe The Manhattan is going to publish my story," I felt myself sobering up by the second.

"Getting your story published in The Manhattan is a life-changing deal! This is going to mean incredible things for you, David. Book deals, magazine deals, movie options. You're going to be famous," Sandy was explaining.

"My God, I'm just in shock," I said.

It was more like disbelief.

CHAPTER TWENTY-SEVEN

The next night I met Carl Greenmam at Gramercy Bistro. Carl was already seated at his table by the time I checked in with the hostess. As I was escorted to the table, I couldn't believe my eyes. There was Karen - *Karen* - sitting with Carl! I felt my heart pounding and my hands started to clam up. Carl and Karen stood up.

"David. Hi, I'm Carl Greenman, and this is my assistant Karen Gold," Carl introduced himself.

I shook Carl's hand and then turned my attention to Karen Gold. Gold! That was the name that had eluded me for the better part of a year. So simple, too. Gold.

"Karen Gold," I strung out the last name for a second or two. "So that's your last name."

"Nice to see you again, David," she said, as I shook her hand.

"I've been trying to find you for the last year. Boy, you are one, difficult lady to track down," I couldn't help myself.

"You two know each other?" Carl asked.

"We met at a New Year's Eve party last year," Karen said, smiling.

"Well, isn't that funny. What a small world. Listen, David, I just have to tell you. We love your story. When Sandy brought it to me I was a bit hesitant at first, but, when I started reading it, I could not stop until I had finished it. It is something special, indeed," Carl admitted.

"Thank you, Carl. I think it is something special, too," I answered.

"We're going to fast track it and have it ready for publication in our next issue that hits the newsstand next month. We really think it's going to generate a lot of interest," Carl said.

"I certainly hope so. I'm tired of living on my sister's air mattress," I said.

"You are very funny, David," Carl laughed. "Certainly no mystery here. You were definitely the person who wrote that story."

Carl complimented me all the way through dinner. Karen smiled a lot, and threw her own compliments in every now and again. Carl then excused himself to go to the bathroom. This was my only chance.

"I didn't know you worked at The Manhattan," I said to Karen.

"I didn't when you met me. I just started here two weeks ago. It's the first job I've had in nine months," Karen said, beaming at me. She was prettier than I even remembered. And she looked younger than I remembered. Maybe I was just comparing her to Sandy. But, now that I was sitting here with Karen, I realized just how old Sandy was. Karen sort of looked like Sandy. She had the long legs, the nice boobs, the pretty face, the blond hair, but Karen was the younger, sexier version.

"Wow, I can't believe this. I've been trying to find you for almost a year. I had a great time with you on New Year's, but you left so soon! I didn't get a chance to even say goodbye, let alone get any info about you."

"I know, I'm sorry. My brother pulled me out of there. He had some other party to go to. And of course he couldn't leave his baby sister by herself at a party," Karen said.

"Am I wrong or did we have something special there that night. I just couldn't stop thinking about you."

Karen took a sip of her water and then put her hand on mine, "I felt the same thing, too."

"I propose we do something about it right here. I would like to take you out tomorrow night. Do you like music? Because I know a great piano bar where we could go." I was babbling.

"I'd love to. But you have to promise me that you won't tell Carl. I really like my job and I don't want anything to blow it," Karen said.

"You have my word." I was psyched.

I had to lie to Sandy, telling her that I was working late doing inventory at the store, but I didn't really care. This bitch was going to show Sandy who had the upper hand in this relationship. If she didn't have to commit, neither did I. More to the point, I had a strong sense about Karen that told me that she had been worth the wait.

I met Karen at The Eighth Note at nine. I loved this place. It was a throwback to the old-school, piano bars where you could request any song. The kicker was, here, you could sing along karaoke-style and an entire big-band would back you up. I got there a few minutes early, found a table off to the side of the stage, and ordered myself a G&T.

I liked that this bar was set up like a cabaret. There were small little tables scattered everywhere, all directly facing the stage.

The few times that I had ventured on the stage, singing, and backed up by that band, I felt like an actual performer, belting it out for my devoted fans.

"Karen, over here!" I yelled, when I saw her walk in. Her straight, blond hair flowed behind her as she strutted over to me. She was confident. I loved that.

Karen sat down, ordered herself a red wine, and then said, "I'm so glad we have a chance to continue our last conversation." She looked me straight in the eye. "So, the last thing you were telling me was the man you subletted your apartment from wanted $2.50 for a shower curtain."

"I can't believe you remember that," I said smiling, as I took another sip of my drink.

"I remembered everything about that night. I still can't believe Sara - that's her name right? - pulled you away like that," Karen picked up my drink, "You don't mind if I have a sip do you? I'm so thirsty."

Someone was singing. It wasn't that bad. But, how could anything sound that bad with an orchestra behind you? And, it was an orchestra, with ten musicians on the stage. The musicians were dressed in tuxedos, and before each, stood a blue podium with two giant letters on them: E and N. It was a professional set-up, the likes of which would have made any singer proud.

The cocktail waitress walked over with Karen's wine.

"Anyway, I'm glad we finally had a chance to get together," Karen said.

"I was thinking the same thing," I said. "Nine months is a long time to look for someone."

"You should have looked harder," Karen laughed.

After a few more drinks, and a funny lecture on the finer points of trying to locate someone that you're interested in, I built up the courage to sing. "Do you like to sing?" I asked Karen.

"If you're asking me to duet with you, I'm game," she said. "Do you like old standards?" Karen said flipping through the karaoke songbook that was sitting on each table. The songbook listed songs that people could choose from to perform.

"Pick whatever you want,'" I said. "I'll give it a whirl."

Karen was on her third glass of wine by this time. She ran up to the piano man and requested our song. Before we knew it, he called our names.

"David and Karen! Come on up, it's time for you two to croon,'" he called, before launching into a salsa-rhythm introduction. The band followed along.

Karen sauntered up to the stage, stumbling a bit. A few drops of wine spilled from her glass as she tottered up to the stage. I followed the crumbs, er, wine-drip, footpath Gretel left for me, and met her on the stage. Karen took the microphone out of the stand and began the first verse. Then I joined in, our voices colliding, resulting in an utter disaster.

Karen is an absolutely horrible singer. I think she's awesome and hot, but the girl can't sing. At least she was trying. It was kind of endearing. On the other hand, I can kind of sing on key. It's the high pitched, nasally, singing voice that's my downfall. Otherwise, I would have been a rock star by now.

I moved my hips a little, in a feeble attempt at dancing. I'm terrible - at least I know it.

"Whoops," Karen said, laughing and stumbling, as her wine flew out of her glass into the crowd. I guess she was dancing, too.

"You got wine on me, bitch!" someone screamed from offstage.

Hey, pal. Don't fuck with the talent.

Karen provided the big finish. Totally trashed, she accidentally threw her wine glass across the stage when she flailed her arms Broadway style, attempting to hold the last note of the song forever. She was giving the crowd all she had.

"Goodnight, everybody!" I yelled as we finished.

I hugged Karen, "That was great," then threw the microphone down on the floor like the rock star I was.

"We rocked," Karen hugged back.

I leaned in and went for the kiss. Our lips met, and we kissed for what seemed like hours right off to stage left. It was great.

The audience applauded, but I think they were applauding the kiss. There was no way they were clapping for our horrendous singing.

We had a few more drinks, got to know each other a little better, before I took Karen home in a taxi. I walked her to her apartment building's door.

"You know, you are really talented," Karen slurred, "Your story is really great. Thank you so much for taking me out. I had a wonderful time".

"Thanks. I had a great time too. You're a lot of fun," I said, going in for another kiss. "You know we're going to have a lot of time to work on our duets. I intend to ask you out pretty much every day."

"Well, if that's the case we should have our act down in a couple of months," she said.

"I'll call you tomorrow," I said, walking away.

"If I don't call you first," she said, and she closed the door to her building.

I saw Karen every night after that for a week. I even slept over at Karen's apartment one night. Things were going great. What was I doing with someone who looked at me like another toy, when Karen seemed to actually care about me?

There were a few things that I was conveniently leaving out of my conversations with Karen. Namely, I was basically Sandy's bitch, and living in the apartment that she bought for me. I would eventually have to come clean, but for now, I figured, why spoil all the fun? I still thought that I could somehow end my relationship with Sandy gracefully, and just pick up with Karen. But, of course, it is common knowledge that things don't always go as smoothly as planned.

CHAPTER TWENTY-EIGHT

The Manhattan hit newsstands on October 15th with my story 'Sh*t.Falls.Up.' as the featured piece of fiction that week. I took the day off from Sneaker Heaven to celebrate the event. I went to the bodega on the corner of 72nd and Lexington and bought myself ten copies of the magazine. I looked at the ten and thought to myself, "How could ten copies possibly be enough?" so I walked over to the Charles and Boles bookstore on 56th and bought eight more. I couldn't contain my excitement. I made a pit stop at Michelle's and dumped off all the magazines.

My cell had been ringing since I woke up. I ignored it to bask in my own private celebration. Finally, I picked it up.

First my mom called: "David, oh, this is so exciting. Dad and I are so happy for you. So now does this mean that you're going to go back to practicing law? I mean, we really think you should reconsider it. Sneaker Heaven is no life for someone with a law degree."

After that debacle, I received call after call of congratulations. Michelle called to tell me, "You actually made something of yourself. I didn't really think you had that in you."

Thanks for the vote of confidence.

Karen gave a ring from California and offered me congratulations on the story. The magazine sent her there to preview the fall movie season. Two seconds later, Carl called to tell me that I was invited to Hut 17 - an exclusive club - tonight for a private party celebrating the release of 'Sh*t.Falls.Up'.

"Why don't you bring, Sandy?" he said, "I think she'll get a kick out of it. After all, she had a hand in getting the story published."

Yeah, thanks Carl.

I called Sandy to see if Carl had already gotten to her.

"Hello, Sandy?" I said when she picked up.

"This is exciting! You did it, honey! Did you see it yet?" She asked.

"Yes, I bought 20 copies."

"That's it! I bought 50-something, I think," I heard her counting to herself, "53, to be exact. Listen, I spoke to Carl. What time do you want to meet for this thing tonight? Carl said it starts at seven. Carl picked a perfect day for the release since Jim is out of town on business. We can play all night. How about I come by 72nd Street at six? Okay? . . . I've got to run. Oh, those look great," Sandy was talking to someone off in the distance, "The sales lady here just brought over six more dresses. Bye," She hung up.

I sat down on my air mattress and decided that I had to break up with Sandy. This couldn't continue. I had to start clean. Today was the day I was going to change my life. Tonight would be the last time I would speak to Sandy. I hoped.

By the time Sandy got to 72nd Street, I was dressed and ready to impress. I was looking pretty hip, if I don't say so myself, with my custom, form-fitting, tailored black suit, courtesy of Sandy, checkered shirt and thin, 60's inspired tie. We took a limo provided by The Manhattan to the festivities – apparently, success had some perks.

When the limousine pulled up to Hut 17, Sandy and I got out and walked to the entrance. Hut 17 was located in the middle of the Meatpacking District, surrounded by old, abandoned warehouses. There was a velvet rope outside the club to keep any crowds penned in and a separate, mini-velvet rope blocking the door. A line had formed with young, star fuckers trying to get in. Occasionally, a long, black car would drive up to the entrance. One or two people would exit, strut straight up to the bouncer, who would remove the mini-velvet rope, open the door and usher them in. There was a small group of photographers huddled on the edge of the sidewalk about five feet from the entrance, calling out the names of those they recognized and taking pictures. So far, I hadn't seen anyone that I recognized. But, I'm not that up on the celebrity scene. Someone screamed Sandy's name a couple of times and was snapping shots of her with a camera.

"Don't worry about them," Sandy said, "God Damn paparazzi. Happens all the time. They never leave me alone. But I have to tell you that secretly I love it."

"Sandy, over here," one called out.

"Who's the guy you're with? Where's Jim?" Another screamed.

Sandy just ignored them.

"It's weird," I said, as we approached the bouncer, "people taking your picture all the time."

"Comes with the territory, honey," she answered, then,

turning to the bouncer. "We're here for The Manhattan party. Two, under Michaels, he's the guest of honor. Just had a story published in The Manhattan."

It was amazing how she could say anything with an air of pretension.

The bouncer, a massive man wearing an earpiece, searched his list and found us, "Okay, Mr. Michaels, and guest, enjoy your evening." Then he removed the mini-velvet rope and opened the door.

I heard some of the wannabees in line start to make a stink, "Who was that?" One said.

"How come that guy got in? And who's the old bitch with him?" Another commented.

Sandy didn't hear the 'old bitch' comment. Thank God. She was too focused on the fact that she was listed as a guest. "Guest, huh? That's the first time I've ever been referred to as 'guest'."

Though Sandy did not like that she was referred to as 'guest' she seemed very attracted to me. She grabbed my arm and let *me* escort *her* into the party. Apparently, the balance of power was shifting.

Carl met us at the door. "There they are. The genius writer, and his beautiful muse," Carl said, shaking my hand, and then giving Sandy a double cheek kiss.

"Oh, Carl, you say that to all the ladies," Sandy dryly retorted.

This place was unreal. There was real sand on the floor, and the walls resembled the grass walls of typical island huts. There were tiki torches, string lights, palm trees and little VIP cabanas all over the club. Carl took Sandy's hand and led both of us around to meet the guests. He introduced us to every intellectual and pseudo-intellectual (the pseudo-intellectuals were usually the assistants), who worked at The Manhattan. Everyone was singing my praises, telling me how wonderful my story was, and how they expected great things from me in the future.

Everyone here must be really important. You don't end up at parties like this unless you know the right people, correct? I was never invited to anything like this, but here I was. According to the Manhattan, I was now important.

Every guy was dressed in some sort of suit, and every woman was dressed as if they stepped off the runway. I didn't even know these sort of parties existed. It wasn't the most exciting party in the world. It was more like a giant cocktail hour with people forming little groups, drinking and laughing. I did see a couple of people just aimlessly staring into space. Hey, everyone can't be a star. Every party needs its share of wallflowers, too. Sandy was busy mingling. She fluttered from publisher, to editor, to curator, to actor. There were all sorts in this club. Older actors were around, the ones you don't see too much of anymore. I sort of recognized them, but couldn't place their names, or what show or film I had seen them in. I wasn't quite sure who some of the other people were, but judging by their demeanor they had to be important. Plus, Sandy wasn't going to waste her time with nobodies. She knew how to work a room. She was a pro.

After I thought that I had met everyone there was to meet, Carl introduced me to Jason Hoffman, a publisher of new fiction at King Life Press, one of the largest publishers in the world.

"Jason, here is the guy I've been telling you about," Carl said.

"Well, Mr. Michaels, it is indeed a pleasure to meet you. I read your story, and was thoroughly impressed. It's been a long time since we've had someone who could really write in this town," Jason seemed smitten.

"Thank you, so much," I said, shaking Jason's hand, "That is quite a compliment."

"Well, it's true. Look, I would love to talk to you about turning this story into a full-length novel. I think it would be fantastic."

"Wow, I don't know what to say," I was nearly speechless, "Sure, thanks. I mean, yes, I would love to turn it into a novel."

"Great, then give me a call tomorrow morning and we'll discuss the details," he said, handing me his business card.

"I will. I definitely will." I repeated myself. "Thanks." We shook hands again.

Meanwhile, Carl got up on the stage and started to speak, "I want to thank everyone for coming out tonight to celebrate the launch of a bright new career in the world of literature. We, at The Manhattan, are thrilled beyond words to bring you one of the finest stories of the year, perhaps the last ten years . . . Mr. David Michaels' brilliant story, 'Sh*t.Falls.Up.' David, come up here and read a few pages to us."

I didn't know this was part of the bargain. I tried to hide behind Jason, but Carl just kept pointing at me, and saying, "come on up and read a few pages for us." I had a sick feeling in the pit of my stomach.

The applause continued, and Carl persisted, so I got up to read a few pages. However, I ended up reading the entire story to thunderous applause and praise. Maybe *this* story really *was* that good. Maybe I had actually done something worthwhile. I was so excited when I left Hut 17 that I decided to give Sandy a reprieve and not break up with her that night. Quite the opposite. We slept together.

CHAPTER TWENTY-NINE

The next morning I woke up to fifteen messages on my cell phone. It appears that I had made my way right on to the dreaded "Page 9" of the Daily Story. It was a great picture of me, looking as sexy as ever, standing outside Hut 17 with Sandy by my side. The caption under the photograph read, "Writer David Michaels accompanied by socialite girlfriend Sandy McBride at last night's Manhattan party".

Message one. 7:17 AM. Sandy. "Fuck!! Fuck! Fuck! Shit! Fuck! (Inaudible rambling)"

Message two. 7:19 AM. Sandy. "Fuck! Did you see the paper yet?"

Message three. 7:21 AM. Sandy. "Wake the fuck up! (Banging the phone on something) WAKE UP!!"

Messages four through thirteen sounded frighteningly similar.

Message fourteen. 8:36 AM. Sandy (calm). "Jim finally saw the picture this morning and confronted me about it. I told him everything, David. Everything. I even told him about New Year's. I told him it was just a matter of time before he drove me away, and that I have wanted to leave him for years, and being with you finally gave me the guts to do it. He told me not to wait one more second.

He'd give me a divorce if I wanted it. I told him I wanted it."

(Message cuts off)

Message fifteen. 9:06 AM. Karen (happy). "Hi David. I can't believe

I'm up so early. I'm at the airport. I can't wait to get the hell out of

LA. I'm so sorry that I couldn't be with you last night on your big

day. I hope you had a good time at the party. I'll be back in town

tonight. Why don't we get together and celebrate on our own? I

should be back in the city by five, so why don't you stop by my

apartment around eight. Bring us a couple of bottles of wine. We

have a lot of celebrating to do."

Oh, shit. I didn't know what to do next. Should I call Karen

back and tell her to skip tonight? She was probably on a plane by

now. Fuck. Should I call Sandy back and see what the hell happened

over there? That was going to be some scary stuff. I didn't really

want to call anyone back. This is the problem with being a

procrastinator; you keep putting off stuff until it all catches up with

you. I should have just stuck to my plan - break up with Sandy. Not

take Sandy to a swanky party and then sleep with her. Everything

was so clear last night before that party. Fuck you, party.

But, I still had other things to do today. I had to call Jason Hoffman back, negotiate a book deal, and get over to Sneaker Heaven and actually go to work. My cell rang again. Unknown. God damn it. I hate those unknown numbers. Doesn't everyone know by now that I have a screening problem? I picked it up in haste.

"Oh, is this the prince that finally woke up from his precious slumber?" Sandy was on the line.

Fuck you, unknown.

"Yeah, well – "

"Did you even bother going through your messages?" She asked, pissed at me.

Didn't she realize this was too early in the morning for me?

"Yeah, I heard them. I can't be-" she cut me off.

"I'm coming over, I'll be there in five minutes," Sandy said. Then I heard the dreaded click.

I sat down and took a look at the article written around my picture. I was pretty impressed:

New Writer Makes Debut In This Month's The Manhattan Magazine.

New York – Mr. David Michaels was spotted yesterday with socialite girlfriend, Sandy McBride, at Hut 17 on the same day that his short story 'Sh*t.Falls.Up' hit the stands in this month's The Manhattan magazine. Sources have linked the pair for the past few months, despite McBride's long-term marriage to businessman, Jim McBride. The couple has also been seen on numerous occasions in Chinatown, and gallivanting about the Upper East Side.

I could not believe what I was reading. I was becoming tabloid trash. Wasn't it bad enough I was someone's bitch? Did I have to sink to tabloid trash as well? I didn't even have a chance to read about anyone else when the doorbell rang.

"Let me in," Sandy barked, pushing at the door.

I opened the door and got ready for some fireworks. "So, Jim knows everything. That's it. He's moving his shit out and heading over to our house in the Hamptons to live until things are settled," she explained.

"I'm sorry. I can't believe we got caught because of the Daily Story. Page 9 is the last place I ever expected to find myself this morning. Before yesterday, I was a manager at Sneaker Heaven.

Today, I'm Tabloid Trash," I said.

"I'm kind of glad this happened. I mean, I knew some picture of us would show up somewhere. I'm not that naive. But, to actually write about our affair like that, for the world to see. That put everything in perspective. It was time to leave Jim. That's what I realized this morning. This mistake gave me the strength I needed to finally end things with him. Now, we can finally be together. We get to start our own life now," Sandy said apprehensively, trying to convince herself what she was saying was true.

Here is where it got a little tricky. I obviously wanted to dump Sandy on her ass, leaving me free to be with Karen. The problem was, Sandy submitted my story to The Manhattan and, as Carl pointed out, she had a lot to do with any success that may follow. Sandy, basically, ushered me in as a writer. But, I was the one who wrote the story. On the other hand, because of my new-found celebrity, Sandy was losing her marriage. I wasn't quite sure what the time frame was for dumping someone whose marriage you helped end. I was guessing it wasn't a couple of hours. I needed some help.

"Sandy, I have to use the restroom," I bolted to the master

bathroom, and quickly dialed up Jon on my cell.

"Dude, did you see Page 9 this morning?"

"Yeah. Holy Shit! Jim is going to freak," Jon said.

"I got news for you. Jim already freaked. Jim and Sandy are getting a divorce," I said.

"What -!?"

"But, here's the thing. I have Sandy in my apartment right now. She says she wants to be with me, but I really like someone else that I've kind of been dating on the side," I said.

"What -!?" This was too much for Jon.

"Dude, I want to get rid of Sandy. How long do I have to wait until I can dump her?" I was grasping for straws here.

"What's wrong with you? You're sick. Sick! You know that. Oh, man - ," Jon just kept babbling.

"I have to go," I hung up the phone. Jon was no help. I quickly dialed Lisa.

"Hobart and Klein, Lisa Thompson speaking."

"Lisa, it's me. I'm in the bathroom of my apartment and I have a big problem," I started.

"What's the problem?" Lisa was confused.

"You know how me and Karen are kind of dating?"

"Yeah," Lisa sighed, already exasperated with me.

"Well, there is sort of a problem" I was trying to get to the point, but I also was very confused. "I'm kind of seeing someone else. Well, I was seeing her before I met Karen, and then-"

"Do we really have to go into this right now. I'm in the middle of some important stuff. We're not all big-time writers and have all day to – "

"Can you kill the dramatics? I need help! I have to dump this other woman, but I'm not sure how or when to do it."

I couldn't dump her right now that was for sure. I could probably dump her next week. That would be more than enough time, I thought.

"No time like the present. Just dump her. You say, 'This isn't working out. We're through'. Seems pretty simple to me," Lisa said, half listening. I could hear her typing on her keyboard.

"Well, obviously you didn't see Page 9 this morning. The girl I'm seeing is Sandy McBride," I said.

"You're on Page 9!"

"That's not the point," I said. "The girl I am seeing is Sandy McBride!"

"Sandy McBride, the socialite? Isn't she like 50?" Lisa was floored.

"Yes, the socialite," I said, ignoring the dig.

"I thought she was married to Jim McBride, the business guy," Lisa deduced.

"Well, she was until this morning when the two of us showed up together in the newspaper. Now she's leaving him to be with me," I said.

"Is everything okay in there?" Sandy called in the bathroom.

"Everything is fine. I'm just finishing up," I called back.

"Is that Sandy?" Lisa said.

"Yes that was her," I was whispering. "I have to go."

"I can't believe it, Sandy McBride is right out –" Lisa was star struck, but I cut her off.

I hung up the phone, and stood there looking at the Roman tub. What was I doing? I flushed the toilet, threw some water on my face and headed back into the lioness's den with absolutely no help from any of my friends.

Five steps out of the toilet, Sandy threw her arms around me and hugged me, whispering in my ear, "We're finally free, David. We're finally free."

I just stood there shaking inside when I formulated a new, life theory: Hugs Kill.

Sandy eventually left to get in some therapeutic shopping. For the time being, she was still Sandy McBride, which meant she could buy anything and everything that suited her fancy and charge it to Jim's account. Shortly, she would be "finally free" of Jim. Maybe she wanted to have some new clothes for divorce court. I'm sure that wasn't going to be any fun.

I still had some things to take care of. I tried to stop and think about what I needed to do first. Okay, priority number one. I had to call Jason Hoffman. I moseyed over to the kitchen where I poured myself a small glass of scotch to calm my nerves. I looked around for the business card Jason gave me. I finally found it buried in the back pocket of the swanky, black suit pants that I wore last night.

I dialed the number. "Jason Hoffman speaking,"

"Hi, Mr. Hoffman. It's David Michaels."

"David, glad you called. I just got out of a meeting about turning your story into a full-length book. We were all very excited, and we have some great news for you. Could you come in around three today so we can chat about things?" Jason explained.

"Sure, I just have to stop in at work for a little while. I'll try not to be late," I said.

"David, after today you probably won't be heading to your old job any more. Make sure you get here at three. There are some people I want you to meet," Jason explained.

"Okay, I'll try my best. See you at three," I tried to sound professional, even though I was bouncing off the walls at this news.

I hung up the phone and called Carl. I needed some advice before I showed up at my King Life appointment.

"Carl, it's David," I said, as he answered his phone. "David Michaels."

"David," he said. "Hi. Great party last night."

"I had a blast. It was great. Look, Carl, I spoke to Jason Hoffman a minute ago and he said he wanted to talk to me at 3 o'clock about a book deal. Is there anything I should know? Could you come with me?"

"David, I have been getting calls all morning about you," Carl, who was an older man and who always spoke calmly, was getting very excited, "At least five publishers called trying to get your information so they could offer you a book deal. They were throwing seven-figure numbers around. I wouldn't sign anything with King Life just yet. There might be a better way to go about finding the right publisher for you. Maybe you could run a silent auction for the rights to your first novel. That way you can ensure that you get a fair price for the book," Carl said.

"Silent Auction? Where? How?" I said. How was I going to run a silent auction?

"It's not all that complicated. Look, I can help you if you want. I have a good friend who's an agent. I've worked with her for the past twenty years. She's more than capable. She can run it for you. She'll call back the interested publishers, tell them to prepare a written bid for your novel and submit it to us by 5:00 p.m. tomorrow. The highest bid wins."

"Wow, okay. Can we have the bids sent to your office?" I asked, shaking with excitement.

Carl laughed, "Sure. Look, I'll call my friend and have her

run the auction from here. Don't worry about it. You head over to King Life at three, and let them know the deal. This will be very exciting," white haired, blue-eyed Carl had to be brimming with excitement.

"Are you sure I shouldn't sign anything with them? What if it's too good to pass up?"

"It's up to you, but it seems to me you have some options and you might want to explore them all. I've been around publishing for a long time, they'll probably try to get you on the cheap. Dangle some cash in front of you I don't think you can do any harm waiting."

"Okay, I'll talk to you later. Thanks, Carl," I said and hung up the phone.

I still had to head over to Sneaker Heaven and check up on things. I was neglecting my job, and that was unacceptable. I took a shower, put on my khakis, threw on a referee shirt and headed over to the mall.

When I walked in the door, the employees looked at me like I had ten heads. Peaches ran over to me and pushed me into the back office.

"Where the hell have you been?" Peaches said.

"I know, I know, I've been neglecting the store," I said.

"Neglecting the store? Damn, David, you haven't been here for days, and when you did come in it was like you weren't even here," she said, pointing her finger in my face and shaking her head back and forth.

"I'm sorry. But things got nuts," I started to explain the whole story thing.

"You know what's nuts? You getting paid for work you're not doing, and I'm working my ass to the bone here every day," Peaches was pissed, her head was weaving all over the place.

"But I – " I didn't even have a chance to speak.

"But you're the manager, and that's cool, and we tight, so I made sure no one knew what was going on. I covered for your sorry ass," Peaches said.

I almost welled up with tears, "I can't believe you did that for me. That was so nice."

"Well, you are a good guy - I guess. And, I saw you on Page 9! You're famous!"

"Oh, Jesus," I mumbled.

"Can I get an autograph?" Peaches winked at me.

"Sure," I walked over to the register to pick up a piece of paper and a pen.

"I'm kidding! I don't want your autograph!"

I walked back over to Peaches and pulled her in for a hug.

"Damn, what you doin'?" she said mid-hug.

"Come on, give me a hug, you know you love it."

We embraced. I really had a lot to thank Peaches for. After all, she saved my ass and didn't rat me out to Corporate.

"All right, now get back to work," I said.

"Damn, I should have had your ass fired when I had the chance," she smiled slyly and returned to the sales floor.

I sat in the back for a good three hours. I had a drink, played a few games of Madden. Some quiet me-time. It was nice to be away from everyone for a spell, but I was having trouble taking it easy. I couldn't just sit here. I walked out to the floor and took a peek over at Coffee Kiosk. Not much of a line. Since this was going to my last day here I broke my rule and left the store. I walked over and mingled with the MILFs.

A good-looking woman behind me in line tapped me on the

shoulder, "Was that you on Page 9 this morning?"

"Yeah, well, yeah," I said.

"I thought that was you!" Some other ladies in the line must have heard. They started pointing. Maybe a little notoriety wasn't going to be so bad.

"Home wrecker!" shouted one lady.

On second thought, maybe fame wasn't going to be so great.

CHAPTER THIRTY

It was a beautiful, sunny, crisp autumn day so I decided to walk over to the King Life offices through the park - hoping to see some colorful leaves still left on the trees - over to Columbus Circle. The offices were located in the sort of building that tourists gawk at with their heads back, trying to see the top of it through the clouds.

"David, glad you could make it, follow me," Jason Hoffman said, meeting me outside the elevator on the 41st floor. He shook my hand.

"Jason, this is pretty exciting," I said as we walked.

"Just wait, it's about to get even more exciting," he said.

He walked me into a conference room. The walls were all windows and opened directly upon Central Park. We really were in the sky, so high up that I couldn't see Columbus Circle. I saw only the tops of trees. I was in a giant building of steel and glass, and my view was of this natural haven in the middle of the city. I loved New York. Jason walked me over to the three people seated at the far end of the conference table. They immediately rose to greet me.

"David, I would like you to meet a few people," Jason

pointed around the room, "This is Trinity Campbell, our PR representative. Over here, we have Seth Olive, VP of Marketing, and, finally, this is Christopher Donald, the CEO of King Life."

I shook hands all around, and then we sat down. "It's very nice to meet all of you." I said.

"David," Christopher jumped right in, "We enjoyed your story and would love you to be part of the King Life team. Everyone in this room thinks that your first novel can be a breakout novel."

"Well, that is quite a compliment. Thanks."

"What we are offering for the opportunity to work with a writer of your talent is equally unprecedented. We are prepared to offer you a one-million-dollar advance for your book."

I nearly choked. Carl had told me that there could be a seven-figure offer, but how could I believe it? This was like winning the lottery. That doesn't happen! I wasn't even sure that I had heard Christopher correctly.

I made a fist and brought it up to my mouth, so I could cough into it. Hiding my excitement, mid-cough, I said, "What?!"

Christopher looked at me like he had me reeled in, "I said, we're offering you a one-million-dollar advance for your book."

That's what I thought he had said. One million dollars. I had no idea what to do. Should I take the million and run, or stupidly turn that down and tell them I am going to run a silent auction?

I cleared my throat trying to regain my composure. "Wow, that is a lot of money. A-lot-of-money. But, I have to disclose to you guys that I have been approached by other publishing houses, and it would seem unfair if I didn't let everyone have an equal shot at purchasing the rights." I actually got these words out of my mouth.

"David, we are offering you a chance to be with one of the largest publishers in the world. We are prepared to put a lot of marketing dollars behind your book. Not many other publishers can offer you the same," Christopher said.

"I appreciate that, Mr. Donald, all I am asking for is a chance to see everyone's proposal. This is a big decision for me. Please, put your proposal in writing and send it to Carl Greenman's office by tomorrow at 5:00 p.m. I will make a decision within a day, or so. I'm looking forward to seeing it," I said.

"Well, if that is what we have to do, then we'll have it at Carl's office by five tomorrow. David, thank you for taking the time to meet with us and hear us out. I hope you go with King Life in the end."

And with that Christopher got up out of his seat, walked to where I was now standing, and ushered me out of the room with his hand positioned about an inch from my back. The hand floating behind the back was an old corporate trick. Unbelievable, this world was just as corporate as law. But, this was one corporate atmosphere that I didn't mind being stifled in.

I met Karen later that night at her place. She looked great, having just come off a plane. She had on a faded pink t-shirt, no bra (it was a good look for her) and pink boy shorts. We had gotten to the point where lying around semi-nude was the norm. Less clothes to remove before jumping into bed - if we even made it out of the living room. We were cuddling and sipping some wine, when Karen turned to me, and asked, "Did you really think I wouldn't know?"

"About the auction?" I asked.

"No, not about the auction. About Sandy McBride!"

"Oh, that..." shit, I was caught. "That was nothing. Just the tabloids making shit up."

"Don't give me that!" Karen said. "If it was nothing why

didn't you say anything?"

"I wasn't even thinking about it," I said. "That's why I didn't say anything,"

"Bullshit!" Karen yelled. "How long have you been seeing her?"

"I'm not seeing anyone," I said. "Well, I'm seeing you, right?" Maybe injecting a little humor into the situation would diffuse this nightmare.

No response from Karen. I was going to try not to dig my own grave.

"I'm not seeing Sandy. I took her to the party, that's it! Carl invited her, for God's sake. I can't control the paparazzi. I can't control what they write in the paper."

"Is that the truth?" Karen was skeptical.

"The whole truth, and nothing but the truth," I lied.

"There better be nothing going on, or I'm going to kill you."

"Would you still kill me if I told you I just got offered one million dollars for my story by King Life?"

"That's old news. I work at The Manhattan, remember?!"

Karen joked, informing me that we had successfully concluded our first fight.

"I hope you know what you're doing," she added.

"No. I don't know what the hell I'm doing," I said. And I wasn't just referring to the book deal. Lying to Karen probably wasn't the best idea, either.

"We'll see, shortly," Karen hugged me and kissed me on the top of the head. "Everything will work out. You know, I just can't believe all of this. Everything is happening so quickly. Meeting you again, getting your story published, and now this," she kissed me softly on the lips, "I'm falling in love with you, David."

"I already love you," I said. And I meant it. I had fallen in love with Karen in the short time that I had known her. I couldn't imagine my life without her. I thought to myself how odd this felt. Karen just made me feel different. I can't explain it. I just knew it was right.

We had some more wine and talked about the auction. Then we passed out on the couch in each other's arms. Most people would think that this night wasn't much of a celebration, but to me it could not have been more perfect.

The next day I arrived at Carl's by 4:30 p.m. I sauntered into the office and into the conference room, where Carl and Karen were seated next to a woman who I had never met before. Carl stood up and made the introduction. "David, this is Elaine Kirsch, your new agent."

Elaine was in her late fifties, with black bobbed hair and blue eyes. She had on a smart, fitted, navy-blue pant suit, with a white, button-down blouse on underneath her jacket. Her face had a serious, 'I mean business' expression on it that you could read in her eyes behind rimless glasses that were sliding down her nose.

"So nice to meet you, Elaine," I said shaking her hand. "I can't really believe this is happening." I actually was brimming with excitement.

"Bids have been coming in all day. I have seven of them right here in my hand. Two from publishing houses I never even talked to," Elaine said, equally as excited.

"Did you go through them yet?" I asked, taking a seat at the conference table where Elaine laid out the seven proposals like cards.

Carl chuckled, "Not yet, we are waiting until five. Did you think we'd open them without you?"

"Is there a proposal here from King Life?" I asked.

"We haven't received a bid from them yet," Elaine said.

"You haven't? It's 4:45pm, what are they waiting for?" I was getting worried.

"What did they say to you yesterday?" Carl asked.

"Well, they offered me one million for the book, and then I told them we were having the auction," I said, nervously.

"You turned down $1,000,000 for a book! Are you nuts? That's an insane amount of money for a first-time author!" Carl yelled at me.

"But you said 'silent auction' –" I said.

"Who cares what I said? King offered you one million dollars! What's wrong with you?" Carl said.

Karen looked over at Carl, confused by what she was hearing. Last night, Karen acted as if she knew about the million, but Carl must have just told her that I was going to turn down the King Life offer - not realizing they were going to offer me $1,000,000. Now, it seemed as if her faith in Carl was waning.

"I trust you. I didn't think that you would steer me wrong, I mean, you've been so nice to me since I met you," I said.

For the first time in his life, perhaps, Carl was rethinking the advice he had given out regarding the publishing industry. I could see the uncertainty in his eyes. He didn't think King was going to submit a bid.

"Okay, I know it's getting late, but let's not jump to any conclusions. I'm sure King is just getting their numbers together. I'm sure they aren't mad about you turning down their offer. Well, I hope they're not mad. We'll just have to wait and see," Elaine said, trying to calm everyone down.

I liked her.

The clock struck five and there was still no sign of King Life anywhere.

"Well, looks like this is all we're going to get. Let's take a look at what we have," Carl said.

I looked around the room. Carl was hiding his disappointment and his face by shuffling papers. He had possibly just lost me one million dollars. Shit! I knew that was a lot of money! I should have taken it! What the fuck was I thinking?

Elaine was all business. She was laying out the bids in front of her. What did she care? She was going to get a small percentage of whatever I brought in. This was all found money to her. And Karen. Well, she was just staring at me, trying to calm me down with her eyes. It's not working, Karen!

"All right folks. Let's open the first proposal," Elaine said.

Suddenly, a knock at the conference room door. A messenger arrived with a letter.

"I have a letter for David Michaels," he said.

I stood up. "I'm David."

"Can you please sign for this," the messenger, asked as he handed a King Life envelope to me.

"Here it is," I said, "I never doubted you for a second, Carl."

"Okay, let's look at these bids already," Karen said.

Elaine went methodically through each proposal. The first one was not that great. Mid six figures. Not great? Have I lost my mind? Six figures was a shit-load of money. The second and third were about the same. It's funny how in the course of twenty four hours your perspective can change. A few days ago, six figures would have been unimaginable. Now, I was looking at it like I was being ripped off. I need to stop thinking like a crazy person. Six figures will change my life forever.

"Can we look at the King Life proposal already?" I pleaded.

"Hold on, we have one more," Elaine said.

We opened the proposal and it was from Michael S. Publishing. They offered a $1.25 million advance for the book! Holy crap! They also offered guaranteed marketing money bringing the proposal into the mid two-million dollar range. I was floored. Elaine gasped.

"Let's try to get our composure here. Michael Publishing's offer is impressive. But let's continue with the process. You guys ready to open King Life?" Elaine asked, trying to regain her own composure.

Then we opened the King Life envelope. Elaine slowly ripped the manila folder top open. Then she blew the envelope open. (C'mon, Elaine, let's cut the drama, I thought) She slowly took out the proposal, held it up and showed it to us, brought it back down to eye level, read it, looked up at all of us and then re-read it.

"C'mon, Elaine! What does it say!" I said.

"Well, I don't believe it. They're," she coughed, " offering a package including promotion

of the book in excess of three million dollars. Including an advance

of $1.75 million."

"YES!" I jumped out of my seat, screaming. "YES!! $1.75

million! I can't believe it!"

"I don't believe it! I have never seen a proposal like this for

an unknown author! Congratulations!" Elaine was ecstatic.

I ran over and gave Carl a high-five.

"David, this is amazing! Congratulations!" Karen hugged

me.

"I never doubted you for a minute Carl. Thank you so much

for everything. This is unbelievable!" I said.

Carl joked back, "I hope this means we can have the first few

chapters for publication in The Manhattan."

"Don't worry about that Carl, we'll work that into the

contract somewhere," Elaine said.

"I'll tell you what, I'll write you stories for the rest of my life

for free!" I said.

"I won't forget that!" Carl laughed.

CHAPTER THIRTY-ONE

I accepted the bid at 5:12 p.m. that same day, calling Christopher Donald, personally. We were both really excited and couldn't wait to get started working together. By the next day, the media had gotten wind about the amount of the advance. I was all over the news again.

I got a call from Christopher, "David, have you seen the news?"

"I've seen the news and read the papers. I'm all over the place. What happened?" I asked.

"Well, that's an easy one. I leaked it to the press. Figured we'd get a little advance buzz for the book. I would also like to book you for the "Today's Morning" show to talk about The Manhattan story and the upcoming book. Can we book you for tomorrow?" Christopher asked.

"Um, sure," I said. I'm going to be on a national television show? I felt a little sick to my stomach.

"I'll have a driver pick you up and take you to the Lux Hotel. We'll have a reservation waiting for you. After the show, spend a few nights just relaxing. We need you fresh to start that book."

"How will I know when to go over to the studio?" I asked, not yet thinking clearly.

"The show is taped around the block. The driver will give you all the details. David, we're really excited about this. Have a good show, buddy," then Mr. Donald hung up.

I had Karen staying with me at the Lux so we could spend some quality time together. After all, we were in love. For the past few days I had been hiding from Sandy, and staying over at Karen's apartment. I definitely was not answering my phone. I had to formally end things sooner or later with Sandy, but in the back of my mind I was hoping that if I ignored her long enough she would eventually go away - my sure fire method for ending relationships in high school. However, I tended to think that a woman who leaves her husband for another man might be a little more persistent than a fifteen-year-old girl.

The limousine taxied Karen and me to the set of "Today's Morning," a few blocks down the street, at 5:45 a.m. I was exhausted. Karen and I were ushered into the Green room, to wait for my turn on set. I had a cup of coffee and was greeted by Sam Blauer, the host of the Today's Morning show.

"David, thanks for coming," said Sam. "We're excited to have you on the show. If there's anything you need, just let, Cindy, my assistant know and she'll get it for you."

"Thanks, I will. Boy, you look shorter in real life, uh, . . . I mean," I stammered. What the hell was I thinking?

"Haha, everyone says that. Well, not to my face, but I hear it often." Sam had a bit of a confused look on his face, "And who is this?" Sam pointed to Karen.

"Ah, this is Karen, my girlfriend," I said. "She works at The Manhattan."

"Yup, I'm the girlfriend, Karen Gold," Karen said, shaking Sam's hand.

"Well, it's a real pleasure to meet you both. We'll see you around seven," Sam said, as he walked out.

As the door closed, Karen slid between my arms. "Girlfriend, huh?" she said, "I like that."

Around 6:55, Cindy, Sam's assistant, pulled me out of the Green room while I still had a chocolate chip cookie in my hand, and sat me in a chair on the set. She pulled the cookie out of my hand.

"No eating on set," she scolded me. I was a bad boy. "This is where Sam's going to sit," Cindy pointed to the chair sitting across from me. "Remember, speak clearly and don't kick Sam in the leg. You two are seated very close together."

"Okay," I said.

Sam finished delivering the news on camera, then walked over and sat down across from me, "You ready?"

"Yup, let's do it." I was as ready as I ever would be. "Oh, one more thing, Sam, can you bring Karen out at some point. I have something planned."

"Yeah, Mel, over there," he said, pointing to the producer standing near the camera just off set, "told me all about it. You still want to do it?"

"I do."

Sam looked at Mel and shouted, "We're still on?"

Mel gave a thumbs up.

"Okay, we'll bring Karen out," Sam said. Then it was 'go' time.

The camera panned in on Sam: "My next guest has taken the

literary world by storm with his recently published short story 'Sh*t.Falls.Up' a big hit with readers of The Manhattan. He also has a book to be published next fall that, according to today's papers, fetched the author a reported $1.75 million advance. Wow. Please welcome, David Michaels, to the show."

The camera pulled back to Sam and me sitting face to face in our comfy chairs. My heart almost bounced out of my chest. I tried to hold down the vomit that was slowly rising up my throat. Come on, David, get a grip, I told myself. Who knew I had stage fright? I was on the "Today's Morning" show. This was my chance to change my life. I took a deep breath, pushed the lump of vomit back down my throat and said, "It's a pleasure to be here, Sam."

"Is it true that you just received a $1.75 million advance for rights to your first book?" Sam asked.

"It is. I mean, it's just unbelievable. I never expected any of this."

"You just had your first short story published, 'Sh*t.Falls.Up,' and now all this. It must feel like a roller coaster."

"It's definitely surreal. I mean, I was working at Sneaker Heaven and sleeping on my sister's floor on an air mattress and now this. It's just unbelievable."

"That's some story. For anyone who hasn't read 'Sh*t.Falls.Up' I suggest you go out and get a copy of The Manhattan magazine. The story is brilliant. Why don't you tell our viewers a little bit about the story."

"The story is about a guy a bit down on his luck who finally makes it big. He works at Sneaker Heaven at the Mall and lives on his sister's air mattress."

"Sounds a little autobiographical," Sam said.

"Sam, if I didn't write about my situation I would still be crying about it."

Sam laughed. "You actually lived on an air mattress?"

"Not just any air mattress, Sam. It was the SuperBed. It inflated in less than sixty seconds. I mean, I would stand in front of my sister's air mattress with the inflate button pressed and think to myself, every night, 'what the hell am I doing with my life?' You know inflating a bed every night is a very humbling experience."

Sam laughed again. I couldn't believe I was killing on "Today's Morning."

"Are the stories about the women true?" Sam asked,

changing the tone.

"Now, Sam, I can't comment on that. I don't kiss and tell," I answered.

"Is there anyone special in your life right now?"

"Actually, there is. In fact, she is here this morning. Would you mind if we brought her out?"

"Not at all," Sam said.

Sam waved Karen over. I saw Karen offstage, mouth open, stunned, embarrassed as all hell. A producer walked over to her, whispered something in Karen's ear, and then gave her a little push. Karen resisted, but Sam was waving her along to come out and sit with us on the set. Karen took a couple of steps, and before she knew it she was on camera heading over to us.

I stood up, and let Karen have a seat in my chair.

"So, you are the special someone?" Sam asked, as the "Today Morning" crew started to come a little closer, still off camera, including, the co-hosts, Carole Samuels, the co-anchor of the show and, Bill Stoker, the jovial weather man.

"Yes, I'm Karen," she answered, shrugging a bit, her cheeks turning red.

"You are certainly very attractive. And you are sure you are not any of the women in the story?" Sam joked.

"I hope not," Karen smiled.

"Sam, you're killing me," I added.

"Okay, I'm just kidding. So how long have you two been together?" Sam acted the part of a schoolgirl trying to get the gossip.

"We haven't been together very long," Karen said.

I bent down, and gave Karen a hug and a kiss on the check.

"Sam, since the day I met her, I have been in love with her. She has made every day better than the next," I moved from behind Karen and over to a position just in front of her. I continued, "I know we have only known each other for a short time, but I can't see myself with anyone else but you," I bent down on one knee, overcome by the fact that I was in love. I reached in my pocket, "You make me smile each day that we are together and make me feel like the luckiest man in the world. And even though all I have is this plastic ring that I stole from the Green room, Karen Gold, will you marry me?"

Sam, Carole and Bill went nuts. They were applauding along with the crew. I looked over at Karen and almost fainted. I had actually done it. I had asked Karen to marry me on national television! I had thought about it the night she had come back from LA, but I couldn't muster the courage. This morning I was determined to do this, and I had asked the producers to arrange it so that I could bring her out on the set with me, but I couldn't believe that I had actually gone through with it.

Karen was about to fall apart. She was crying, shaking, trying to compose herself – and doing a poor job of it. I took her hand and tried to steady it so I could put the ring on her finger. With the camera focused directly on Karen's hand, I slipped the plastic ring on Karen's finger. She answered, "Yes!"

I thought I saw a tear well up in Sam's eye. I have always loved these spontaneous, television moments. I was happy to be a part of one. I was trying to control my shaking by hugging Karen, now surrounded by the majority of the crew who were applauding.

"Congratulations, you two," Sam said.

Carole and Bill, not to be outdone by Sam, chimed in, "Yes, congratulations you two."

"Fabulous!" Carole added that quip all by herself. What a professional. She was patting me on the back, and then ran over to give Karen a hug.

Sam continued, "We'll be right back, with the newly engaged David and Karen, right after this," Sam went to commercial.

In high school things were easier. You would just avoid the girl's phone calls when it was over. This always worked. Sure, the girl would call a few times and try to establish some form of contact, but if you didn't answer the phone there was no problem. Well, unless you bumped into her at school or at some party. Problems did arise when your parents weren't aware of your situation and answered the phone by accident, but with caller ID, the odds of Sandy catching me on the phone were slim to none. I would not answer the phone. I liked this plan. This was something I could get behind.

Now, I know that asking someone to marry you on national TV might make your other girlfriend a bit jealous. It may even throw her into fits of rage. I didn't want this to happen. What could I do? I can't postpone my life forever because Sandy was getting a divorce.

When I got back to the Lux after the show, I listened to the message she left.

"You mother-fucking, lying, son of a bitch. I can't believe that you just got engaged on fucking national TV. Who do you think you are? You are going to be one, sorry, little prick when I get my hands on you. You fuck. No one does this to Sandy McBride. No one. You'll be –" Sandy was a little upset. Hey, that's understandable. There are always angry threats when a couple breaks up. I'm sure it will get better with time. I hit the delete button. I'd deal with Sandy when I was ready.

CHAPTER THIRTY-TWO

Besides the Sandy dilemma, things couldn't have been better. Karen and I were now engaged, I had just earned a lot of money doing something that I loved, and one would think that I had some sort of blossoming career on my hands. To top it all off, Karen and I had a chance to stay at the Lux for an entire week after the taping of the "Today's Morning" show.

Karen and I were enjoying every minute of our extended work vacation. Carl gave Karen the week off from The Manhattan so we could to spend some quality time together in my fancy, complimentary suite. King Life knew how to treat their authors. If this was the beginning, I couldn't wait to see what was in store for me ten years down the road. Karen and I went for massages, spa treatments, and long lunches. Manhattan was a very different place once you had some money to spend. I still had a problem believing I could afford anything.

One day, Karen took me shopping on Fifth Avenue. There are always a lot of Pink Piggies running around Fifth Avenue, dressed in their beautiful designer clothes, carrying their $5,000 bags. Of course, many of these Piggies are barely old enough to afford any of the clothes they wear or the bags they carry, but that's what Papa Piggy is for. Pink Piggy screams 'I want it' and the Papa Piggy caves, credit card in hand. These Piggies will never understand that they can dress up in $10,000 worth of clothing, but they will still always be the man-sniffing, Cosmopolitan-drinking, reconstructed-nose bearing, insecure girl dressed in pink. I was over wanting a Pink Piggy for my very own. I had my very own, woman now, who was caring, loving, and, most of all, perfect for me.

I called my sister and told her to meet us. I wanted to pay her back for all she had done for me, and to introduce her to Karen. Michelle met up with us at Jean Michelle. The outside of the store was decorated with a clear wrapping of interlocking JMs, and shapes in different blues, reds, yellows and greens that replicated one of their insanely expensive bags. Michelle deserved something nice for putting up with me for the past year.

"Michelle, I'm so glad you could meet us," I smiled, "Michelle, this is Karen."

"Well, it's nice to finally meet David's fiancé. Hi, Karen," Michelle walked over to Karen and gave her hug.

"It's nice to meet you, Michelle," Karen said.

"Oh my God, you're so pretty, Karen," Michelle said, looking Karen up and down, "And I love that coat! We're going to get along just fine!"

Karen was blushing, "Thanks, Michelle. David never told me how pretty *you* are!"

"Then you tell me - how have I not met a guy yet?" Michelle asked.

"Oh, I'll help you fix that. I know plenty of guys." Karen said. "But, first, let's get you a wardrobe to die for."

"And who's paying for that?" I asked.

"You are," Karen and Michelle answered simultaneously, pointing at me and giggling.

"Oh, boy."

We finally walked into the store. Michelle was being sarcastic, as she looked at all the handbags on display, just begging to be bought. "Mom is going to kill you. She's been trying to call you for a week. Don't you think you should call her? You just got engaged on national television and got a book deal!"

"I'll call them in a few days. I need time to just enjoy things before they ruin it," I explained.

"How are they going to ruin it?" Michelle asked.

"Do you even need to ask that question? They'll find a way," I said.

"You're right. Sorry." Michelle caught a glimpse of the ring on Karen's finger. "Oh, my God! Karen, are you still wearing that plastic ring? David, what is wrong with you?"

"Are you going to analyze everything today?" I asked Michelle. That was my only defense.

"David, aren't you going to get your fiancé a real engagement ring? You can't let her walk around with a plastic band on her finger! I can't believe this, Karen? This is my sick brother. Get the girl a ring!"

"Okay, okay, we'll get a ring this week."

"That's better," Michelle said.

"The reason I wanted you to meet us, Michelle, was I want you to pick out any bag that you want and I'm going to get it for you," I said. "Then, apparently, we're going shopping for a new wardrobe."

"Really? *Any* bag??" Michelle was flabbergasted. "You're

kidding right?"

"I mean it. Anything, get anything you want in the store. And after you clean out Jean Michelle's, we are hitting every store on Fifth Avenue. This is payback for all those months of dealing with me on your floor."

"Michelle, look at this one," Karen already had a bag in her hand.

"Oh, my God, I love that one. Everyone needs a good shoulder bag. Oh, God . . . but look at this clutch!" Michelle said.

"That one's great. But it's really just for going out. How about this top handle? You can't go wrong with a Jean in classic white." Karen said.

"Gorgeous!"

Shopping usually killed me slowly, but I was enjoying this. I wanted to make Michelle happy. I also wanted to make Karen happy. Looks like they were both happy, and shopping was quickly becoming a family sport. We ended up with three bags for Michelle and one for Karen. Next stop: Every God Damn expensive store on Fifth Avenue.

By the end of this shopping marathon, Michelle had amassed

a wardrobe that would make any Pink Piggy proud. She gave me two air kisses, thanking me for all of her gifts, as I sent her home in a taxi, carrying no less than ten giant-sized shopping bags. There were so many bags that the cabbie was forced to stuff most of the bags in the trunk. Oh, and I paid for the cab, as well. Ain't I a sport!

After our little shopping excursion, Karen and I took a walk around Central Park. It was the perfect end to our perfect week together. We were running into a bit of a problem, though. People were stopping us on the street, telling Karen how excited they were for her and asking to see her ring. The problem was, as Michelle pointed out, she was still wearing the plastic ring that I had stolen from the Green room. Actually, now that I got a good look at the florescent-green band, Karen's hand was sporting one, sad-looking, ring finger. I think the saddest part of the whole story was that I hadn't even thought about buying a real engagement ring, until Michelle mentioned it. I know, very sad. But thanks to the frightening, star-obsessed individuals who watch morning talk shows, I was now reminded on a minute-by-minute basis that Karen needed an engagement ring. And believe me, I know she needed one fast.

We continued to stroll around the park until we found ourselves back on Fifth Avenue. Now was my big chance to right my wrong. I spotted Rose's, and led us both right up to the door with the iconic ROSE & CO. awning above the entrance. I turned to Karen and said, "Let's find you a ring."

Karen bolted, I mean, *bolted*, to the diamond section. Which was kind of funny, as the diamonds were located on the 3rd Floor. We met up at the elevator.

"Wow, someone's excited," I said.

"Are you kidding, this is Rose's! I'm only human!"

When the elevator opened we were tossed onto an entire floor of diamonds and rings. This was absolutely crazy. How does one find a ring in this place? The selection is overwhelming. Karen pulled me over to one display case with 50 or so rings and a number of loose stones. Jacques, the salesperson, strolled over.

"Beautiful, aren't they?"

"Oh, my," was all that escaped Karen.

"These are cushion-cut diamonds. Would you like to see one?"

Karen nodded.

"First time looking at diamonds, sir?"

"I bet you say that to all the boys," I joked.

"Well, actually, yes," he chuckled.

Jacques took out a tray of diamonds and started pointing out some of the various sizes, colors, carats, clarity. They all had the same cut. Jacques was educating me on the 4 C's of diamond shopping. As he was explaining the finer points of the 2.5 carat, cushion-cut diamond in Karen's trembling hand, he handed her a jeweler's loupe. Then he interrupted his spiel, and turned to me, "Are you that writer?"

"Yup. That's me. This is my fiance, Karen."

"I didn't want to be rude - though we get famous people in here all the time - but I read your story."

"And? What did you think?"

"I liked it. Not my favorite story ever, but it was fun."

Wasn't this guy supposed to lie? After all, he's trying to sell me a diamond ring.

"I will tell you this, I'm excited to meet you. You've got talent, and that's something that 90% of the celebrities that walk into this place don't have. Keep up the good work. Now, Karen, how does that look?"

"Beautiful!"

"Don't make up your mind just yet, my dear," Jacques said. "I've got some stones over here that will have you positively drooling."

After we spent two hours examining various stones and settings, we finally found the right diamond and the right setting. Now came the mock-up of the ring. Jacques put the three-carat diamond in the middle of the setting with a one-carat trapezoid diamond on either side of the massive stone. Jacques gingerly placed it on Karen's finger.

"Isn't that just divine? It looks stunning on your finger," Jacques said.

Of course, it's beautiful. It's fucking huge and fucking expensive.

"It's beautiful," Karen held out her hand in front of her face and was mesmerized by the sparkling stone. "Isn't it beautiful?" Her eyes were glazed over.

"It is," I said, "We'll take it."

"Oh, my God!" Karen screamed, "Oh, my God! Oh, my God!

Oh, my God!"

After three 'Oh, my God's!' I got down on my knee for the second time in less than a week, and asked Karen to marry me. This time I did it the right way, with a three-carat diamond ring on her finger.

As if I needed more attention, folks in the store started applauding.

"Hey, that's David and Karen from the TV!" One hillbilly tourist screamed out.

Yup, that's us all right.

When we finally made it back to the hotel, we collapsed on the bed.

"That was the most shopping I have ever done in my life," I said. "How do women do that all day?"

"Presents. That's how. Look at all the pretty presents I have," she stopped dead in her tracks and stared at her ring, "This is the most beautiful present of all."

"Besides me, you mean," I teased.

"Of course, besides you. I'm so excited. What a week. I can't believe we got engaged. I never thought it would happen so soon," Karen was drunk from all her shopping.

I looked at the beautiful new ring on her finger and said, "You're telling me? It's been crazy. I can't believe you said yes."

"You make me very happy. I truly can't imagine being with anyone else," Karen said. "Did you really plan on asking me to marry you before we got to the show?"

"Well, I planned on asking you, but not on the "Today's Morning" show. That idea hit me when I was backstage." I had to chuckle, "I wasn't sure I could do it."

"I don't want to go back to real life. I just want to pass my time here with you."

"I can't wait to get back to our real life. It's only going to get better," I said.

"That's what you think. The next step is planning the wedding. You'll want plenty of time apart when we get back to our real lives and my mother gets involved."

"You're wrong, I can't wait," I claimed.

"Did you ever see a Jewish mother planning her only daughter's wedding? I have. It's frightening. Before you know it, it's her wedding. You'll see."

"Great."

Oh shit.

CHAPTER THIRTY-THREE

We checked out of the Lux the next morning, and walked up Park Avenue to Karen's apartment. Karen was stopped by something terribly frightening staring us directly in the face. Somehow, we had made it to the front cover of every tabloid.

The Starlight had a picture of us at Tiffany's with the headline: MCBRIDE'S LOSS IS KAREN'S GAIN. DAVID AND KAREN'S $100,000 EXPRESSION OF LOVE.

The Snoop actually had a picture of the ring on Karen's finger with DAVID PONIES UP $100,000 TO WIN KAREN'S HEART.

Star Fer magazine had us hugging on the cover with the headline: TV's SURPRISE ENGAGEMENT GETS REAL.

"Why the fuck is Sandy McBride's name in the same headline with mine?" Karen was pissed.

"Karen, it's the tabloids. They make shit up," Karen believed this line once, so I went with it again. "I'm more concerned about how they got pictures of your ring. We bought it yesterday!"

Apparently, Karen again accepted my bullshit answer about

the tabloids and moved on, "Who knows? The paparazzi must be everywhere. This is New York. People are constantly taking pictures. On top of it, everyone has a camera on their cell phone. We'll never spot these creeps. It was just a matter of time before they got to us and we wound up on the cover of this trash," Karen explained.

"But we were on one, morning TV show," I pleaded.

"Well, I guess one is enough. Anyway, at least it's not bad."

"Yet . . . " I said, as I felt my stomach drop.

We spent the next couple of days unwinding at Karen's apartment. Well, I spent the next few days unwinding. Karen had to go to work. I did have some unpleasant things to take care of back in the real world, and one of those was the Sandy situation. I still hadn't figured out how to handle that one yet.

I eventually made my way over to Sneaker Heaven to officially quit, though I'm sure they had figured it out.

"Hi, guys," I waved, as I strolled onto the sales floor of Sneaker Heaven for the last time as manager.

"Well, nice of you to join us," Kim said.

"Um, I've been a little busy lately," I said.

"No shit! I wasn't sure if you were ever coming back. The store just doesn't run itself," Peaches said.

Touche, Peaches, touche.

"Well, I'm here now," I said.

"Yeah, I can see that. Taking time out of your busy TV schedule - yeah, we saw you on TV, David. How come you didn't tell us you had a girlfriend?" Peaches asked.

"Never got around to it, I guess." It was more like, I just wasn't around.

"Wow! That was some ring you bought Karen," Kim said. "The picture of it almost blinded me."

"Quit playin'," Peaches laughed.

"So what's been going on here?" I asked.

"Nothing. Everyone has just been coming to work and doing their thing like we always do. If anyone got out of line they had me to answer to."

"Hey, Peaches, come in back with me for a minute," I opened the office door, and motioned Peaches to sit down.

"Damn, look at this office," Peaches was shocked. There were half-eaten, scum-ridden, skanked bowls of cereal all over the place not to mention some broken glass by the G-Circle from one of my last games of football.

"You didn't come in here when I wasn't around?" I was stunned.

"No way! Why would I? This is your space," Peaches said, a little defensive.

"I'm not accusing you. Relax. I can't believe you didn't peek in. I would have. Look, Peaches, I want to ask you something."

"Go ahead."

"You know I'm leaving this job, right?"

"I sure hope so. Nobody wants to be at Sneaker Heaven unless they have to be."

"Well, it's not the worst job in the world, but anyway, look, you're the best employee they have here. Hell, you were much better than me. I just went to law school, that's all. That's why I got the manager job. But I was a terrible manager. I didn't exactly give it my all while I was here, and that's wrong. You care about your job, and you're good at it. That's why I want you to take over as manager here. I think you would be great at it. I'm going to talk to Corporate about it later today. They'd be crazy not to give the job to you."

"Manager?" Peaches looked at me dazed.

"Yes, manager. You would do a great job. I mean you've certainly been here long enough," I said.

"Damn right," Peaches said, as she started to tear up. "That would mean a lot to me, David."

"I know, Peaches. You deserve it. You're great at what you do and you're going to be great at whatever you do in the future," I said. "You're a special person."

Peaches started crying, "Thank you, David. Thank you so much."

"So, I'll take that as a yes?" I said.

"Yes!"

I walked over and gave Peaches a hug.

"And one more thing. I want an invitation to your college graduation," I said.

"Of course, of course," Peaches hugged me even tighter.

CHAPTER THIRTY-FOUR

A few months later, on an unseasonably warm February night, King Life arranged my first major reading in New York. It was at the flagship Charles and Boles on 14th Street and Union Square. Carl, Karen, Elaine, and Jason Hoffman, my book publisher, were going to be there. Supposedly, big-wigs representing all facets of the publishing world would also be in attendance. They would hear me, a former manager of Sneaker Heaven, read my short story in person. I also found out, when I arrived, that the local, public access show "Bookworms" was going to film this event for an upcoming show.

The room was set up for about 100 people, but there were at least that many people waiting outside in line as I walked through the main entrance to rousing applause.

"This is amazing," I said to Michael, the manager of Charles and Boles, when he met me at the front of the store.

"It certainly is. We've never had a response like this to one of our readings. We are thrilled you decided to do this."

"It's my pleasure. I can't wait. It's going to be a blast."

I prepared in the stock room, alone, so I could relax for a few minutes before they brought everyone in to be seated. I was sipping on some bottled water when Carl, Jason, Emily, and Karen entered the room.

"It's a madhouse out there," Karen said.

"This has been some ride," I said.

"You deserve it, kid," Carl said, "They love you."

"I hope they love him this much when the book comes out," Jason cautioned.

"Even if the critics don't love him, I always will," Karen cooed.

"Look David, if things get tough you can always sell that ring Karen's got on her finger," Carl joked.

Not ten seconds later, Michael walked into the room. "Are you ready?" He looked in my direction, and I nodded my assent. "All right. Let's go."

We followed him to where there were chairs set up for us. As soon as I came into view there were screams from some young ladies in the audience.

"We love you, David," one girl shouted.

"I love you, too," I shouted back.

"You're so sexy," another girl yelled.

Karen was laughing behind me. What was next? Girls throwing their panties on the stage? Perhaps I was some kind of nerdy Tom Jones.

Michael was at the microphone. "Continuing with our dedication to excellence, Charles and Boles is thrilled to bring you one of this year's best new authors. We have all read his wonderful short story 'Sh*t.Falls.Up' in The Manhattan magazine, and we are delighted to have him here to read that story for us tonight. So without further ado, please join me in welcoming David Michaels. David, come on up."

Embarrassed by the applause, I nevertheless bellied up to the microphone, "I want to first thank you all for coming out here tonight to see me. I can't express what an amazing experience this has been. I would also like to thank The Manhattan magazine, especially their fiction editor, Carl Greenman, for taking a chance on me. Carl is right behind me here. Carl, please stand up and take a bow. You deserve it," I paused for applause, "I would also like to thank my fiancé, Karen - boy, that sounds great to say . . ." I pointed

at Karen, and she recoiled shyly in her chair, " . . . for her support."
When the applause had died down, I added, "And now I will
continue to bore you with my reading!"

I opened my copy of "Sh*t.Falls.Up" and began to read. My
voice is so goddamn nasally. And high-pitched, for that matter.
Despite my whiny voice bothering me, it was an exhilarating
experience. I was caught listening to my own words, as though I
were reading them for the first time. I watched as the audience
reacted to my canvas of words, laughing at the jokes, and
thoughtfully stoic at the life-lessons. I never dreamed there would be
a moment as touching as this. Then I came to the last line, "I reclined
the airplane seat, took out the miniature pillow, placed it against the
window, and closed my eyes."

When I finished, the crowd sat silently for a moment, as the
emotion I had brought to the reading sank in, and then the applause
spontaneously erupted. Moments later, everyone was standing,
including Carl, Jason, Elaine, Michael, and Karen. My first standing
ovation!

I soaked in the moment, thanked everyone and stepped aside
to let Michael address the crowd.

"David, thank you. That was truly wonderful, a story and a reading that none of us is likely to forget any time soon. Now, David has agreed to take some questions from the audience. So, if you have a question, please step up to one of the microphones located on either side of the stage."

The crowd bustled for a few moments, but then some people actually lined up.

A young lady asked, "What gave you the inspiration for the story?"

That was easy enough. Sheer and utter disgust for life. Desperation. I answered, "Boredom. That and sleeping on my sister's air mattress." I didn't want to freak out the poor lady.

A few other questions were proffered, ranging from the main theme of the story to whether or not I liked pizza. When it appeared that there were no more questions, a woman stepped to the microphone.

"Do you remember me, asshole?"

This was no ordinary woman. After the baseball cap and the sunglasses were removed, it was clearly Sandy. I immediately kicked into damage-control mode.

"Of course, of course. Hi, Sandy," I nervously tried to diffuse the situation.

Soft murmurs rippled through the crowd. Everyone was already a little thrown with the whole 'asshole' comment.

"I don't think you do because you haven't called in months." Sandy seemed a little peeved.

I was thrown into a full-blown panic. I tried to rationalize with Sandy.

"Sandy, this really isn't the place for this –"

But Sandy had come here to make a point. "This isn't the place? This is the perfect place to let everyone know what a fucking jerk you are."

I heard Karen asking, "Why is this bitch here?"

"How about I let everyone know that you were fucking me for nine months . . . well, until you became a star. That I was the one who submitted your story to The Manhattan. That I was the one who convinced Carl to give your story a chance. That I was the one who got you out of that dead-end life of yours and made you famous. And how does he repay me?" She slowly surveyed the room. "What does this genius of a writer do? He leaves me without an explanation and runs off with some floozy bitch to get engaged on national television," Sandy was steaming.

At that point, management thankfully killed the microphones. But that didn't stop her. She was screaming at the top of her lungs and approaching the stage, slowly at first, but soon I realized she was just a few feet away from me.

Karen was more than horrified at the accusations coming out of Sandy's mouth. She looked confused, and kept saying aloud, "Is this true?" then "Who is she calling bitch?"

"Nobody walks out on Sandy McBride. Especially not some two-bit writer who thinks he's some kind of celebrity," Sandy ran up to me. "Fuck you asshole," she screamed, and then she hauled off and cracked me with a solid, left hook to my right eye.

I fell backwards, hard. Michael was still standing at the podium shaking like a schoolgirl watching her boyfriend get his ass kicked on the playground. From the floor, I heard security rustle up Sandy as she tried to run away through the shocked crowd. Karen darted over to me lying on the floor.

"Oh, my God! Are you all right?" She asked bending over me. Her face was angelic. Maybe it was the celling light shining into my face.

"Yeah, I'm okay. Can you help me up?"

With Karen's help, I made it to my feet.

Meanwhile, the "Bookworms'" cameras were rushed in to make sure they could capture every moment of this disaster. I believe a cameraman jumped from behind the camera and started reporting as if he were in the middle of breaking news.

"You were fucking her? I thought the tabloids made that up?" Karen asked.

I had finally arrived at one of those defining moments of my life. I could lie, and tell Karen that Sandy was just some lunatic out for attention - or I could actually tell the truth for once in my life. Maybe I should embrace this moment and accept the notion that relationships aren't based on lies, that I shouldn't have hidden my nine-month relationship with Sandy, that I shouldn't have dated both women at the same time, that I treated Sandy like shit, but all the while I was still Sandy's bitch. That would be the mature thing to do. Hell, that would even be the right thing to do.

I turned and looked Karen in the eyes, "Yeah, it's true," I said and it felt great. Our love was stronger than this simple little speed bump.

"You fucking asshole!"

Apparently, Karen didn't see this as a speed bump. I guess, to her, it was more like Mount Everest. She then proceeded to punch me square in the one good eye that I had left. Great, two black eyes, I thought, as I hit the floor for the second time. I struggled to make sense of what had just happened. Then the ring hit me in the face. Yeah, Nance, some girls certainly want a chance to spoil things. Sandy had made that abundantly clear. I didn't struggle much after that.

Jason walked over to me with Carl.

Jason said, "At least you have an ending for your book."

CHAPTER THIRTY-FIVE

Once again, I had made the tabloids. Whoop-tee-fucking-do. This time the television tabloids. I sat with Michelle at the apartment we were once again sharing, watching Sandy and Karen punch me over and over again on network television. They actually had some really nice footage. This must have been "Bookworms'" crowning, fucking moment. First, they would show Sandy cracking me with the left hook, followed by Karen with the right. The piece de resistance was a close-up of the ring hitting me square in the middle of my face. "Bookworms" certainly had their crack technical team out that night.

"Wow, that was some punch," Michelle said.

"Which punch? They both hurt," I said.

"I bet. Looks like Sandy really knew what she was doing. Who punched harder?"

"Sandy, she's a fucking beast. She works out."

"I can't believe you were dating them both. Why wouldn't you just end it with Sandy first?" Michelle asked.

"I don't know. I tried, but things got weird. Sometimes you

make bad mistakes."

"I'd say, getting punched by two girls, and smacked in the face by a boulder in the same night is pretty bad."

"Yeah, it's pretty bad," I said, dejected. I looked like the loser of a prizefight.

"So, now what?" Michelle asked.

"I don't know. Karen's not talking to me. And judging by the 50 replays we just watched of her throwing the ring in my face, I'm guessing the odds of her talking to me anytime soon are pretty slim. Jon told me that Sandy is in jail, waiting for Jim to bail her out, but I'm sure he'll just leave her in there until they release her. And to be honest with you, I'm scared of her. I'm also back on your air mattress until I can find an apartment to rent. So I guess the only thing I have left is my book deal. At least until they take that away from me, too."

"Are you going to give up that easily?" Michelle asked, "I think you and Karen still have a shot. I think she just needs some time to think things over."

"Did you see her punch me in the face? I'm not sure how much thinking she needs," I sighed deeply. "I guess, I'll give her another call." I picked up the phone and called her.

Ring. Ring. Ring. Ring. Voicemail. "Hi, you've reached Karen. I'm not available, but leave me a message and I'll get back you right away. Ciao."

I left a message, "Hey Karen, it's me. Look, I really want to work this thing out. I know I was a jerk, but I love you, and want to be with you. Anyway, give me a call when you get a chance. Bye." I hung up.

"That's it?? I think you are going to have to do a little more than leaving a nice message. You need to dazzle her. You have to show her that you want to be with her. It's going to take more than a phone call," Michelle explained.

"Dazzle her? Are you kidding? First, I ask her to marry me on a morning show, and then I bought her a $100,000 ring from Rose's. Now you want me to dazzle her?? I don't know how much more dazzle I can muster," I said.

"All those things are nice, but you were sleeping with another woman. I don't know how you can do it, but you better start thinking of some way to win her back, or you're a goner. It's up to you. Plus, I love Karen. She's great, and I need a sister!"

Again, Michelle was right. I had to win her back. But I had no clue as to what to do. All I could think about was putting ice over both eyes, unpacking the air mattress, plugging in the pump and inflating the fucker. Within one minute, I would be able to put this day behind me – God, I fucking hope so.

For the past week, I had tried to talk to Karen on a daily basis. I would call her apartment, leave a message. Call her at work, leave a message. Call her cell, leave a message. All of this, to no avail. The calls were gradually increasing with alarming frequency. I needed something else to focus on, so I decided that I had better start working on my book since I had deadlines to meet. I decided to meet with Carl for some advice. Subconsciously, it was a ploy to see what Karen was up to.

Carl agreed to meet me for lunch to talk about the book. We met in midtown at Brasserie, a nice French restaurant.

"How's the book coming along?"

"Not so great."

"Where have you gotten to in the plot?"

"Nowhere."

"Do you have something in mind?"

"How's Karen?"

"That doesn't sound much like a plot?" Carl said.

"I'm serious, Carl. How's Karen? She hasn't spoken to me in weeks," I said.

"Put yourself in her shoes. That was some bomb that you laid on her at your reading. You weren't exactly telling her the truth," Carl started.

"Well, I wasn't exactly lying to her, either," I said.

"But you didn't tell her you were sleeping with Sandy. You didn't tell me that either, by the way."

"Sorry. But that's beside the point."

"No, David, that's exactly the point. Let me share something with you about women. Listen up, because this might be something you may want to use in your book. Women are different than men. Women base a relationship not only on love, but also on trust. Karen had your trust and you had hers, until that night at Charles and Boles. Once she learned that you were keeping things from her, she lost her trust in you. And, once that was gone, so was she. There's no doubt she still loves you. It's all just a matter of trust now. She has to learn to trust you all over again. Better yet, you have to get her to want to trust you again," Carl finished.

"What should I do?" I asked. Carl seemed to have all the answers today.

"I don't know the answer to that. All I can tell you is this would make a great plot twist," then he took a bite of his steak. "Mmm, good steak."

How was I supposed to get her to trust me again when I couldn't even get her to talk to me? This was beginning to look more and more like a losing battle. On the bright side, I did have plenty of time to work on my book.

CHAPTER THIRTY-SIX

I spent most of the days that followed looking for an apartment, writing a little, and doing most things by myself, including walking around aimlessly like a homeless person. I had forgotten what it was like to walk around by myself with no one to talk to. Being alone was hard enough. Being alone without the woman I loved was devastating.

It was on one of these sad days when I decided to take a walk over to The Manhattan offices. Just to stop in and say hi to Carl. All right, I'm lying. I wanted to talk to Karen so desperately that it drove me to confronting her at work. Another low point for me. Is anyone keeping track?

Getting past the front desk was a snap. After all, I'm pretty famous around the office. I hopped in the elevator bank and hit number 25. When I got off the elevator at Karen's floor, Carl met me at the door.

"She's not here," he said.

"How did you know I was coming up?" I asked.

"Security called," Carl said.

Damn you, security.

"Anyway, I didn't come to see-"

"She's not here," Carl repeated himself.

"Oh, she's not," I tried to sound smooth, "Where'd she go?"

"She's in London, helping to edit a piece for next month's issue."

I obviously looked like a beaten dog.

"I'm actually beginning to feel sorry for you. You know, in an emergency we can give out the whereabouts of our employees," Carl winked.

"Funny you should say that. There's been an emergency, and I need to find Karen immediately," I said.

"You don't say? Wait right here. Let me see if I can get you that information," Carl reached into his pocket and pulled out a piece of paper with Karen's info written on it, "She's at the Piccadilly Hotel. Room 602."

I was so grateful that I just stood there like a statue in front of Carl.

"Well, what are you waiting for? Go get her!" Carl yelled at me.

I arrived at the airport as fast as I could, considering the cab driver recognized me and took the long way there.

"Why are you on Lexington? I told you to take 2nd down," I said.

"Listen, my friend, 2nd is murder this time of the day," the Indian cab driver told me.

"Yeah, but it's completely out of the way. I'm in a hurry."

"We'll get there, my friend."

I'm not your friend.

"I know you," the cab driver began.

Here we go. I stared at his Vishnu air freshener and dreaded the conversation that was about to ensue.

"Na, I just look like someone you know," I said hoping to end this.

"No, I know you. You are on TV, no?"

"No."

"Give me a minute, my friend. I'll figure it out."

Good luck.

We were now on the Van Wyck on our way to JFK going 50

miles per hour. Thank God, this journey was coming to an end shortly, albeit slowly.

"I know who you are. You're that guy that wrote that story. Haha! I've got a celebrity in this taxi," my Hindu friend said.

"I'm hardly a celebrity," I said.

"I saw you on TV. That makes you famous, my friend. I saw your girlfriend, too -"

"She's my fiance. Well, technically, we're kind of nothing right now." Why was I discussing this with the cab driver?

"You know, that girlfriend of yours is very pretty."

"Thanks."

"You know . . . " He said in a way that made you think something weird was going to come out. His voice rose a bit. I didn't like where this was heading. ". . . do you have any nude pictures of her?"

"What?!" Was this guy serious? "No. Why the fuck would I take nude photos of my girlfriend?" I questioned why I was even justifying this question with a response.

"Easy, easy my friend. I take pictures of my wife all the time. I love my cell phone. We have a lot of fun."

By this point, I'd had it, "OK, enough. Stop fucking milking the meter and step on it. I have a plane to catch."

When I finally arrived at JFK I ran to the ticket counter. I needed to book myself a flight to London.

"When's the next flight to Heathrow?" I asked the stewardess behind the counter. Are they still stewardesses if they are not on the plane? Are they flight attendants now? Who knew the airport could be so confusing. I'm going with stewardess. I like it better.

"It leaves in an hour. They're boarding soon, but you can still make it. The next one leaves tomorrow morning at nine."

"I'll take a ticket for the next flight."

The stewardess hit a few keys on her computer. "Very well sir, we have one upper class seat." She had a sweet, British accent. "That will be $2,862.20." Somehow, that price didn't seem so outrageous when delivered in a British accent, plus I deserved to travel in style.

Luckily, I also could now afford the ticket price of $2,862.20. I paid the lady, and after being frisked going through security - seriously, do I look like a fucking terrorist, asshole? - I made it to the gate with plenty of time to spare. I boarded the plan without being recognized and settled into my seat next to a smartly-dressed, older woman. I saw her eyeing me as soon as I walked through the cabin door. She had that worried look on her face like 'please don't sit next to me'.

The cabin doors were locked and we were ready for take-off. About an hour into the flight the woman next to me tapped me on the shoulder.

"I hate to be rude, but, are you David Michaels?"

Shit. Busted on the five-hour flight.

"Yes, that's me," I said in a monotone drawl trying to quickly appease her curiosity and dismiss the conversation so I could partake in the thrilling in-air entertainment. After all there were three very bad movies on that I had to watch.

"I loved your story! Very funny. The ending even made me cry."

I always have some time for adoring fans, "Well, thanks. I'm glad you liked it."

"I read that you're turning it into a novel. I can't wait. When will it be out?"

"I don't know yet. Should be a few months. I'm still working on it."

"Can I be in it?"

"What?"

"Well, since I'm a big fan, I mean, do you think you could you make me one of the characters in the book?"

"What kind of character would you like to be?"

This woman was smartly dressed in a cream colored, one-piece, casual-dress. From what I could tell, she had a pretty good body for some lady in her late 50's. However, I believe I was wrong about her: she must have been thinking 'I hope this guy sits next to me' when I walked in. Especially after, I caught her gingerly brushing her thigh with her finger and moving the hem of her dress every so slightly up her leg, "I don't know. Maybe an older woman that seduces David on a plane." She kept moving her dress up her thigh. "What do you think?"

What did I think? At any other time in my life I would have jumped on this opportunity in an instant. But not today. Not now. I love Karen.

"I'm flattered, but I'm engaged." I said.

"That's not what I heard," she said. Suddenly, her hand was rubbing my shoulder, and she cozied up to me.

"Yeah, well, I'm working on that. That's why I'm on this flight." I moved her hand off my shoulder.

"Tell me more, stud." She returned her hand to my shoulder and tried to lean her head there, as well.

"Lady! I'm on my way to get Karen back. I'm not looking to meet someone new." I said, sternly. I delicately removed this woman's head and hand from my shoulder.

I saw the rejection in her face. That's not a very attractive look, especially on an older woman.

"I was only trying to give you some ideas for your book," she was trying to save face.

"I'll tell you what. I'll write something about this *incident*. But, don't worry, in the book it will work out."

She smiled. "You are cute. Thanks."

When did I become such a stud? Good for me!

The lady chatted my ear off for the next four hours and, to be honest, I reciprocated in good fashion. I told her the whole Karen and Sandy ordeal and she listened, then she offered this advice, "I think you need to show her how much you really love her. Women like to be shown how much they are loved."

"But, how can I do that?"

"Well, that's up to you. Showing up out of the blue is a good start, but you need to honestly tell her how you feel. Not just apologize for what you've done. You have to be honest, and then, the best you can hope for is that she believes you."

She did give me some good advice, but our chatting kept me from achieving my goal of catching a few hours of shut-eye before I confronted Karen. I haven't been sleeping well since she left me. Plus, I would be arriving in London when I normally went to bed. Needless to say, I was exhausted by the time we arrived at Heathrow. As we touched down I thought of the old adage: 'Who needs sleep? I'll have plenty of time to sleep when I'm dead.'

I found myself leaving Heathrow Airport in a taxi heading for Piccadilly Hotel in central London. And, oh yeah, it was three in the morning - London time.

When I got to the hotel, I was met with a bit of resistance in the lobby. Apparently, these unfortunate Brits didn't realize who I was in their country.

"Sir, where are you going?" asked the concierge in a snooty, British accent. I had inadvertently run right past him.

"Oh, I'm sorry. I'm just heading up to room 602. Thanks for checking," I said, and I waited for the elevator.

"Excuse me sir. I'm afraid that won't be possible. Room 602 has only one registered guest, who appears to be a female," he said.

Ummmm, no shit, Sherlock.

"I know. I'm her fiancé. I just got in from New York. I was going to surprise her. You know, keep a little magic in the relationship."

"Well, there isn't going to be any 'magic' here at the Piccadilly at 4 a.m.. I'm afraid that since you are not a registered guest, we'll either need to wait until 7 a.m., at which point we can contact her, or we can call the authorities right now and see if they would be willing to contact her for you."

What a dick. I would have to wait.

"Can I wait here? It's only three hours," I asked.

"You may wait here, but you may not sleep here. We do not allow sleeping in our lobby."

Again, what a dick.

"Okay, then. I'll wait," I said.

The lobby was quintessentially English. Ornate, classy and stuffy all at the same time. The entryway was checkered white and black marble that led to a beautiful pine-wood floor with a giant Persian rug in the center. The check-in area was to the left, with the staff working behind a long, art-deco, reception desk. Above me, were 40-foot ceilings with four stained-glass, dome-skylights. There was an abundance of crown molding along the ceiling and pilasters that made the lobby look quite stately. I moved over to the right-hand side of the lobby, directly across from reception desk, and pulled up what looked like the most comfortable chair that they had in the place - a tapestry-upholstered club chair. My other options were a few, scattered arm chairs. I concentrated on staying awake for the next three hours.

There was a copy of the paper on the coffee table, so I took a gander at that. Seems the Brits aren't very fond of the Prime Minister these days. I tried getting through an article about the economy, but I started feeling my eyes getting very heavy. Before I knew it, I started to dream.

Karen and I were riding horses through an open meadow.

The sun illuminated the high sky as we rode. First, a light trot, then a gallop. We were somewhere in the west. I looked at Karen, beautiful as ever, her long, blond –

"Sir. Excuse me, sir," someone was speaking to me.

"Shut up, you dick," I said in my dream. The serene scene disappeared. Something or someone was making noise.

"Sir," I felt a tap-tap on my shoulder, "Excuse me, sir. Please wake up, sir. I would like a word with you if you don't mind. Sir? . . ." he kept tapping me until I opened my eyes.

"Yes," I finally mumbled after being tapped back to reality by the glorified doorman.

"Sir, you were sleeping. I indicated to you earlier that you may wait here, but you may not sleep here. You, sir, were sleeping. We cannot have this unfortunate incident again. Is that understood?" The concierge asked.

Holy shit, I was being browbeaten by a doorman.

"I wasn't sleeping," I said, even though I knew I was.

"Sir, your eyes were closed and you were snoring. I distinctly heard a grumbling, nasal sound followed by a whisper of 'Puhhhhh' coming from you as you exhaled. This would indicate to me you were asleep."

Smart chap, even for a concierge.

"Maybe I dozed off for a minute. I apologize. You have to understand, I've been up all night. I just arrived from New York and I can barely keep my eyes open," I tried to plead with him, but quickly found myself yelling. "Please! Just let me rest!" My nerves were on edge. I was never any good on no sleep. I was getting frantic. I tried to relax, and I knew that yelling at this guy wasn't going to get me anywhere.

"That's quite a shame, sir. But the hotel policy is no sleeping in the lobby. Thank you for understanding." He returned to his post behind the counter.

Apparently, I was his number-one priority this morning. I pulled out my cell and sent Jon a text message. He should be up. It was only eleven back home.

I'M IN LONDON TRYING TO GET KAREN BACK. ANY ADVICE? A few seconds later, I received Jon's reply.

YEAH, COME HOME!

That wasn't very encouraging. Seconds later, I got another message.

KIDDING. JUST MAKE SURE YOU ARE REAL. GOOD LUCK.

That was the extent of Jon's good advice, I guess. To sum up, I had to dazzle Karen, according to Michelle. Get Karen to trust me again, according to Carl, and be real, according to Jon, and be honest according to that chick from the plane. Shouldn't be that hard to accomplish in London with no sleep.

The text messaging didn't take very long, and I was running low on how to occupy my time. Now what? I still had three long hours to go. I figured I would get some writing done while I waited. I asked the concierge for some paper and a pen. To my surprise, the prick was ready to help. He gave me a legal pad and a nice pen. Thanks, prick – at least he's a helpful prick. Minutes later, I was again sleeping.

Tap. Tap. "Sir! Please wake up," The doorman again.

"I'm up, I'm up," I mumbled trying to focus out of a deep sleep.

"Sir, please –" he wasn't going to ask again.

"Okay, I'm up. I'm exhausted."

"Tragic," he said, and then walked back to his post at the

desk.

I yawned, and got back to writing. Now, the time really started to fly by. I was well into the story when I noticed sunlight coming through the window. The time was quickly approaching when Karen and I would be reunited. I dug in my pocket and pulled out a mint. Fresh breath would be very important this morning.

I decided not to ring Karen at seven on the dot. I thought it would be better to let her get ready without the major distraction of me suddenly thrust into her life. That way, she would have a normal start to her day and, hopefully, be nice and calm when I actually got a chance to see her. My plan was to catch her on her way out of the hotel. Minutes later, the elevator door opened - and there was Karen. I jumped out of my chair and waited for her to recognize me. To be honest, I wasn't looking very good. I had even grown a two-week-old beard.

As she got closer, my heart was pounding through my throat. When she did recognize me, the color left her face. "David," she was nearly whispering. "Is that you?"

"Yes. It's me," I said.

"What are you doing in London?" Apparently, she couldn't

believe I was standing here in London in the lobby of her hotel.

"I came to get you. I mean, tell you I love you, and that I want to be with you forever, and that I want you back," I was babbling.

"You came all the way here to tell me that. You could have just stopped by my apartment."

FUCK!!! APARTMENT!!! I NEVER THOUGHT OF THAT!!!

"How did you know I was here, anyway?" The look on her face belied confusion.

"I stopped by your office, but you weren't there. I made Carl tell me where you were, and I ran to the airport to get here as soon as I could, but the concierge wouldn't let me go up to your room, and I had to stay here in the lobby until seven, but here you are now and I just want to be with you. I don't want to spend any more time alone without you," I was speaking a mile a minute. When I finished, I reached for Karen's hand and added, "I love you."

Karen stared back at me and sighed, "Oh, David." She took a deep breath. "I love you, too." I pulled her closer and kissed her.

"I want to go home with you," she said.

"You must have read my mind," I replied.

We both hopped a taxi on the first leg of our journey back to America. Then I opened my eyes. Was I dreaming? Where am I? Fuck! I'm in the fucking hotel lobby. No! What time was it? I looked over to the concierge desk. I did not recognize the man standing there. Oh, Fuck! I couldn't have been asleep. As I was told on numerous occasions, there is no sleeping in the lobby. I may wait in the lobby, but I must not sleep in the lobby. But I had definitely been sleeping!

"What time is it," I called over to the concierge.

"Good morning, sir. It's half nine," he said.

Good morning? Shit. I had fallen asleep. I did feel rested, though.

"Was I asleep?" I asked.

"Sir, you were asleep for hours," he replied.

"I thought there was no sleeping in the lobby," I said.

"Usually there is no sleeping permitted in the lobby, sir. But this morning, when I arrived, Nigel told me to let you have a rest. He felt bad for you. Said you had a rough day, flying in from the States and all."

What the fuck? Nigel wakes me up twice, and then lets me sleep when I needed to be up. I had to put the absurdity of all this aside and try to focus on my situation. At least I was up now. I got off the chair, and hustled to the front desk.

"Can you ring Karen Gold, please, in room 602," I asked, politely.

"One moment, sir. Let me see if she is in," he checked the computer for a moment and then said, "There is no one by that name in room 602, sir."

"That's impossible. A few hours ago there was. Karen Gold. That's G-O-L-D. Can you check if she is in another room?"

"Surely," he tapped on the keyboard for a few moments, then said, "Miss Gold was indeed in room 602 as of 8:35 this morning, but it appears as if she has checked out of the hotel."

"What?" Oh, no.

"Karen Gold checked out of the hotel this morning at 8:35."

"Shit."

"Is there anything else I can help you with?"

"Why didn't you wake me up? That's the whole reason I was waiting in the lobby. I needed to see Karen Gold. Shit!"

"I wasn't aware, sir," polite as ever.

"Fuck!" I screamed. I ran out of the hotel, and flagged down a taxi.

"Where to sir?" The taxi driver said.

"Heathrow. And step on it," I said.

"American, eh? We don't step on it here, but I rather fancy your John Wayne American swagger. I'll get you there as soon as possible, sir."

I like these British cab drivers. They're efficient. They know their way around - unlike my Hindu friend in New York - and these cabbies will actually get you there 'as soon as possible'.

"Are you from New York? What is it with your mayor? Sending the city to piss, eh?"

And, they're informed.

"How did you know?"

"You've got a bit of an accent," he said.

"Yeah, I'm from New York. The city has already gone to piss. It's even urinated on me a few times."

He laughed, "Here on business or pleasure?"

"I wish I could say pleasure, but it hasn't been very

pleasurable."

"Have you taken in a show on the West End?"

"I've only been here a few hours."

"And you're heading back already?" He was concerned.

"I've got no choice. I'm trying to win my fiance back and she just left for New

York," I was still holding onto the illusion that Karen and I were still engaged.

"Things will work out, ol' boy. Just hang in there."

I liked this guy.

Twenty minutes later, we were at Heathrow. After paying the driver, I scrambled out of the cab and into the terminal. It looked just like JFK. Airports suck. The stewardess behind the counter was cute, though. Short, bobbed, black hair in her purple outfit, complete with neck scarf. I bellied up to the counter.

"Can you please tell me when the next flight to New York is leaving?" I asked the lovely lady behind the counter.

"Let me see . . . that would be flight 14 leaving at half ten this morning, sir. That would be in fifteen minutes. Would you like me to go ahead and see if we have an available seat? I'll see if they can hold the plane."

"Can you tell me if Karen Gold is on that flight?" I asked - OK, I begged.

"Sir, I'm sorry I cannot release that information to you."

"But, I'm her fiancé."

"Sir, I'm sorry, but it's airline policy not to release passenger information."

"You don't understand. I just flew here from the States seven hours ago. The woman I love broke up with me, and for the last month I haven't been able to do anything. I can't eat, sleep, work - it's killing me. I know she is somewhere in this airport and she is going to fly home without me telling her how much I love her. I need to see her. Can you please help me?"

The attendant looked at me with pity in her eyes, leaned over towards me and whispered, "She's on this flight."

"God bless you. Can I get a seat on that flight?"

"Let me see," She was trying to help, "It appears that this flight is completely sold out. I'm very sorry."

"Oh, no. When is the next fl-"

"Wait a minute! It looks like we have one seat left, but it is an upper-class ticket."

I now travel in style, I thought to myself, "Okay. How much is that?"

"That would be £1,880.30 sir. Would you like me to go ahead and book that for you?"

I paid the nice lady, got my boarding pass and headed over to the gate. Thank God, I didn't have any luggage with me. I passed through the metal detector and it went off. Of course. I tried it again, and it rang for a second time. Now, I got noticed.

"Sir, please step over here," the security officer said.

They pulled me over for a spot check. Why, Lord? Why do you toy with me so? I was patted and scanned up and down - I passed the security check. All the while, valuable time was being lost.

Then I heard, "Final call for flight 14 non-stop from Heathrow to New York."

"That's my flight," I said to the security officer, as he finished the pat down. "I have to make it."

The security guard got on a walkie-talkie and spoke to the gate. "Let's go," he said to me and we ran over to a motorized airport cart. I like those things. I have always wanted a ride in one - who hasn't? Off we went, speeding along between three and five miles per hour.

This was like an inside-the-airport limo. As we rode, I observed all the other travelers walking, jogging, rushing along. Not me, I was riding in style.

We got to the gate with no time to spare.

"Oh, my God! Thank you so much," I said to the security guard, and then took off towards the terminal hangar door and onto the plane.

"Mr. Michaels?" The lovely stewardess asked.

"Yes?"

"I'm glad you made it. Your seat is right this way." She escorted me over to the second

row and into my plush seat. "I'm glad you're flying with us today." Then she whispered, "I know who you are. I saw you in the paper the last time I was in New York. If you need anything just let me know. My name is Charmane."

"Well, there is one thing you can do..."

A minute later, the door was shut, and Charmane's voice

filled the airplane, "We apologize for the brief delay, but we are now quite settled and ready to begin our flight."

I took a minute to catch my breath.

I wanted to run back and find Karen, but I couldn't get up until the seatbelt sign was turned off and we were free to move about the cabin. One false move these days, and you would find yourself on the evening news, being escorted to a holding facility, where miscreants waited to be interrogated for terrorism. So, I sat there and waited, with the words of Michelle, Jon, Carl and of course, the cougar from the plane ride over, running through my head. Once we were at cruising altitude, I called Charmane over.

CHAPTER THIRTY-SEVEN

When we were free to move about the cabin, Charmane's voice once again filled the plane, "Will Karen Gold please come to the upper-class portion of the aircraft? Will Karen Gold please come up to the upper-class portion of the aircraft?"

Charmane and her co-flight attendant, Carmel, had taken rose petals - don't ask me how or why they had them on the flight - and placed them all over the front of the first-class cabin. They dimmed the cabin light, and stood behind me with mini flashlights, setting a romantic mood for me when I begged for forgiveness. I stood in the middle of the rose petals, the cheap flashlight beams accenting me in cool, white light. When Karen finally made it through the upper-class divide, I said, "Hello."

"David?" she said. "What the hell are you doing here? I mean, how . . . why . . . what's going on??" Karen could not believe her eyes, which were now wide open. She was about two feet from me, in the front of an airplane with the guy she hasn't seen in weeks standing before her. She was becoming a little freaked out.

When we planned this little encounter, Charmane asked if I

wanted the handset that broadcasts over the plane's speakers. She thought that apologizing so that everyone could hear me might be more endearing. I figured, why the hell not? Nothing was private anymore.

"Yeah, it's me," I answered over the loudspeaker.

"But how did –" Karen started to speak.

"It's not important," I pulled Karen over to me, "I want to tell you how sorry I am for everything that has happened. This month has been the worst month of my life. All I can think about is you, and how much you mean to me, and what a mess I made of everything. I want to apologize for not telling you everything that was going on when I met you. I know it was stupid and inconsiderate and disrespectful. I didn't want to bother you with all the sordid details. I know that I was wrong. I know lying to you was wrong. I'm begging for your forgiveness. I'm pleading for your forgiveness. I know I can't go back and change anything that happened, and saying I'm sorry isn't going to make things go back to the way they were, but . . . I just want a second chance. I just want a chance to start over with you. I just want a chance to feel your love again. Can you give me that chance, Karen?" I poured my heart out in a torrent.

Karen listened, then pulled away from me and took a few steps back. Shit, that's cold. She was standing stone-faced, her arms folded tight to her chest, avoiding my eyes. That's never a good sign. Then she spoke sorrowfully, almost in tears, "I don't think I can do that."

The rest of the airplane could not hear Karen's answer, but everyone in upper class surely had. They held their breath. My heart sunk. I nearly fainted. I had tears welling up in both eyes. I must have looked like a total sucker standing there in the middle of the rose petals with the crappy flashlights behind me.

Then she continued, "You lied to me," Karen said, "That's what hurt me the most. That's what I can't forgive."

Holding back tears, I tried to speak, my voice was cracking, "I want to earn your trust again. I never stopped loving you. I want to earn your love back."

"I didn't stop loving you, David," Karen said. Was this an opening, I thought?

"Can you give me another chance?" I begged.

Then there was silence. I could hear passengers yelling from coach:

"Give him another chance."

"He loves you."

"Give him a shot!"

"Don't be a fool."

"Yeah, don't be a fool. Once a liar, always a liar!" There's always one in the crowd.

Charmaine leaned in. "C'mon, Luv, give the bloke another shot. He really loves you."

"Karen, listen to the nice, airplane people. Well, not the one who called me a liar - you're wrong lady!" I said into the handset. "I love you, Karen Gold."

"I just don't know," Karen said, "But, I love you. I do. I want *us* to work. But-"

"No buts. Please, let's give this another chance. We can make it work. *I* can make it work."

Karen started to tear up, her hands fell to her sides and then moved to shield her face so that we could not see the tears that started to flow, "I . . ." she mumbled. "I love you, David." She ran over to me and threw her arms around me. "I love you," she said louder. "I love you, I love you, I love you."

The handset fell from my hands, as I stood there with Karen in my arms for the first time in weeks. I felt complete. "I love you Karen," I was choked up with happiness. "I love you." And then, in an apparent subconscious attempt to sabotage myself, I whispered into her ear, "Do you *really* think we can make this work?"

"Shut up and kiss me," she demanded.

So I did.

ABOUT THE AUTHOR

David Deutsch is an author, sarcasm guru, and wannabe rock star, not necessarily in that order. He is the author of romantic comedies, crime fiction, mystery, thriller and suspense novels. When he's not busy writing you can often find him chasing the sun. He lives in warm weather with his wife and children.

BOOKS BY DAVID DEUTSCH

Max Slade Thrillers:

Murder.com

The Killing Green

Other works:

Sh*t Falls Up

Life In Super 8

* * * * *

SNEAK PEEK

If you enjoyed Sh*t.Falls.Up, check out this sneak peek of David

Deutsch's Max Slade Thriller:

MURDER.COM

* * * * *

CHAPTER ONE

I had just walked through the door of my house, kicked off
my shoes, poured myself a generous four finger scotch, and sat down
on my couch when there was a knock at the door.

"Did you see what happened?" my neighbor asked, pushing
her way into the house.

"No, I—"

"What? How could you have missed it?" she asked, staring
and waving her hands at me.

I excused Imogen's rude behavior mainly because she was dressed in a slim-fitting outfit accentuating her fantastic body, and, more importantly, she had a lovely English accent. Not to mention I was in love with her.

"Missed what?"

"Max, the house down the block. The police are all over the place."

"What the heck happened?" I asked, taking a sip of Glenfiddich 18.

"You really are clueless sometimes."

"Well, I need a bit of liquor in me before I'm thinking clearly."

"What happened? How could you have missed it? Something big, around the corner!"

I let this information pour over me as my second sip of scotch warmed a path down my throat.

"Did you hear what I just said?" Imogen asked.

"How do you know?"

"I live here. It was hard to miss the screeching sirens. Come on!"

Imogen pulled my arm, almost making me spill my drink. I grabbed my coat and my drink, threw a leash on my black lab Jabber, and we all strolled down Seymour Drive. When we came around the corner, about a quarter of a mile down the road, I saw police tape boxing in the understated colonial mansion. How had I missed this? There were official emergency vehicles everywhere, flashing lights, and uniformed men darting every which way. A white van was in the process of unloading an empty gurney.

"Looks like we just made it," I said, standing with Imogen behind the police tape.

Do you know whose house this is?" Imogen asked.

"Ted Baxter's."

"You know him?"

"You could say that. I've had a history with him over the years."

I indeed had a history with Ted. We were both venture capitalists. Very good ones. And ones that ran in the same circles. Although I tried to limit my circle time with him.

Imogen and I, along with a few other neighbors, milled

around just outside the yellow-taped perimeter. After chitchatting with some people whom I had never met, nor seen before, nor had any desire to see again, I waved over one of the uniformed police officers.

"What happened?" I asked.

"There was a death in the house. You a neighbor?" he asked, walking over, one hand resting on his holstered weapon.

"Yes, I live around the corner. Is there anything that I should be worried about?"

"As I have told some of your other neighbors, nothing you should be concerned about."

"Well, I see some guys running around here in suits. I'm no cop, but they certainly look like detectives to me."

"Move back, sir." The cop sternly directed me with his words and his hands. This conversation was over.

Every time I'd ever asked a cop what had happened, they have never answered. It was always *nothing to see here, move along.* They were all the same. They never wanted to open up.

We hung around for a few more minutes, saw a gurney—no doubt the one that we saw when we arrived, now with a white sheet covering a body being loaded into a white van. One of the neighbors had told me that a man had died. Apparently, he had gotten further with the police than I had. I knew that had to mean Ted. He had lived there alone with his wife. We watched the door shut. The show was over. I wasn't going to hang around and chat with the neighbors any more than I already had, so we decided to head back to my place.

When we arrived home, I let Jabber off her leash and poured myself a drink.

"What do you think happened?" Imogen asked, concerned, watching me fix my second scotch of this short evening.

I took a sip.

"If I had to guess, I'd say that Ted was murdered."

Once they threw the sheet over your body and you were loaded into one of those white vans, you usually didn't make it out for dinner. I was confident we wouldn't be visiting Ted in the hospital anytime soon. And I could not care less.

"Oh my!" Imogen raised her hands to her mouth. "Why in the world would someone do that?"

"I could give you ten reasons off the top of my head," I said, walking over to my couch, ready to sit down.

Imogen glared at me. "Max, you're such an asshole sometimes. Don't you care?"

"Sure I care. But I figure he's out of his misery."

Imogen stared at me as if bewildered. Just about to sit, I decided to head back over to the bar in the corner of my living room.

"Would you like a drink?" I asked.

"How can you just stand there stone-faced? You said you knew the guy."

"I know a lot of people, my dear. Scotch on the rocks?"

I knew her drink. After five years of dating, I should. But I liked to ask. I liked the banter. It kept the romance alive.

"Scotch and soda."

"Ah, yes." I mixed the drink and brought it over to Imogen. "Have a seat," I said, motioning over to the white Italian leather art deco couch adorning my retro living room.

Money could buy you a lot of things. Not all of them nice. The one thing it couldn't buy you was taste. Luckily for me, I had both. But some of the people around here were lacking on the taste front. They decorated their homes like they lived in manor house. I couldn't stand stuffy, stately looking rooms. Never could. I was not landed gentry. I didn't have a valet, footman, cook, and scullery maid. No use pretending that I was. I wouldn't be fooling anyone.

Imogen sat, took a sip of her drink, and put her feet up on the ottoman while staring at the pitch-black television screen. I sat down next to her, put my feet up, and took a long sip of my scotch.

"Who would do such a thing?" Imogen asked.

She looked puzzled. She looked concerned. There was nothing to worry about. Ted was dead. And, I hated to say it, the world was a little bit better of a place.

"Perhaps things will become a little clearer in the morning. Care to discuss it over breakfast?" I asked.

My phone rang. I answered it, excusing myself from Imogen's company, and walked into the kitchen.

"I need your help," the voice on the other end of the phone said.

Kitty. She was alive. Which meant it was indeed Ted who was dead. Why on earth would she be calling me? I would assume she'd be a tad occupied at the moment. Considering her husband had just died.

"How did you get my number?"

"I saw you outside of my house. Can you help me?"

"I'm not sure what kind of help you need, but surely you need to talk to the police first."

"I already did that. I need to talk to you."

"Then go ahead and talk."

"Not on the phone. Can I come see you?"

"Not tonight. I have company."

"Same old Dutch."

Dutch. She never called me by my name. I took a sip of my drink. It was much better than this conversation.

"I'll be over tomorrow morning," she said, and disconnected our call.

I strolled back into the living room.

"Who was that?"

"Work."

"Oh."

"You staying a while?"

I didn't know why I bothered to ask. That was typically what lovers did. They spent the night. But I liked to pretend I was still on the chase for her affections. She liked to play hard to get.

"I guess."

"Well, why don't you kick off your shoes and get comfortable." Imogen was halfway through her first drink.

"Max, you're terrible."

"I know you mean that in the best possible way, my dear." I leaned over and gave her a kiss.

CHAPTER TWO

Imogen woke me around nine in the morning. I was lying soundly in my bed, wrapped in my down comforter—a cozy cocoon. I was barely awake, quite content to make this morning a leisurely one.

"I've made breakfast, luv."

"That means I have to get out of bed to eat it."

"If you think I'm bringing you your breakfast in bed—"

"I wouldn't have it." I started to rise. "Certainly not after you took all the trouble to make it."

I figured that French toast, eggs, bacon, and hash browns were best eaten at a table.

Jabber was standing by the side of the bed, nose cold as ice, nuzzling my leg, tail wagging. I reluctantly pushed the covers off me, exposing the inner sanctum of my warm sanctuary to the elements. Rolling into a seated position and wiping the sleep from my eyes, I gave her a pat on her head as I stood.

I met Imogen in the kitchen. Jabber followed me.

"Cereal? That's what you cooked up?"

"Who said I cooked anything?"

Annoyed that I would be dining on cereal with soy milk, since Imogen forbade me from bringing dairy into the house due to her dairy allergy, I sat down at the table. She joined me.

I'd gotten used to soy. Or maybe I'd just convinced myself that I'd gotten used to soy. Imogen has claimed that I could, indeed, bring dairy into the house. She's even gone so far as to purchase it. But why bother? If she was allergic to it, I didn't need it. Sure, soy didn't taste like milk. And it certainly didn't taste like cream in my coffee. But we all must make sacrifices for love. Mine just came at the expense of an enjoyable breakfast.

"I did make coffee," Imogen said.

"Gold star for you."

Coffee and cereal with soy milk does not a breakfast make. I would have prepared a proper meal. Pancakes. Breakfast burrito. Fried eggs. Something that requires fire. Cooking. Maybe that's because I liked to think of myself as a chef, but without formal training I was more like an advanced home cook. That was why I'd outfitted my kitchen with top-of-the-line appliances, including a top-of-the-line double oven. It wasn't just there to look pretty or to prove that I could afford one. I actually used it. And I cooked a mean lasagna.

Imogen walked over to the coffee pot on the counter by the oven. She prepared my coffee the way I always took it at home, with soy and two sugars. I needed the sugar to offset the soy. She knew that about me. All the more reason to propose one of these days.

"Here you go." She placed the coffee down in front of me. Hers was already sitting at the table, with a dash of soy.

"Thank you, Imogen."

"So, is anything clearer this morning, Max?"

"The only thing I can focus on right now is trying to ingest some caffeine as soon as humanly possible into this old body of mine."

"Since when is forty old?"

"Since I turned forty."

"Bloody hell, speak for yourself, Max."

I ate my cereal and soy while Imogen peppered me with questions about Ted, none of which I could answer. My phone buzzed, and it was a text message from Kitty saying she'd be at my place in five minutes.

"You might get some answers to this thing in a few," I said.

"Why do you say that?"

"We're going to have a visitor shortly. Why don't you stick around?"

"Sure. It's not like I have anything else to do today."

That was true. Besides being a total knockout and having a lovely English accent, Imogen was loaded. Family money mixed with her own hard-earned cash. Like me, Imogen was an investment banker. But unlike me, she'd worked at a proper investment bank before she'd retired five years ago at the ripe old age of thirty-five. I, on the other hand, had made my money from selling dotcoms. Then, once I had some money to play with, I'd started a venture capital firm, and now I spent my days with twenty-somethings that were busy asking me for money to fund the next big thing while Imogen got to work on her tennis game. I was a bit jealous. But I couldn't seem to walk away from work.

"I suggest we both put on some clothes. I don't think anyone wants to see me in my skivvies. But I'm sure plenty of guys would love to get a glimpse of you right now."

"As Moneypenny would say, I'm for your eyes only, Max."

We both threw on some clothes. The best I could muster up was a pair of creased khakis and a blue polo shirt. Imogen was remarkable. She always managed to look like she had just stepped off the runway. Within seconds she had on beautiful cream-colored tailored pants and a white button-down blouse that looked like it must have been specifically designed for her. Just another reason why I loved her—the art of the quick change and her willingness to allow me to grace her well-dressed arm.

"Where did you find that outfit?" I asked, since it was different than the clothes that she had on last night.

"Seriously, Max, you really are clueless sometimes. I've taken over half of your closet, or haven't you noticed?"

I hadn't noticed. I didn't know what that said about me. The doorbell rang. In walked Kitty Baxter, all five feet ten of her picturesque frame. She had long blond hair, piercing blue eyes, and was dressed in a cream skirt and blue button-down blouse that made her look like a walking Chanel display window. Apparently skirts, pants, and blouses are the uniform of beautiful, well-to-do ladies. I, in stark contrast, looked like a schlep.

"Dutch!" Kitty exclaimed as she grabbed my shoulders and gave me two air kisses.

"Hello, Kitty!" I said, feigning excitement.

Kitty immediately noticed Imogen standing off to her left. She looked at her mischievously, like a kitten sometimes looks at a ball of yarn.

"Allow me to introduce my friend Imogen Whitehall," I said.

"Friend?" Imogen asked.

"Lover?" I asked.

"Getting there."

"Girlfriend," I said, playfully.

Kitty didn't need any insight into my romantic life.

"I guess. For now."

"Kitty Baxter, please allow me to introduce my *girlfriend* Imogen Whitehall."

Imogen, seemingly shocked by the revelation that this woman was married to the recently deceased Ted Baxter, froze for a moment, staring into space.

"Well that was certainly awkward," Kitty joked. "Pleasure," she said as she extended a hand to shake.

Imogen, now back to her charming self, extended her hand. "He's incorrigible," Imogen said, shaking hands.

"He's just Dutch."

"So you two know—"

"Kitty, I'm terribly sorry about what happened last night," I offered.

"Thank you, Max. It was certainly a shock."

Kitty was composed as ever as she tried to convey some semblance of sorrow.

"I should say," Imogen said.

"I knew you had to have some idea what had happened, because I saw you and Miss Whitehall standing right outside of the house last night."

"I don't know very much. The police were pretty tight-lipped."

"They saw you two while they were busy questioning me. Me! Of all people."

"They, as in the police? Why wouldn't they question you? You're his wife, or had you forgotten?"

"Oh, Dutch. Ask me a few questions, sure. But to question me all night? I hardly think I deserved that. There are only so many ways to say I didn't kill Ted."

I was more concerned about why the police would care about me. Yes, I had known Ted. A lot of people had. But I didn't want him dead. Sure, I had wished it once or twice. He was a nasty man. And one who didn't respect anyone's personal boundaries. But I certainly wouldn't have killed him. They didn't have scotch in prison.

"So, the police saw me—why would they care about me?" I asked.

"I'd prefer to chat without the presence of Miss Whitehall. No offense, my dear." Kitty turned toward Imogen.

"You can speak freely with her here."

"But—"

"Kitty, Miss Whitehall stays. Why don't you have a seat?" I motioned for her to pull up a chair.

Kitty glared at me, not happy with my response. Possibly

jealous of Imogen as well. Imogen found a place on one of the chairs next to me, facing Kitty, who was now seated in a plush chair opposite both of us.

"Ted was murdered last night," Kitty said, this time emitting some emotion, perhaps even a tear. But her frozen expression made clear that it was disingenuous. Maybe it was just the plastic surgery.

"Oh my!" Imogen gasped.

"Jesus, Kitty, that's horrific," I said. "I'm sorry."

This comment elicited a bit of a smirk from Mrs. Baxter. There was the Kitty I used to know.

"I see you're terribly broken up about it," I said.

"I'm not going to lie. I'm not that upset. We've had our troubles over the years."

"And he's had some women?"

"You could say that."

"Any in particular that stuck around?"

"He was seeing one for a while. I think it was getting serious with her, but you could never tell with Teddy. One minute he loved you, the next he never spoke to you again. He was a fickle sort of bastard. I don't have to tell you. You knew him."

"Well, that was a long time ago."

"Seems like yesterday to me."

"You're surely not here for a walk down memory lane. So, what do you need to talk to me about?"

Jabber strolled around the living room, brushing past Kitty before settling down in the corner.

"The police were asking about you."

"Yes, we've established that. Now why would they be asking about me? I don't have a relationship with Ted. Hell, I haven't even been alone with him in years."

"They know about you and me and Ted."

They knew about me. Kitty. Ted. What was to know? That I hated him? Plenty of people did. He was an asshole. One of those guys that you wanted to punch in the face every time that you saw him. Maybe it was his nose that drove you to rage. It was always turned up at you. Like he thought he was better than you. Like he could own anything that he wanted. Even your fiancée.

"Yeah, well, that's ancient history," I said.

"Well, the police don't seem to think so. They were pretty

interested in my story."

"So you're telling me the police think that I could have killed Ted?"

This was outrageous. There was no reason for me to kill Ted. He had nothing that I wanted. Nothing that I needed. And, on top of that, he wasn't even on my social radar. I never thought about him. If last night had never happened I wouldn't have even remembered that he was alive.

"I'm not sure, but they're not ruling you out as—"

"Wait a minute. You think Max killed Ted?" Imogen appeared shocked.

"I'm not saying that, Miss Whitehall. I'm just telling you what the police told me. They found it curious that Max used to be my fiancé—"

Imogen seemed visibly annoyed at the fiancé revelation. I had kept that under wraps until now.

"Even if he was your *fiancé*," she said with an edge to her voice, "what would that have to do with Ted?"

The jig was up.

"He was the one who stole her away," I said before Kitty could beat me to the humiliating punch.

"Stole her away?" Imogen asked.

"I'm afraid so, Miss Whitehall. Ted swept me off of my feet," Kitty said.

"After we were engaged, Kitty," I reminded her.

"Yes, I know that, Dutch—"

"Why do you call him Dutch?" Imogen asked.

Kitty laughed. "It's an old nickname. When Max and I used to go out to dinner, we'd go dutch. We were both just starting out. So we used to split the bill. It became kind of joke, so I started calling him Dutch. It stuck."

"Jesus, Kitty. Thank you for that," I said, annoyed that she had introduced this nickname into Imogen's consciousness.

Imogen just sat and listened with a big grin on her face.

"Anyway, Max, it still bothers me to this day that I did that to you. You didn't deserve that. No one does."

You could say that again. No one deserved having their love stolen from them. But Kitty wasn't a saint. She had allowed herself to be swept off her feet—fancy clothes, fancy cars. I, on the other hand, had been in love. But if money had been enough to capture her heart, it was clear that she wasn't the one for me. The trouble was, knowing that hadn't made it feel any better at the time.

"Believe me. He's over it," Imogen added in my defense. Yet another reason I loved her.

"Of course he is. He's got you," Kitty retorted.

I smiled at Imogen. She caught my gaze and shot me a smirk back. I was glad that she seemed to be taking this well.

"Now that you've dropped a bombshell on Miss Whitehall, is there anything else that you want to talk to me about?"

"I want you to help."

"Help what? Write his eulogy?"

"No, Dutch. Help me figure out who did this."

"Kitty, I'm a lawyer, and barely one at that, not a detective."

I had graduated law school and had taken the bar but had never practiced. Kitty had met me when I was a poor law student.

"But you're smart and you run in the same circles as Ted. Maybe you could poke around?"

"I'm not a detective, Kitty. I don't work for the police. I'm a venture capitalist."

"I don't think the police are going to solve this. And I'm worried."

"What? You think you're the main suspect? Did you kill Ted?"

"No."

"You sure? If you give me a dollar, you can retain me as counsel and we'll have attorney-client privilege," I said, joking.

"Dutch, I didn't kill Ted!"

I could believe that. She was cold, manipulative, and a heartbreaker, but a murderer? I found it hard to believe that a woman could kill her husband.

"I'll take you at your word for now, but listen, Kitty, I can't help you."

"Dutch, I'm not worried about me. I'm worried about you."

Worried about me. Well, that was a first. She hadn't been too worried about me when she'd broken off our engagement and I'd had to face our friends and family with the news.

"Why?"

"The police scared me. They might think that you did this!"

"Kitty, that's absurd. I didn't kill Ted."

"I know that. But they seem to think you might have had something to do with it. And I'm scared that they are going to come after you."

"Kitty, I appreciate your concern, I really do, but let them come. I've got nothing to hide. I didn't do anything. I'm not a murderer."

"I know that, Dutch. Listen to me. The way they were talking last night, I'm just scared, that's all. I think you need to do something. Poke around, see if you can find out who really killed Ted. I don't want you to wind up being arrested for something that you didn't do because of our past."

"But—"

"Just promise me that you'll think about it. It might be the only way to prove your innocence."

I explained to Kitty a few more times that I didn't kill Ted, that I had an alibi and that the police were sniffing around the wrong hydrant and that she was better off cooperating with the police, as I was going to do if they came knocking. She begged and pleaded for me to help for "old times' sake" and for my sake but finally gave in to my desire to stay out of the mess. She got up from her seat, we all exchanged some pleasantries, and off went Kitty Baxter, zipping into the late-morning sun at the helm of her powder-blue Bentley convertible.

CHAPTER THREE

Moments after the door slammed and as we watched Kitty wind her way down my driveway back toward town, Imogen turned to me and asked, "Your old fiancée, huh? Interesting."

I knew that one was going to come back to bite me. But what was I to do? I knew that I should have filled Imogen in on my past. After all, things were getting serious. I had just never found the right time to tell her. It wasn't exactly the kind of thing that popped up during dinner conversation.

"Does it matter? What did you think of Kitty?"

"Does it matter that your ex-fiancée lives around the block, and her husband, who stole her away from you, is dead? Yes, it does matter. I think it matters a great deal, Max. And for the record, I think Kitty is gold digger, if you really care."

She had a point.

"Jealousy does not become you, my dear."

Sarcasm. That was about the only retort that I could muster up. How else could I respond to something like that? Make a joke and hope for the best. Slide it under the rug of laughs. Then quickly change the subject.

Imogen smirked.

"What do you think?" I needed to get her take on what had just transpired.

There was a lot to think about. Were the police coming for me? I wasn't scared. I knew that I was innocent. I didn't kill Ted. But why would they think that I could have? That was troubling. What did Kitty tell them, exactly?

"Well, for starters, I'm not sure that I believe her," Imogen said.

"Believe the story about me, Ted, and Kitty? Unfortunately, that's true. As much as I hate to admit it."

"No. No. That's not what I mean. I'm just not so sure that she didn't kill Ted."

"You think that she murdered her husband?"

"I don't know if it was her, per se, but I wouldn't put it past her. Anyone who is heartless enough to run off with another guy and to call off an engagement isn't a good person. I know that much."

"I couldn't agree more."

I wasn't interested in getting involved in helping Kitty solve the mystery of Ted's murder. If the police came, they came, and I'd deal with it then. At the moment, there were two things that did interest me. Having dinner with Imogen tonight and fixing myself a scotch.

"Dinner tonight?" I asked, fixing my cocktail. Halfway there.

"Jesus, isn't it a little early for a drink?"

"It's not every day that your old fiancée stops by asking to help solve the murder of her husband," I said, and took a sip.

"You do realize we're not on the set of *Mad Men*, right?"

"Why must you keep reminding me of that? I'd make a great Don Draper."

"You've certainly have got the drinking part down."

We went on with our day. Imogen went home for a spell, most likely napped, showered, and changed. We hadn't done very much sleeping last night. I played a little tennis—after all, I needed all the practice I could get in order to beat Imogen—showered, then had a pre-dinner drink while relaxing and listening to some music.

When I finally got around to checking my phone, there were several text messages, two of which were interesting or desperate, depending on how you were looking at the situation.

Dutch, I realize our past wouldn't exactly prompt you to cooperate but I could really use your help.

What is your email address?

I decided to answer and sent Kitty my email address.

Halfway through my drink, Imogen knocked on the door. I fixed her a drink and we exchanged some small talk, none of which included discussing Ted or Kitty. After about an hour, we hopped in my black Audi RS 7 and headed off to dinner.

We were dining at Circle this evening. A very upscale French fusion restaurant. Imogen looked fabulous in a black dress. Her green eyes were glowing, accentuated against her straight black hair and the dress.

"Charles," I said, extending a hand, greeting the maître d'.

"Ah, Max and Imogen, lovely to see you both. Give me a minute and I'll find you a table."

We ate out a lot.

"No rush, we'll wait at the bar."

Imogen and I walked over to the bar and proceeded to embark on our first drink of the evening. Technically, our second. But who was counting?

"I've been thinking…"

"Never a good thing," I retorted.

"Nevertheless, I've been thinking." Ginny, as I was apt to call her on occasion, especially when she was looking sexy, turned toward me, crossing her legs and revealing a bit of exposed thigh.

"About?"

"Things."

"How about you elaborate a bit, my dear? *Things* is a bit broad."

Just then, Charles walked over to us and informed us that our table was ready.

Saved by the bell.

He escorted us off to the left of the restaurant into a private booth.

We picked up the menus and scanned them briefly.

"Red or white, my dear?"

"White."

The waiter took our drink order, filled us in on the specials, and then disappeared. Moments later he returned with our bottle of wine, poured two healthy glasses for us, and then once again departed to give us time to sip our wine and to decide on dinner. Imogen and I always put our phones on vibrate when we arrived at a restaurant in order to make sure that we would not be distracted by them. No checking Facebook, Twitter, texts, or email during dinner. Any message, email, or status update could wait until after.

"As I was saying, Max, I was thinking." Ginny looked intensely into my eyes.

"Yes, I believe we have covered the fact that you've been thinking." I took a sip of my wine.

"I've been thinking about us."

"I think about us all the time," I said.

"Isn't it time?"

"Well, it's about nine."

"You're such an asshole."

"What?"

"I wasn't asking the time."

"I know. I'm sorry. Go ahead. You were thinking about us, and what did you come up with?"

"Well, we've been together for a while and I love being with you and spending…"

At that moment my phone went off with a notification that I had received an email. Normally I would not have cared, but Kitty's text had me a little curious. I couldn't help myself.

"Hold that thought," I said, reaching for my phone.

"What are you doing?"

"Give me one second," I said, viewing the notification on my phone that I had received an email from Kitty. I opened my email, and this appeared:

From: Kitty Baxter
Subject: Fwd: *CONFIDENTIAL* SCV
To: Max Slade

Thought you should see this. See below.

Regards,
Kitty

Begin forwarded message:
From: Mike Miller
Subject: *CONFIDENTIAL* SCV
To: Ted Baxter

I've discussed this with Clarke, and Overlord is a go. With or without you. ACAE. For your own well-being I would suggest that you reconsider our last conversation.

—MM

Mike S. Miller, Esq.
Partner
Baxter, Miller & Clarke Capital Inc.

"Dinner's on you," Imogen informed me.

She was right. Dinner was indeed on me. The rules of our game stated anyone who picked up their phone during dinner also picked up the bill.

"You're worth it. Get a load of this."

I read Imogen the email.

"Kitty sent you an email?"

"Yes."

"How'd she get your email address?"

"She texted me earlier. I sent it to her."

"Your ex-fiancée is now texting you? I'm beginning to really not like this woman."

"Jealousy does not suit you, my dear."

"Didn't we cover that already? Deal with it."

"Forget about Kitty for a second. What do you think about the email?" I sat back in my chair, sipping my wine.

Ginny thought for a moment. "Possibly a veiled threat, that's, um, not so veiled."

"Possibly. What do you make of 'Overlord'?"

"Not sure. I think that was the code name for D-Day. Maybe Mike or someone at Baxter, Miller & Clarke has a World War Two obsession?"

"Yeah, maybe. Who knows? Could be a threat, could just be work stuff. The tone's a bit strong. I certainly don't send emails like that, but that doesn't really mean too much," I said.

"I don't either. At the very least there was some disagreement at the office. But would that lead to murder?"

"Who knows? I am sure that whatever Overlord is it must be worth a whole lot of money. Men have killed for a lot less than that."

"I guess. Can we get back to dinner, Max?"

"So, you were saying…"

One thing was for sure: something was going on. Something odd. And Kitty was in the middle of it. And, thanks to her, I just might have been as well. Damn Kitty.

Printed in Great Britain
by Amazon

70080516R00220